BLUE
BOOK

TOM HARLEY CAMPBELL

Cayuga Street Press

Cayuga Street Press

Trumansburg, NY USA

Blue Book
by Tom Harley Campbell
(tomharleycampbell.com)

Copyright © 2022 Tom Harley Campbell
ALL RIGHTS RESERVED

First Printing – October 2022
ISBN: 978-1-68111-477-4

Cover Art by Gregory M. Dearth
Copyright © 2022 Gregory M. Dearth
ALL RIGHTS RESERVED

Author photograph by Jason Koski

Printed in the U.S.A.

0   1   2   3   4   5   6

This book is dedicated to the memory of Karl Quintanilla
Rest in peace, my friend

"I used to receive a hundred calls a year from people who wanted me to get into the Green Room at Wright-Patterson Air Force Base, because that's where the Air Force stored all the material gathered on UFOs. I once asked General Curtis LeMay if I could get into that room, and he just gave me holy hell. He said 'Not only can't you get into it but don't you ever mention it to me again.' Now, with millions of planets that we know are up there, it's hard for me to believe that ours is the only goddamn one that has things that can think walking around."

– Former U.S. Senator Barry Goldwater,
1964 Republican Presidential Candidate
(From *The New Yorker* April 25, 1988)

In your heart you know he's right.

– 1964 Goldwater campaign slogan

PROLOGUE

Clovis Army Air Field, New Mexico
July, 1947

"What's in the crates, Sarge?"

"Shut the fuck up, soldier. Ain't nonna yer goddamn business." The sergeant cuffed the private on the ear. "Ain't nonna my business either. Just get 'em loaded up."

It was the middle of the night and the Douglas C-47 cargo plane had landed an hour earlier. Clovis AAF had been shut down and put on deactivated status two months ago. A couple of officers and a skeleton crew of NCOs and enlisted men had been assigned to keep an eye on the base until further notice. But the base had been reactivated for this one night, for this one mission.

"Jesus, Sarge! That hurt." The soldier rubbed his ear. "Why didn't they fly right into Roswell? This shit was already there. What the fuck did we drive it all the way up here for? I thought they closed up this shithole base."

Roswell Army Air Field was two hours southwest of Clovis. Its status was highly active, a little too active at the moment in the opinion of certain members of the Central Intelligence Agency, formerly the Central Intelligence Group. The CIA was part of the newly formed National Military Establishment, soon to be called the Department of Defense. They'd determined that there was too much public interest being paid to the material in the crates, and too many loose lips. Under the cover of darkness, the crates – several of them packed on ice in custom-built tubs – had been loaded onto a pair of Army *deuce-and-a-*

half cargo trucks and driven up to Clovis AAF. In the morning – in broad daylight – similar looking decoy crates would be loaded on to another C-47 and flown to Fort Worth Army Air Field in Texas.

"You boys just get this shit off the trucks and into the plane." The sergeant started to walk away, then stopped. "And be careful with it for fuck's sake. Any snafus and your asses will rot in the guardhouse."

"I heard this stuff has something to do with all that bullshit about 'flying saucers' crashing on a ranch down south of here," the private whispered to another soldier when the sergeant was out of earshot. "Little green Martian men . . . that's what I heard."

"I heard that too," said his buddy, as they dragged a heavy wooden crate off the tailgate of the truck. "One of the flyboys bummed a butt from me. He said they're flying this stuff to Wright Field, out in Ohio."

They passed the crate off to two airmen who hauled it into the plane. "Little green men," he snickered.

"Women too. That's what I heard," said the private. "Gimme a cigarette."

1

Dayton, Ohio
July, 2012

Through the mid-morning summer haze, Alex Johnson was not impressed by his first view of the Dayton skyline. Not as inspiring as Nashville or Cincinnati, he thought, more like Jackson or Birmingham. Yawning, he stretched, then slumped back into the stained fabric seat as the bus approached Dayton from the south on I-75. Starting in Hattiesburg, Mississippi, Alex had been on one bus or another for almost twenty-four hours, with stops or changes in Jackson, Meridian, Tuscaloosa, Birmingham, Huntsville, Nashville, Louisville, and Cincinnati. Before yesterday, he'd never been north of Jackson in all of his eighteen years.

Alex had managed to sleep on the bus, off and on, and now he was hungry. The sandwiches and apples he'd brought with him from home were long gone. Bus station snack bars had provided him with beef jerky, peanuts, and Coke.

Nobody knew where he was, not even his mother. She'd cried when he left, hugging him and begging him to be careful.

"I'll be all right, Mom," he'd promised, assuring her that he wasn't involved in anything illegal. "It's something I have to do, and it's better if nobody else gets involved."

"I don't understand why you can't tell me," she pleaded. "It's about your father, isn't it? Please, Alex, just tell me."

"I just can't, Mom. It might not be safe."

The bus exited I-75 at Rt. 35 and soon pulled into the Dayton terminal on Longworth Street. Alex grabbed his backpack and thanked the driver, bought some coffee and a pack of small powdered donuts, and sat on a bench outside the station. He'd been too cold on the air-conditioned buses, and now the warm sun was a relief – not *too* hot – and nicer than the scorching heat he'd left behind in Hattiesburg. He unfolded the Google Street map of Dayton that he'd printed out from his laptop at home. His backpack held several days' worth of clean clothes, his Dopp kit, and the four-year-old plane ticket that he'd stumbled across just over a month ago while leafing through one of his father's aviation books. The book was titled *To Conquer the Air: The Wright Brothers and the Great Race for Flight.* The unused airline ticket had been issued to Charles A. Robinson – round trip – from Hattiesburg to Dayton.

Alex took out his wallet and removed a small scrap of paper. He'd copied down a name and address from a business card that was thumb-tacked to a small bulletin board near his mother's computer in Hattiesburg. The card had been stuck there for the past four years.

Captain John Burke
Homicide/Assault Division
Dayton Police Department
335 West Third Street

At first, Alex was going to take the card, but he wrote down the information instead. He was afraid his mother might notice the card was missing and figure out where he was going, and he didn't want to get her involved. He'd already been warned not to go.

"Stay out of it, son." That's what Charles A. Robinson had told him when he'd asked him about the ticket. Alex had tracked Charles down, in Hattiesburg, the month before. "You've got to trust me," Charles had said. "This is way over your head. You and I could both end up like your father. Just leave it alone – I'm begging you."

Alex put the address back in his wallet, finished the doughnuts, and started walking the eight or nine blocks to the Dayton Police

Department. He called his mother on his cell phone and told her everything was okay. He didn't say where he was, and felt bad leaving her in the dark, but he thought it best – at least until he figured out what he was getting himself into.

Alex easily found the police station, near the corner at Perry Street and Third. Everything looked just as it had on Google Maps. He brushed away the powdered sugar from the front of his shirt, took a deep breath, and went in through the front entrance of the building. In the brightly lit lobby, a uniformed officer was seated at a desk next to a walk-through metal detector. The cop was an older Black man, and that made Alex relax a bit. His nametag read *Smith*.

"Morning, son," Smith said, giving Alex and his backpack a quick once-over. Alex was wearing a light-blue polo shirt, cargo shorts, and leather sandals. *Definitely not a gangbanger*, Smith thought. "What can I do for you?"

"I need to see Captain John Burke," Alex explained, nervously gripping and twisting the straps of his backpack.

"Well, I'm afraid you're about – oh, let's see – maybe nine months too late," said the cop, smiling.

"Damn!" Alex put his hand over his mouth. "Sorry, sir."

"That's okay," said the cop, still smiling.

"Is he *dead*?" Alex asked.

"Good God no!" laughed the cop. "He retired. Back in October or November, I think."

"Damn. Retired?" said Alex, and again quickly apologized. Smith just nodded his head.

Alex couldn't believe that he hadn't even *considered* the possibility that Captain Burke might have retired. Or died. Or moved away. Hell, four years is a long time, he thought. Anything could have happened. *God, I'm such an idiot!*

"But, sir, I *really* need to talk to him," Alex implored. "It's very important. Do you know where he lives?"

"Look, son, I'm afraid I can't tell you that," said the cop. "Even if I *knew* where he lived, we can't give out that kind of personal information. What's this all about anyway?"

"I can't tell you," said Alex. His shoulders dropped and he let the backpack slip slowly to the ground. He bent his head and stared at his feet.

Officer Smith watched Alex deflate. "Listen," he said, "Cap's son, Kevin, he works here. He took over the homicide division when his Pop retired, and now *he's* Captain Burke. Could you talk to *him*? I'm pretty sure he's in the building."

"Can he tell me how to find his dad?" Alex looked up hopefully.

"I don't know. That'd be up to him, I guess."

"Sure," said Alex. "Yes sir. I'd like to see him."

Smith picked up the receiver from the desk phone and punched the line for the homicide/assault division. A detective answered and passed the call on to Kevin Burke.

"Hey, Kevin," said the desk cop, "This is Smitty, down at the front desk. There's a young man down here looking for your Pop. He said it's real important."

"Hell, Smitty. Did you tell him Pop retired?"

"Oh yeah. You should've seen the look on his face."

"Did you ask him what it's about?"

"I did, but he won't tell me. He's kind of mysterious," Smitty said, nodding and winking at Alex.

"Okay, let him in. I'll be down in a minute."

"Captain Burke will be down shortly," said Smitty, hanging up. He inspected the contents of Alex's backpack and waved him through the metal detector.

"Have a seat in the lobby right through there. Good luck, son."

2

Charles Robinson

That same morning, down in Alex's hometown of Hattiesburg, Mississippi, Charles Robinson wheeled his motorized wheelchair out through the front door and onto the wide screened porch. He looked both ways – a nervous habit – pushed open the screen door and rolled down the ramp to the concrete driveway. Again, he looked up and down the street before retrieving that morning's edition of the *Hattiesburg American*, lying in a plastic bag at the end of the driveway. He put the newspaper in his lap and hurried back up the driveway, up the ramp, and across the porch into the air-conditioned comfort of his house. The temperature was going to hit 100 degrees again today.

Charles was sixty-five years old and lived alone in the house he'd inherited from his father – a craftsman-style bungalow on Adeline Street in the old Historic Oaks District. The house had been completely retro-fitted to accommodate the needs of a paraplegic, and parked in the garage behind the house was a tricked-out handicap van. Charles didn't use the van too often, mostly staying home except to shop for groceries. He still taught a history class at Xavier University in New Orleans, and once a week he drove there and back.

Between his Xavier paycheck, his military disability checks, and an inheritance from his father, Charles had all the money he needed. He'd never married, and although there'd been a few girlfriends over the years, none of them had been able to commit. *To me and my wheelchair*, Charles knew.

He poured a cup of coffee, made some toast, and opened the newspaper at the kitchen table. The *American* was owned by the Gannett Company, and like all of the Gannett newspapers around the country, it had been in decline for years. It was mostly ads, and much of the content was reprinted from *USA Today*, or the Associated Press or the other wire services. Charles sipped his coffee and was wondering why he even bothered with the paper, when a small headline in the *Nation/World* column caught his eye –

Arafat May Have Been Poisoned

Charles leaned forward and read the article with great interest. According to *Al Jazeera*, traces of a radioactive substance – *polonium-210* – had been detected in high concentration on some of Yasser Arafat's personal belongings, eight years after the Palestinian leader's death. The article noted that *polonium-210* was the same substance that had been linked to the death of Alexander Litvinenko, the journalist and former KGB agent who fled Russia and had sought asylum in London, where he died in November of 2006. According to the article, many Palestinians now suspected that the Israeli government had murdered Arafat, and they were calling for his body to be exhumed for further testing.

Curious, thought Charles, as he wheeled himself into the small room that he used for an office. Bookcases lined two walls, and Charles had to push himself up from the wheelchair to reach a book on an upper shelf. He opened the book at his desk – *Modern Nuclear Chemistry* – and found the letter he was looking for among several others that he'd hidden there several years before.

Charles wasn't really sure why he'd saved the letters. They were remnants of his own investigation into the mysterious death of his father, retired USAF Lieutenant Colonel Henry Robinson, back in 2004. The investigation had produced more questions than answers about his old man's past, and created an odd level of paranoia in Charles that he'd lived with ever since. Worst of all, it had left another good man dead: Michael Johnson.

Now, his curiosity piqued by the article about Yasser Arafat, Charles read the letter again, skipping to the final calculation and the last several paragraphs. The rest of the letter was total gibberish to him—

AFIT

Air Force Institute of Technology
2950 Hobson Way
Wright-Patterson Air Force Base, Ohio 45433

Dear Charles,   *December 21, 2006*

I was intrigued by your question and did some calculations. Please indulge an old professor. The biological half-life only has meaning for a living organism. Once an organism dies, the amount of radioactive material remaining in the body is determined by the physical half-life, 138.38 days in the case of polonium 210. The activity, A, of a radionuclide, or the number of disintegrations per unit time is given by

$$A = \lambda N$$

where N is the number of radionuclides present, and λ is the decay probability per unit time (e.g. per second) of the nuclide. $\lambda = \ln 2 \, / \, T_{1/2}$, where $T_{1/2}$ is the half-life, and $\ln 2$ is the natural logarithm of 2. (The activity at time t is also given by $A(t) = A_o e^{-\lambda t}$, where A_o is the activity at time $t = 0$. Thus $A(T_{1/2}) = A_o e^{-\lambda T_{1/2}} = A_o e^{-\ln 2} = A_o \dfrac{1}{2}$, and hence the origin of half life.)

Now a "large" activity would be 1 Curie, or 3.7×10^{10} disintegrations per second. (One Curie is defined as the number of disintegrations per second of one gram of radium 226 that has a half-life of 1600 years.) So, lets take 1 Curie of $^{210}_{84}Po$. The number of polonium nuclei N_{Po} is

$$N_{Po} = \frac{A}{\lambda} = \frac{3.7 \times 10^{10} \times 138.8d \times 86,400 \sec/d}{\ln 2} = 6.38 \times 10^{17}$$

Now, 210 grams of Po contains Avogadro's number $\left(6.022 \times 10^{23}\right)$ *of atoms, so that* N_{Po} *corresponds to*

$$210 \times \frac{6.38 \times 10^{17}}{6.022 \times 10^{23}} = 0.222 \text{ milligrams.}$$

Now, 99+% of the $^{210}_{84}Po$ *disintegrations decay to the ground state of* $^{206}_{82}Pb$, *lead 206 which is stable, by the emission of a 5.4 MeV* α *particle. That is,* $^{210}_{84}Po \rightarrow ^{206}_{82}Pb + ^{4}_{2}He$ *(The emitted helium 4 is known as a* α *particle.)*

Now the thing about alphas is that the dead layer of our skin readily stops them. However, if alpha-emitting material is ingested, or somehow placed into a body, the alphas are very dangerous because the kinetic energy they carry is deposited locally, and does a tremendous amount of damage to tissue.

Again, taking our 1 Curie of polonium, we have

$3.7 \times 10^{10} \, \alpha's / \sec \times 5.4 \, MeV / \alpha \times 1.6 \times 10^{-13} \, joule / MeV = 0.032 \, joule / \sec$ *deposited in tissue. Since the range of 5.4 MeV alphas in tissue is about* $5.2 \times 10^{-3} \, gm/cm^2$, *and the irradiated area is a few square centimeters, say two, the energy is deposited in* 10.4×10^{-3} *gm, or* 10.4×10^{-6} *kg. Thus, the absorbed dose rate is*

$$\dot{D} = \frac{0.032}{10.4 \times 10^{-6}} \, joule / \sec / kg = 3077 \, joule / \sec / kg.$$

One Gray (Gy) corresponds to an absorbed dose of 1 joule/kg. A whole-body exposure of the order of 10 Grays leads to death within a very short time-few weeks. So, one would not need 1 Curie, one millicurie or less would do the trick. (I wonder if the amount given to the Russian is known?)

Now, as to detection of the activity. Unlike gamma rays, alpha particles are a little bit harder to detect. For gammas one only needs a sodium iodide crystal mounted on a photomultiplier plus appropriate electronics, and the activity can be detected from several feet away. For alphas one needs a plastic scintillator mounted on a photomultiplier with appropriate electronics, and the very thin sample has to be placed very close to the detector in order to avoid energy degradation in air. So, if there is any remaining tissue, one would have to take very thin slices and place them next to the alpha detector.

While the organism is alive, the effective decay constant λ_{eff} is given by $\frac{1}{\lambda_{eff}} = \frac{1}{\lambda_{phys}} + \frac{1}{\lambda_{bio}}$, or $\lambda_{eff} = 1.44 \times 10^{-4} \ 4.25 \times 10^{-8}$ per sec, compared to 5.78×10^{-8} per sec. So if the organism lives for say three weeks, the initial activity is only reduced by 7%. After death, the remaining activity decay is governed by λ_{phys}.

*So, if the initial activity was one millicurie, at the time of death, three weeks later it would be 0.93 millicurie or 3.44×10^{7} disintegrations per second (dps). After three years, it would be 1.43×10^{5} dps, easily detectable, and after **6 years**, 5.92×10^{2} dps- possibly detectable, depending on whether or not remains of the tissue stuck to bones etc.*

Just as an aside, in the late 1970's I spent a sabbatical in Paris at the Institute du Radium, Marie Curie's old institute. We lived in Sceaux, where both Pierre and Marie Curie are buried. My friend and colleague, who was a student of Joliot Curie, told me that people from the institute have used a gamma detector over the Curies' grave, and the activity there is very noticeable. Of course, the Curies used mostly radium 226 that has a long half-life and whose daughters emit gammas that are easily detectable.

More to the point, dear Charles, let me say this. I am assuming your question has something to do with your father's death and the similarities between the symptoms that Henry suffered and those of the Russian who died recently in London. I admit that I, too, took an interest. As to your desire that we not communicate about this by email or telephone, I think you may be exaggerating the necessity for that, but I am happy to comply. I do urge you to tread carefully down this path.

Should you decide to proceed, as far as testing goes, I would not recommend exhumation at this point. It seems that it would be impossible to keep such a thing out of the news. I believe that discernible levels of polonium-210 would be detected on any of your father's personal items such as a toothbrush, hairbrush, hat, etc. Did you keep any such items after your father was buried? If so, I could put you in touch with a particular lab in Lausanne, Switzerland, that I'm sure would be happy to help you out. Let me know, and I will send you the contact information. Again, I urge caution.

All the best,
Martin

Dr. Martin Novak
Professor Emeritus of Nuclear Chemistry
Air Force Institute of Technology
Wright-Patterson Air Force Base, Ohio 45433

Charles noted that Martin's calculations had extended out to only six years. According to the article in the newspaper, Arafat had now been buried for almost *eight* years. *It'll be interesting to see what the Palestinians come up with*, Charles thought. He folded the letter carefully, put it back into the book with the others, and placed the book on the shelf where he'd found it.

With a deep sigh, Charles settled back into his wheelchair. He thought again about his father's mysterious death. He thought about his friend, Michael Johnson, who had *also* died mysteriously, in Ohio, just four years ago. And he thought about Michael's son, Alex, the young man who'd visited him last month, asking for his help. He'd sent Alex away with a warning, and prayed that he wouldn't hear anything more from him.

3

John Burke

John Burke's cell phone rang.

"Burke," he answered automatically. Then, "Hello."

Maggie looked up from the newspaper she was reading, lowered her glasses a little, and looked at her husband. *Stop answering the phone like a cop* – it was one of the small things she'd been trying to get Burke to work on. Old habits die hard, but her Johnny was no longer a cop.

"Morning, Pop," said Kevin. "I'm glad I caught you. What are you doing?"

"Well, let's see," said Burke, sitting back in the chair and removing his reading glasses. "Right now, I'm having a second cup of coffee and trying to finish up today's crossword puzzle. Your Mom's reading the paper, and, and let's see . . . it's a beautiful day, so we might play some golf, or I might just hang around and read a book. The lawn needs mowing, the front windows need washing, and . . . oh yeah, I see my shrink at 4:30. You know, same old shit. How about you?"

Burke and Maggie had both been retired for less than a year, Burke from the Dayton Police Department, and Maggie from the Dayton School District. After living separately for many years, Burke had recently moved back in with Maggie at their house in North Dayton. Since his retirement, he'd been seeing a shrink, trying to work through some of the issues – *his* issues – that had split them up in the first place.

"Nice," Kevin laughed. "Very nice." He could hear music playing in the background as they talked. *Up on Cripple Creek*. Levon Helm was one of Maggie's favorites.

"You at work?" Burke asked.

"Yeah. I'm here in the squad room. Same old shit is right. Well, mostly anyway."

"So, what's up?" Burke asked.

"Well, Pop, there's this kid down here – a Black kid – maybe seventeen or eighteen, and he won't tell us his name. He just showed up out of the blue, and he's looking for you. Nobody's ever seen him before, but he says he knows you."

"Jeez, Kevin," said Burke. "What does he want with me?"

"He won't say, Pop. Said he can only talk to you. He said he needed your help."

"And nobody knows him? Nobody's seen him around before?"

"Nope."

"Christ almighty," said Burke. "Okay. I guess if he said he needs my help, I'll come down. Hell, it's been a while since I dropped in anyway. I'll be down in, oh, say twenty minutes."

As Burke hung up, Maggie fixed him with a curious look.

"What was that all about?" she asked.

"I'm not sure." Burke shrugged. "Some kid down at headquarters looking for me. Said he knows me and wants my help."

Burke changed out of a T-shirt and shorts, and into a golf shirt and jeans. He kissed Maggie on the cheek, told her he didn't know how long he'd be, and climbed into his Inferno Orange Metallic 2011 Chevy Camaro convertible, the first car he'd personally owned in over forty years. He'd been driving one unmarked DPD cruiser after another, and he bought the Camaro as a retirement present to himself. Maggie thought it was a little much, *a bit too macho*. She referred to it as the *mid-life crisis car*, but she enjoyed their long country drives, and she was happy with Burke's delight in his new acquisition.

With the top down, Burke headed out of their old North Dayton neighborhood and turned south onto North Dixie Drive. He tuned into an oldies station on the radio, and before long was singing along with Aretha Franklin –

...R-E-S-P-E-C-T Find out what it means to me ...

Burke had begun singing again. For years, his complete aversion to any kind of music had been a great mystery to Maggie and Kevin. It had been one of Burke's *issues*. But things were different now. Just before he retired, Burke had found himself personally involved in a case that had forced him to step back into a deep, dark, debilitating past. The case involved the discovered remains of a long-dead Catholic priest who had once been the choir director in the parish where Burke grew up. *But that was then. It was what it was.* Now in therapy, Burke's demons were slowly, but surely, being dispelled.

His life was much different now than it had been when he was Captain John Burke, head of the homicide/assault division of the Dayton Police Department. Since then, he and Maggie had been doing a little travelling, something they'd never done before, and playing a lot of golf, which they both enjoyed. They often played with Jim McGowan and his wife, Kathy. McGowan was a retired Air Force general and had been involved in Burke's final investigation.

Dixie Drive crossed over the Miami River and became Keowee Street, crossed over the Mad River, and took Burke all the way to Third Street. He sang along with the Rascals –

…there will be children and robins and flowers, Sunshine caresses each new waking hour…

Burke had to admit that he sometimes missed going into the police station every day. He missed the squad. His work had pretty much been his life for many years, ever since Kevin had grown up and Maggie had asked Burke to find his own place to live. What he didn't miss was the tedium of the never-ending office paperwork, and he *certainly* did not miss the often-grim reality of the job.

Burke parked in the back lot, then walked around and entered the DPD building through the front door. He no longer had access to the rear and side door codes.

"Cap!" exclaimed Smitty, grinning and coming around from behind the desk to shake Burke's hand. "It's been a while."

"Hey, Smitty," said Burke. "It's good to see your smiling face."

The two men caught each other up on what they'd been doing, and then talked about golf. They'd played more than one round together over the years.

"You've got a visitor here, you know," Smitty finally said.

"Yeah, Kevin called me," said Burke, nodding. "And you've never seen this kid around before?"

"Nope, and I know *everybody!*" Smitty said shaking his head and laughing. "He looks pretty clean-cut though. Polite, too."

Smitty apologized for having to ask him to walk through the metal detector. Burke waved dismissively and climbed the stairs two-at-a-time up to the squad room.

4

Martin Novak

What's this? Eighty-eight-year-old Martin Novak spied the headline on the back page of the front section of the morning's *Dayton Daily News*. He was standing next to the dining room table with a box of corn flakes in one hand and a quart of milk in the other. His wife, Sylvia, had read the paper earlier, and there it was, open on the table. Martin leaned closer to the table and read the headline –

Al Jazeera Reports Arafat Poisoned

He began to read the article from where he stood, but when he saw the word *polonium,* he quickly put his breakfast on the table and sat down. The article mentioned the Institute of Radiation Physics at the University of Lausanne in Switzerland. It was the same lab Martin had recommended to Charles Robinson over five years ago. Martin knew some of the scientists at the lab, and in fact had once collaborated with one of them on some research.

Now, according to the article, the Swiss had detected levels of *polonium-210* on some of Arafat's personal belongings – levels that far exceeded those that occur naturally in the human body. Martin remembered that the lab had come up with similar results back in 2006 when they tested some of Henry Robinson's belongings. The cause of Henry's death in 2004 had completely stumped the doctors in Mississippi.

Martin's appetite quickly faded. Henry had been Martin's best friend. The article brought to mind the unpleasant period – June, 2006 – when an investigation by Charles Robinson into the cause of his father's death had ended abruptly with another mysterious death. Since that time, Martin had not been in touch with Charles, and he'd never had the chance to tell him what he knew about Henry's visit to China in 2001.

Martin pushed the paper away and sat back in his chair. He missed his old friend Henry. They'd met at Cornell University in 1948 and had been reunited in 1963, when Henry, a United States Air Force major at the time, had been appointed the new director of *Project Blue Book*, the U.S. government's study on unidentified flying objects. The project had begun in 1952 and was housed in several highly secretive and restricted buildings located in Area B at Wright-Patterson Air Force Base. Officially, the purpose of Blue Book was twofold – to determine if UFOs posed a threat to national security, and to scientifically analyze any UFO-related data. While the general public was led to believe that Blue Book was an Air Force Material Command project, it had always been directed by the Central Intelligence Agency. Blue Book was preceded by *Project Grudge*, and before that *Project Sign*, the earliest UFO program. *Project Sign* and the CIA had both been created in 1947, not long after a flurry of unexplained UFO activity alarmed the Pentagon, most notably the reported crash of a UFO near Roswell, New Mexico. Project Blue Book was eventually tied into the Foreign Technology Division, which later became the National Air and Space Intelligence Center.

In 1963, and up until his retirement, Martin had been a civilian researcher and professor of nuclear chemistry at the Air Force Institute of Technology, also located in the vast Area B at WPAFB. He and Henry Robinson had worked together on several projects over the years – Henry's background in physics was often cited as the primary reason that he was chosen by the Pentagon to run Blue Book. The two men remained best friends even after Henry retired from the Air Force as a lieutenant colonel in 1970 and moved south to Hattiesburg, Mississippi, a year after Project Blue Book was terminated.

Martin thought about Henry's son, Charles. He wondered how much Henry had told his son about what happened during his trip to China, not long before his mysterious death. Other than the fact that they were best friends, Martin hadn't been sure, at first, why Henry had shared the unsavory details of the China trip with him. *Maybe he wanted my approval. Maybe he wanted me to talk him out of what he wanted to do – tell him he was nuts – tell him he'd be a traitor to his country.*

Eventually, Martin had learned of Henry's plan, and he'd counseled him to consider the consequences. But Henry died mysteriously, and Martin didn't know what his friend had decided to do in the end.

5

Do You Remember Me?

"Cap!" someone declared loudly, when Burke walked into the squad room. Everyone stopped what they were doing and greeted their old boss – they'd been expecting him. Tarisa Williams gave him a hug, and after a little playful chiding from her, there were more hugs from Tony Renzi and Pete Scoff, man hugs all around. The rest of the squad was either out on the street, or off duty.

Kevin, who had replaced his father as head of the homicide/assault squad, watched with amusement, appreciating the obvious affection the squad felt toward Burke. Kevin and Burke bumped knuckles, and Burke right away noticed the young Black man sitting alone in a quiet corner at the far end of the room. He was looking at Burke.

"That the kid?" Burke asked quietly, nodding in the young man's direction.

"That's him," said Kevin. "Does he look familiar?"

"I can't say that he does," Burke replied, noticing Alex's almost preppy look. "Sure as hell doesn't look like the usual gangbangers you see up here."

"Yeah, and he's very polite. Won't tell us his name, though. Said he was sorry, but he could only talk to you."

The young man stood up as Burke approached him.

"Captain Burke," he said quietly, extending his hand, "I'm Alex Johnson. Do you remember me?"

Burke seemed to have a very vague recollection of both the face and the name, but nothing he could pin down instantly.

"I'm not sure that I do," he said, studying Alex's face as they shook hands. "Where would I know you from?"

"We met four years ago," Alex said, letting go of Burke's hand. "My dad was Michael Johnson. From Mississippi."

Burke remembered all right. Like it was yesterday. . .

6

... Four Years Earlier: Riverside, Ohio

"There it is, Kevin," said Burke. "Right there, going into the woods." He was leaning forward and looking straight ahead from the shotgun seat of Kevin's unmarked cruiser. Scott Kaminsky, the Riverside police chief, had said to look for a gravel service road, just beyond the cloverleaf, right across from where Springfield Street connected to Route 444. *If you get to the dam, you've gone too far.*

Kevin crossed the highway and drove into the woods. As if choreographed, both father and son quickly removed their sunglasses. The shade was a relief from the brutal August sun, and the temperature seemed to drop inside the already air-conditioned car. It was just past ten o'clock, but according to a bank sign they'd seen on their way out of downtown Dayton, the temperature was already close to 90 degrees.

"It's too goddam hot out there," Burke said. He was crankier than usual. Having to get *up close and personal* with a dead body was always the worst part of his job, and Burke never got used to it. No cop ever did.

The short section of woods ended and the sun pounded the car again. Both men squinted, and the sunglasses went back on. The service road split in front of a small concrete block building and three tall silos. Burke guessed that they had something to do with Huffman Dam and the Dayton water system.

"Bear right," said Burke. "Scott said there'd be a turnaround at the end of this lane, down by the river."

"There they are," Kevin said, nodding to his right as the lane curved around the edge of the woods.

Two Riverside police cruisers were parked in the turnaround. The area was open, flat and dry, and here and there a stunted chicory plant or Queen Anne's lace poked up through the brown grass. Two spans of Route 444 crossed over the river, just to the west. A uniformed Riverside officer climbed out of one of the cars as Kevin and Burke drove up and parked. The three exchanged greetings, then headed toward the river.

"You guys go ahead," Kevin said, stopping. "I'll grab some gloves."

Maybe fifty yards from the turnaround Burke spotted Scott Kaminsky, sitting in the grass at the edge of the scrubby, tree-lined slope that separated the clearing from the olive drab, slow-moving water. Another officer sat with him, and they both got up when they noticed Burke approaching.

"He's down there, J.B." Kaminsky said, shaking hands with Burke. "Somebody spotted the body from the highway. We took the liberty of dragging him onto the shore. He was tangled up pretty good in a log, right down there at the end of this path. I think people must fish from here."

Burke hadn't noticed before, but now he could see that both Kaminsky and the other officer were wet, almost to their belts.

"Beyond that, nobody's touched him," said Kaminsky.

"Good, good." Burke said. "The coroner should be here soon."

Kevin joined the others, and when he and Burke scrambled down the hard-packed bank they could see immediately that the dead body was that of an African-American male. He was lying on his back, with one arm bent behind at an odd angle. The eyes were open, and the legs were crossed at the ankle, as if the man were sleeping on a couch. He was wearing a light blue dress shirt, partially buttoned, and brown khaki pants. Both were torn, most likely from the broken branches of the bleached driftwood log that the body had attached itself to along the river bank. His shoes and one sock were gone, washed away.

"He hasn't been in this river very long," Burke said, studying the body. "A day at the most, I'd say."

The man was tall, probably over six feet, and well built. The top front part of the skull was caved in, the skin broken in a large gash. All signs of blood were long gone, cleansed by the river water.

Burke sighed loudly and squatted down next to the body. He looked off to his left, toward Huffman Dam, not more than a hundred yards away. The river was low this time of year, and the concrete conduits and most of the spillway of the dam were clearly visible.

"Maybe he took a header off the dam, Pop," said Kevin, following his father's gaze.

"Could be," Burke responded, looking back at the corpse. "I don't see any real obvious bad wounds, other than that knock on the head."

Burke got down on his knees, adjusted the reading glasses that hung around his neck, and looked closely at the back of the one pale hand that was visible.

"Some scrapes here, nothing much," he said, straightening up and removing his glasses. "The coroner's crew should be here any minute – we'll let them do their thing."

Burke patted the front pants pockets of the corpse – nothing there – and then felt under the body.

"Kevin, help me turn this guy over."

"Maybe we should put on the gloves first," Kevin said.

"Good idea," Burke agreed.

The Riverside cops watched as father and son pulled on latex gloves. Kevin got down next to Burke, and they managed to turn the body over. Both rear pockets were still buttoned, and there appeared to be something wallet-shaped in each one. Burke unbuttoned the right pocket and extracted a tri-fold leather wallet. He put on his glasses again, unfolded the wallet, and looked at the driver's license displayed in the center fold.

"He's from Mississippi," Burke said after a few seconds, handing the wallet to Kevin. "Michael Johnson. Same age as you."

Unbuttoning the other pocket, Burke pulled out a wet, neatly folded cloth handkerchief, and what appeared to be another wallet, only thinner. When he opened it, they all saw the badge.

"Jesus Christ!" Burke gasped, looking up. "He's a cop!"

7

New Information

Yeah. Burke remembered all right. Even in retirement, he was still haunted by the Michael Johnson case. A cop from Mississippi died in Riverside. But why? *Accident? Suicide?* No one had thought so. Foul play had been highly suspected, but absolutely no evidence was ever found. Robbery was ruled out. The cop's wallet – cash and credit cards included – was still buttoned into his pocket. Of all the cold cases in the file, this was the one that troubled Burke the most. *The man was a cop.*

"I remember," Burke said, patting Alex on the shoulder. "Yes, of course I remember. How are you doing, Alex?"

"I'm okay," said Alex. "Sir."

Burke had flown to Hattiesburg as part of his investigation into Michael Johnson's death, escorting the cop's body back to Mississippi. He'd interviewed Alex and his mother, who was divorced from the cop. Alex lived with his mom and was fourteen years old at the time. Burke remembered him as a nerdy, polite kid, completely freaked out and mystified by his father's death. *Jesus, was that really four years ago?* Not a single person Burke had talked to in Hattiesburg had any idea that Johnson had even *gone* to Dayton – much less why.

Burke looked around and realized that a high level of curiosity existed in the squad room, even though the detectives had all gone back to their desks and appeared to be busy.

"I'm hungry," Burke said to Alex. He wanted some privacy. "How about we go get some lunch? Are you hungry?"

"Yes, sir, I *am* a little hungry."

"C'mon," said Burke. "I'll buy. We can get a sandwich right down the block."

On the short walk to Lucky's, Burke learned that Alex had spent a long day and night on various buses, having saved up for the ticket from his summer landscaping job, mowing lawns mostly. And no one knew where he was, not even his mother. *Like father, like son*, Burke thought, remembering Michael Johnson's curious presence in Dayton four years earlier.

"You should at least call your mom and let her know you're okay," Burke told him. "Do you have a cell phone?"

"I already did that, Captain."

"You can call me John," Burke said.

"Can I call you Cap, sir?" Alex asked, wide-eyed. "Like up in the squad room?"

"Okay, call me Cap." Burke smiled, opening the restaurant door.

"Cap!" Lucky exclaimed from behind the sandwich counter when Burke and Alex walked in. "Long time no see!" Burke and Lucky high-fived across the counter.

"Let me turn the music down for you, Cap," said Lucky, heading for the kitchen.

"Don't worry about it," Burke said, with a wave of his hand.

They ordered ham and cheese sandwiches, two small bags of Mikesell's potato chips, an iced tea for Burke, and a Coke for Alex, then sat at Burke's favorite table, the farthest back from the front door.

"So, Alex," said Burke. "What's this all about? Something to do with your dad I'm guessing."

"Yes, sir, it is. I was hoping you could help me find out why he died. I mean, I know you never came up with anything before, but I found out some stuff last month. I didn't know who else to talk to. Mom still had your card, and I remembered you said to get in touch if anything ever came up."

"But I'm retired now. Couldn't Kevin help you out with this?" Burke asked. "And why all the secrecy?"

"Well, sir . . . I mean Cap, I trust *you*."

Alex sighed and rubbed the back of his neck. "I thought you were nice to Mom when you came to our house – and nice to me. And now I think there was something going on with my dad that got him killed. I think it might be pretty serious stuff. That's why I don't want anyone to know – not even Mom. I think it might be *dangerous* to know. I'm really sorry to get you involved, but I didn't know what else to do."

Burke could sense that Alex was genuinely frightened. He hoped that for some reason the young man's imagination had gotten the better of him. Whatever the case, Burke was intrigued.

"So why now?" asked Burke. "And what . . . umm . . . *stuff* did you find out last month?"

Lucky delivered the sandwiches to their table, and Alex opened his backpack and rooted through it until he found what he was looking for. He unfolded the airline ticket and placed it on the table in front of Burke.

"This," Alex said.

Burke looked at what appeared to be an unused airline ticket. It was a round-trip fare from Hattiesburg-Laurel Regional Airport to Dayton International Airport with changes in Atlanta and Philadelphia, issued to Charles A. Robinson. The outgoing flight date was August 12, 2006 – departure time from Hattiesburg 6:05 am, arriving in Dayton 12:29 pm – returning August 16, 2006. In blue ink, someone had written *wheelchair assistance* across the bottom of the ticket.

Burke fixated on the dates. He was fairly certain it was right around the same time Michael Johnson's body had been pulled from the Mad River, four years ago. This *is* something, Burke thought. Forget about a young man's imagined danger. This was a legitimate clue.

"Where'd you find this, Alex?" Burke asked, pushing his sandwich aside.

"In one of my dad's books, a book about the Wright brothers," said Alex. "He was kind of an airplane buff. I kept all of his books after he died. Stacks of them."

Burke recalled seeing the rows of aviation books back in 2008 when he'd searched Michael Johnson's little house in Hattiesburg as part of his investigation.

"And you just found it now?"

"Yes, sir," said Alex. "Well, about a month ago, I mean."

Burke looked at Alex intently, and then back at the ticket. "Who's this Charles A. Robinson?"

"I guess he was a friend of my dad's," Alex said with a quick shrug. "I just met him once, but I don't really know him. But his father, Mr. Robinson – Henry – he was a *very* close friend of Dad's. He died a long time ago, four or five years before my dad died. He was pretty old, but he was almost like a father to my dad. *Charles* Robinson wasn't around much then. I don't think he lived in Hattiesburg."

Burke's investigation in Hattiesburg was coming back to him. He remembered being surprised that the head of the Hattiesburg Police Department, Michael Johnson's boss, was a Black man. Burke had hit it off with Chief Luther Banks, and had even been invited to dinner at the chief's house. He recalled that Banks considered Michael Johnson a nice guy, a good cop but a bit of a loner. No close friends that Banks knew of. Maybe he had a few beers with some of the other cops once in a while, that was about it. Alex's Mom had more or less agreed. She and Johnson had already been divorced for many years at the time, and she didn't really keep track of her ex, much less his friends. Everyone Burke talked to in Hattiesburg was shocked by Johnson's death, but no one knew what he was doing in Dayton, and no one knew of anyone with a grudge against him. *Had anyone mentioned an old Mr. Robinson? Or his son, Charles Robinson?* Burke couldn't remember now. He'd have to check the cold case file. Burke pointed to the bottom of the airline ticket. "What about this *wheelchair* business?"

"Charles Robinson. He's handicapped. He was in a wheelchair when I went to his house. I've seen him around town and he's always in a wheelchair, one of those motorized ones."

"You went to his house?"

"Yes, sir, Cap," said Alex. "After I found the ticket. I'm pretty sure it's the same house *old* Mr. Robinson lived in before he died, on Adeline Street."

"Did you show him the ticket?"

"Yes, sir. That's when it got weird. He got pretty upset. I thought he was going to start yelling at me at first, but he didn't. He kind of calmed down and said we had to go outside to talk, like he was afraid to talk in the house. But there was no one else there. We went out to the porch and started to talk, but then he said we better go down to the driveway."

"And what'd he say?"

"Not a lot. He said we couldn't talk about my father's death, just that he didn't know how or why it happened. He said it may have had something to do with his *own* dad's death. But he said he didn't know for sure. He said he'd been warned to stay out of it or he might end up like his father, or *my* father, and he said that probably goes for me, too, if I got involved. He begged me, *begged me* to stay out of it."

"Wait a sec. *Who* warned him?" asked Burke, having a hard time grasping where this bizarre story was heading.

"He didn't say," said Alex, again with a shrug. "I guess I should have asked him that."

"Good lord, Alex." Burke sighed and sat back in the chair, trying to get his head around what he'd just heard. He thought about it for half a minute.

"So, what did you say to Charles Robinson?"

"I told him I would think about it. He asked me for the ticket, but I told him no way. I left him sitting there in the driveway."

Burke sat quietly for several moments, somewhat stunned. Alex had ignored his sandwich, but picked it up now and took a bite. Burke followed suit, and they ate in silence for a few minutes, not an awkward silence, both of them content that enough had been said for the moment.

"You know, Alex, you're a pretty brave young man for coming all the way up here, on your own, to tell me all this," Burke said finally, nodding his head. "Yes sir, pretty goddamn brave. After a warning like *that?*"

"Or stupid," Alex said, with a crooked grin. "So, can you help me, Cap? Can you talk to Charles Robinson?"

At that moment, Burke realized there was absolutely nothing in the world that he would rather do than talk to Charles A. Robinson. He handed the airline ticket back to Alex.

"Here, you hang on to this, and let me think about it."

But Burke already knew that he was going to help Alex. He paid for the lunches and they headed back to the police building where Burke had parked. Alex finished the potato chips as they walked.

"Where are you planning to spend the night tonight, Alex?" Burke asked.

"Well, there's a Motel 6 somewhere on North Main Street. I found it online. I can afford that."

"That's *way* north on Main, probably seven or eight miles from here," said Burke. "How will you get there?"

"I don't know – a bus maybe. Or a taxi," Alex said. "How much do you think that would cost?"

"Too goddamn much," said Burke, grinning. "How about if you stay at my house? I won't charge you a dime. I'll call my wife just to give her a heads up. How's that sound?"

Alex smiled. "That would be great, Cap. That would help me out a lot. But I don't think we should tell anybody about all this. I think anybody that knows could be in trouble. I just have a feeling."

"Well, how about if I at least tell Kevin and my wife who you are, and that I'm going to look a little deeper into your father's death. I can leave out the details. Are you good with that?"

"Umm…okay," Alex agreed. "That's probably okay, I guess."

"And you have to call your mom again and tell her you're in Dayton with me," said Burke, giving Alex a playful shove. "She's probably worried out of her mind by now. I think it'll be okay for her to know."

"Okay," Alex said, sounding relieved. "I'll do that."

Up in the squad room, Kevin was alone now and Burke directed Alex to a quiet corner where the young man could call his mother in private.

"Remember Michael Johnson – the cop from Mississippi?" Burke asked Kevin, with a quick nod in Alex's direction. "That's his son."

"Jesus, Pops. What's he doing here?"

"Trying to figure out what happened to his dad. He has some new information about the case." Burke was instantly aware that he'd already said too much.

Kevin knew his Pop pretty well. They'd worked together as homicide detectives for almost fifteen years. Burke had been deeply affected by the mysterious death of Michael Johnson, a fellow cop. And it wasn't that the investigation had hit a wall. Hell, it never picked up enough speed to even *get* to the goddamn wall, but the whole thing had angered Burke more than any case they'd ever worked on together.

Kevin glanced over at Alex, chatting away with his mother in Mississippi, and then back at Burke. He already knew that this case was going to drag his Pop back into a world he'd happily retired from only nine months ago. Maggie wouldn't like it, and Kevin wasn't so sure he liked it either.

"*New information?*" he asked, his eyebrows arching.

"Look, Kevin, it's probably nothing. Probably a wild goose chase," said Burke. "But I've got to help the poor kid. Hell, he came all the way up here and asked for my help."

"Listen, Pop." Kevin shook his head. "You *know* you should let us handle this. If there's new information we should reopen the case – the squad I mean, not *you.*"

"I know, I know," Burke said. "Just let me check it out first. Do you want me to talk to Claire about it?"

Major Claire Winston was Burke's old boss – now Kevin's – head of Special Investigations. Kevin thought about it.

"No, no," Kevin said. "I'll talk to her if I need to. But, look, let's keep this between us for now. Okay?"

"I was going to ask you the very same thing," said Burke, smiling and giving Kevin a pat on the shoulder. "Now then, can you let me take the Michael Johnson file home for a day or two?"

"Jesus, Pop," Kevin said. "You *know* I'm not supposed to do that. Claire would have my ass if she found out."

"Well then," said Burke, grinning, "she'd better not find out."

Kevin just shook his head and headed for the file cabinet that held the cold cases. Burke made a quick call and cancelled the appointment with his shrink. When Kevin found the file, he took it from the cabinet and thumbed through it quickly. There were a few photos of Michael Johnson's body, his rental car, and the hotel room he'd stayed in before he died. Kevin returned the photos to the drawer, found a white wastebasket bag, put the rest of the file in the bag, and handed it to Burke.

"Not much here," he said.

"Tell me about it," said Burke, hefting the bag.

"The autopsy report's in there. Everything but the photos. Did you want them?"

"No, this should do it. Thanks, Kevin. Now I better call your mother and let her know what's up."

"Good luck with *that*." Kevin rolled his eyes. "Mom's not going to be too happy."

8

Cold Case

"Awesome car!"

Alex was impressed when he saw the orange Camaro, and Burke gave him a quick tour of downtown Dayton before they stopped at a Kroger store and did a little shopping for dinner. Maggie was expecting them when they pulled into the driveway.

She liked Alex right away. *This won't be so bad,* she thought. What she didn't like was what Burke told her about his plan to help the young man. After they set Alex up in the guest room – Kevin's old room – and while Alex had a shower, Burke reminded Maggie of the ice-cold Michael Johnson case.

"Johnny, you are *retired*," she said, rather firmly. "Can't you just let Kevin and the squad handle this?" Maggie remembered the case quite well – and the way it had affected Burke at the time.

"C'mon, Maggie," he implored. "How can I not help this poor kid? And, yeah, I'm curious. This case has been a thorn in my side for a long time. I can always turn it over to Kevin if anything turns up."

Keeping his word to Alex, Burke didn't tell Maggie about the old airline ticket. He told her the same thing he'd told Kevin – that while it was probably a wild goose chase, he somehow felt obliged to look into it for the young man.

"He was a cop, Maggie," Burke said quietly. "He was Kevin's age."

Maggie reached out and took one of Burke's hands, giving it a squeeze. She understood. She always did.

With a Jack Daniel's on-the-rocks in hand, Burke cooked three New York strip steaks on the grill. During dinner on the patio, Alex told Burke and Maggie a little about his life in Hattiesburg. His mother taught at Hattiesburg High School, and his father had been a cop. He didn't have any brothers or sisters. Maggie and Burke looked at each other and smiled, realizing the similarity to their own little nuclear family.

Alex's mom, Michelle, grew up in Jackson, Mississippi. His dad came from the coast, near Biloxi. They'd met in Hattiesburg, as college students at Southern Miss. Michael Johnson played football on a scholarship, and was accepted into the Air Force ROTC program. All of his young life he'd been enchanted by the history of the Tuskegee Airmen, and had dreams of being a pilot himself one day. Unfortunately, a congenital heart problem put an end to both the football and his chances of ever being a pilot. Discouraged, Michael dropped out of school and before long found himself painting houses, banging nails, hanging sheetrock – whatever trade work he could find.

But they had stayed together – *Mike and Michelle* – and were married right after Michelle graduated from Southern Miss, settling in Hattiesburg. Michelle began her teaching career, and after several years and too many dead-end jobs, Michael eventually enrolled at the police academy. That's when the marriage started to fall apart.

"I think Mom had a hard time supporting Dad's career choice," Alex said with a shrug. Burke and Maggie again exchanged glances.

"And then, Mom got pregnant with me," Alex said. "I think that kept them together for a few more years."

Alex was five when his parents finally divorced, and he'd always lived with his mother, spending time with his dad on weekends. From the way Alex talked, both Burke and Maggie could tell that while he was closer to his mother, he loved both of his parents. Burke thought that the young man's current quest was proof of that. He wanted to ask Alex about Michael Johnson's relationship with Mr. Henry Robinson, Charles Robinson's father, but not in front of Maggie.

After dinner, they all watched a Cincinnati Red's game on TV and started a Scrabble match – Alex told them he and his mother often played. He wasn't much of a jock or a baseball fan, he said, but he'd been to some Southern Miss football and basketball games with his dad, when he was still alive. Before long, Burke and Maggie could tell Alex was tired. The long bus trip was catching up to him, and he was grateful when they suggested that he go to bed.

Maggie decided to turn in also, and Burke kissed her goodnight. Alone now, he sat down at the dining room table and opened the Michael Johnson file. The coroner's report was right on top, and Burke read it through. Michael Johnson had probably died from a combination of blunt force trauma to the front of the skull and drowning. His skull was severely fractured, but water was found in his lungs, meaning that he was still alive when he went into the river, if just barely. A serious laceration occurred where the skull had been crushed. There was some bone damage to one shoulder, plus abrasions and some bruising in a manner consistent with what might occur in a fall from a good height. *Like the top of Huffman Dam.*

Burke went through the file, which mostly consisted of his own handwritten notes, and the same notes again, typed up on his computer. Johnson's wallet, containing $182.00 in cash and two credit cards, had been buttoned into one rear pocket, and his police badge was found in the other. The front pockets were empty – no cell phone and no keys – probably washed out in the river. The badge and the wallet had been returned to Michelle Johnson.

It had been determined that Johnson arrived in Dayton in the early afternoon, the day before his body was spotted by a motorist while crossing the river on Route 444. The US Airways flight from Philadelphia had originated in Hattiesburg, Mississippi, with one other stop in Atlanta. The keys to a car that Johnson rented at the airport – he had been alone – were found on the front seat of the car when the car was discovered on the south side of Huffman Dam. Not long after the body was found, the Riverside Police had located the car, parked with the front windows open, at the side of Marl Road, right where the road ended and the Huffman Prairie Bikeway began. Marl Road, just off of Route 444, was once a two-lane blacktop road across the top of the damn, but it had been closed to vehicular traffic for years.

The weather had been hot and dry for weeks around the time of Johnson's death, so no tire tracks were found. There was absolutely no evidence of a struggle – not in or around the car, and not on the bikeway across the dam. In fact, there had been no evidence, *period.*

Burke looked at a copy of the car rental receipt, and another one from the hotel that Johnson had booked himself into. The hotel was just off Harshman Road across from the Air Force Museum, not much more than a mile from where his body was found. A simple check of the local hotels had turned up the booking which had been made from Johnson's cell phone – the phone that was never found. But according to cell phone records, other than three nuisance calls, there were no calls dialed out or received on Johnson's phone that day.

The hotel room had been booked for two nights. An inspection of the room showed that the bed had not been slept in, and one piece of carry-on luggage was found, containing only clothing and toiletries. A return ticket was lying on the bed along with some change, a paperback crime novel, and a few brochures pertaining to the National Museum of the United States Air Force. It was determined that Johnson had flown with only the carry-on bag, and from this Burke had surmised that Johnson did not travel with a weapon. There would have been paperwork filed with the airline, and the weapon would not have been contained in a carry-on bag, but in a checked-through bag.

One hotel employee said that Johnson had been alone when he checked in. Another employee said that a man had called, claiming to be an old friend of Michael's, wanting to know his room number so that he could surprise him. The employee had given the caller the number. Records showed that the call lasted just fifty-seven seconds, and had come from a pay phone in the entrance area of a Save-A-Lot grocery store located on Dayton Yellow Springs Road in Fairborn, at 9:04 in the evening on the day Johnson arrived in Dayton – the day before he was spotted in the river. Burke had sent two of his squad members to check out the Save-A-Lot, but no one there could tell them anything. A plea to the public, asking if anyone had noticed someone using the phone at that time, had also proved unsuccessful, but Burke's gut told him that call was related to the death.

Burke looked through the notes he'd written on his trip down to Hattiesburg, when he escorted Michael Johnson's coffin back home on a commercial flight. According to everyone Burke had interviewed, including Johnson's ex-wife Michelle, his young son Alex, his boss – Luther Banks, the Hattiesburg Police chief – and seven or eight fellow officers and a few other police department employees, Johnson was a bit of a loner, hanging out occasionally with some of the other officers and spending time on the weekends with his son. There had been one friend, an older man named Mr. Robinson, but he had died several years previously. No one knew why Johnson had travelled to Dayton, or was even aware that he'd done so. He'd been on a week of paid vacation leave.

Johnson's neighbors said the cop mostly kept to himself, mowed his own lawn, and was always polite and cordial whenever they saw him in the neighborhood. No one recalled seeing visitors at his house, except for his son, Alex, and an older Black man, years ago, probably Henry Robinson.

With the help of the Hattiesburg Police, Burke had carefully searched Johnson's small house, where nothing of real interest was found. There had been shelves full of aviation related books and magazines, and several expensive-looking aircraft models, some hanging, some on stands. Johnson's computer turned up nothing that seemed to be related to his death, other than a slew of web searches for the Air Force Museum, Wright-Patterson AFB in general, and Dayton and Riverside hotels. There was no land line phone at the house, and cell phone records indicated that Johnson had booked his flight using the missing phone.

Burke now realized that during the initial investigation, there was every indication that Johnson had travelled alone, and no one had really bothered to check this out with the airline reservation office. *Michael Johnson had probably booked two tickets*, Burke thought now, *one for himself and one for Charles A. Robinson that was never used.*

"Man, did we fuck that up," Burke mumbled to himself.

So why *hadn't* Charles gone to Dayton? And what *had* happened to Michael Johnson, a Black cop from the South who'd made the trip

– apparently to visit the Air Force Museum – and ended up dead? There was a lot more to the story. Burke knew it then – but he never found out what it was – and he knew it now.

He read the section in the file pertaining to the questioning of a member of the Dayton Outlaws, a local biker gang with a clubhouse located on the city's west end. The Outlaws didn't like being known as a gang, preferring *club* instead. Years before, Burke had assisted the FBI in bringing down a local white supremacist group with ties to the Outlaws. After the media reports of Michael Johnson's death, and a public plea for help in solving the case from the DPD, Burke had received an anonymous tip that a particularly nefarious Outlaw member – nicknamed "Crotch" – had been bragging around town that he "offed the nigger cop." When Crotch was hauled in and questioned, he actually broke down and cried like a baby as he pleaded his case, saying he made it all up. As it turned out, he'd been in Florida at the time of Johnson's death. That useless, dead-end tip had been the only public help offered in the case.

Finally, Burke looked at the emails that had passed between him and Lamar Presley, the Special Agent in Charge at the FBI district field office in Cincinnati at the time of the investigation into Michael Johnson's death. Presley, whom Burke had gotten to know through the white supremacist case, had initially been eager to support the Johnson investigation, but he'd backed off, suddenly and reluctantly, "at the insistence of his superiors in Washington." The explanation had always mystified Burke.

Burke closed the file and put it back in the plastic garbage bag. *Garbage was right!* Maybe he could track down a number for Charles Robinson and just talk to him over the phone, but he quickly dismissed the idea. *You can't see someone squirm over the phone.*

He called USAirways, reserving two seats on a flight to Hattiesburg for the day after next. Alex had seemed pretty excited when Burke asked him if he would like to stick around for a day and visit the Air Force Museum, so that was the plan.

9

Brian Lopez

Right around the same time that Burke called it a night, Brian Lopez was finishing his third boilermaker and staring myopically across the expanse of the dimly lit gentleman's club. He was sitting where he always sat, at the corner table farthest away from the elevated stage. A naked dancer was writhing on the stage to crude catcalls from a handful of drunken patrons – mostly enlisted airmen and off-duty cops – as they flipped dollar bills onto the stage. *Maybe I should shoot myself,* Brian thought. *Maybe I should go out to the car and get my gun and shoot all these stupid motherfuckers and then shoot myself.*

Three boilermakers down and Brian's brain slipped into a familiar darkness. The darkness came often, when he sat drinking alone in a corner, at this or any of the other Dayton strip joints where he spent most evenings. The club owners and bartenders all knew him by name. So did the girls. Brian had dated one of the girls for a short while, until she'd died the previous summer in a tragic fall from her apartment window. After that, Brian changed. He was a different man. They all felt sorry for him, but no one knew about the darkness.

In fact, no one knew much at all about Brian Lopez. He was handsome. He was from Texas. His mother was Irish and his father was Mexican. He worked at the base for a private contractor. That was about it. Brian had been hanging out in the strip clubs for many years, but that had stopped when he hooked up with Sarah Sheldrake, a young, exotic, Chinese-American dancer who worked in several of the clubs. They were a beautiful couple, everyone agreed. They'd fallen madly in love, and Brian was eventually spending most of his free time at Sarah's high-rise apartment on Dayton's north side. And then Sarah died. Brian had been questioned by the police, but it was easily proven that he'd been working at the time of her death, and his grief was undeniable. The death was determined a terrible accident, a misstep while foolishly trying to wash the outside of a window. A tragedy.

After that, Brian was back in the clubs drinking heavily. He always came in alone, sat by himself, and left alone. He got drunk on boilermakers – Jim Beam and pints of draft – but never so drunk that he couldn't walk out in a straight line and drive himself home – wherever that was. No one seemed to know. He usually quit after three boilermakers.

Actually, there was a *lot* to not know about Brian Lopez. He'd enlisted in the Marines on September 13, 2001, two days after the World Trade Center collapsed into rubble. As a Marine sniper in a Force Recon platoon, he'd served in Iraq, in 2003, and later in Afghanistan. Through a series of battlefield promotions, Brian quickly rose to the rank of staff sergeant, and was honored as the only enlisted Marine who served as an advisor on the creation of the new Special Operations Command in early 2006. Shortly after that he quit the Marines, making the jump from special ops to black ops, when he was aggressively recruited by BlackSnake Security, a civilian contractor funded by the CIA's National Clandestine Service. BlackSnake offered Brian a $125,000 starting salary – plus bonuses – and he'd been stationed at Wright-Patterson AFB since the summer of 2007.

It didn't happen every night, the darkness, but it did tonight. Brian would handle it, just the way he always handled it. Just the way he could always handle *anything*. It's why he'd been recruited by BlackSnake in the first place. He was a hard-ass motherfucker and he did what he was told. He was loyal, perhaps to a fault. He'd done things as a Marine that he wasn't proud of, but he'd been told to do them. He'd done things for BlackSnake. He knew things he wished he didn't know, and sometimes he wished he could shoot himself in the head. But he was a hard-ass motherfucker, and tonight he would walk out of this club in a straight line and take himself home, wherever that was.

10

North Dayton: The Previous Summer

Sarah Sheldrake went to the door and looked through the peep hole. All she could see was a large bunch of yellow roses being waved back and forth. *Brian.* He must have gotten out of work somehow and this was his idea of a surprise – he was always buying her flowers.

When she opened the door, she didn't recognize the man who was standing there. It was not Brian Lopez. The man was wearing gloves, and in one hand he was holding a small stun gun, which he immediately jammed into her stomach, immobilizing her. The man came through the doorway, dropped the roses, and caught Sarah by the head before she fell. Kicking the door closed behind him, he stunned her a second time and then stuffed the weapon into his belt. The gun had been designed to minimize marking, and he knew from experience that the mark it left would be hard to identify. Before Sarah had time to recover, he executed a Marine blood choke to her neck, putting pressure on her carotid artery. She quickly passed out. There was no struggle.

It wasn't the first time he'd been in the 7th floor apartment. The television was on. He carried Sarah across the living room to the dining area just off the kitchen and dropped her limp body on the floor. In the kitchen cabinet under the sink, he grabbed a bottle of Windex, then ripped off some paper towels from a roll on the counter. Opening one side of a large, old-style metal casement window, he removed the screen and leaned out. The window faced a side alley, and almost directly below was a dumpster. He sprayed Windex over the entire outside half of the unopened window, wiped a portion of it with the paper towels, and dropped the moistened towels to the ground below. He looked down at the dimly lit alley and saw no sign of human activity.

Sarah was just coming to. He picked her up, folded her over the edge of the sill with her head hanging out the window, lifted her legs and tipped her out. He held his breath as Sarah fell, but the sound from the impact was not as loud as he thought it might be. He looked out and listened, once again detecting no human activity. Leaving the window open, he placed the Windex and a few paper towels on the inside sill, then took a chair from the dining room and laid it on its side on the carpet in front of the window. He turned off the TV, picked up the bunch of roses, and took a quick look around. The only sound he could hear was coming from the air conditioning. He slipped out, and the door locked behind him. He'd been in the apartment for just under three minutes.

11

Like Father, Like Son

Alex emerged from the guest room at 10:30 the next morning, yawning and apologizing for sleeping so late. Maggie had gone off to run some errands, and Burke offered to cook up some bacon and eggs for the young man. Burke had been up for hours, reading the morning paper, doing the crossword puzzle, and going for his regular three-mile walk through the neighborhood.

"I booked us a flight to Hattiesburg for tomorrow morning," he said, flipping the eggs. "We'll get there around three in the afternoon."

"Us? You mean you and me?" Alex was amazed.

"Yeah, us. I want to talk to Charles Robinson," said Burke, smiling and high-fiving Alex. "Oh, and I called the Air Force Museum. The IMAX Theater is showing a film called *Air Racers*. It's about the fastest airplane race in the world – the Reno National Championships. Should we go see it?"

"Definitely!" said Alex. "Sounds awesome! I've never been to an IMAX movie."

After a top-down drive out to Riverside, Burke and Alex spent the late morning and early afternoon wandering through the Air Force Museum, inside and out. Burke acted as Alex's personal guide, and they lingered at all of his favorite displays. For as long as he could remember, Burke had loved the museum, and he'd passed that love on to his own son. Ever since Kevin was a boy, they came at least once a year – to check out an IMAX film, or to keep up with any new aircraft or displays.

Burke took Alex through John F. Kennedy's *Air Force One*, and they walked around the huge B-29 Superfortress called the *Bockscar*, named after the plane's first commander, Captain Frederick Bock. It was the *Bockscar* that dropped the "Fat Man" atomic bomb on Nagasaki. Alex took a special interest in the Tuskegee Airmen display.

"We have a little museum in Hattiesburg," he said. "The African American Military History Museum. They have a display like this in there. I think that's where my dad met Mr. Robinson – you know, Charles Robinson's father?"

"I've been meaning to ask you about that," Burke said. "How long ago did they meet?"

"*Long* time ago," said Alex. "Like I said, Dad was always really into flying – even after he found out that he couldn't, because of his heart. I think Mr. Robinson had something to do with the military museum – like he was on the board of directors or something. But I think he was in the Air Force once, maybe even a Tuskegee Airman."

"You said they were close friends," said Burke. "How close?"

"Well, he was almost like a father to my dad, who never really knew his *real* father. I think Mr. Robinson helped Dad get into the ROTC program at Southern Miss. Dad was pretty sad when Mr. Robinson died."

After a quick lunch in the museum cafeteria, Burke and Alex watched the forty-minute film on the IMAX screen. Alex seemed pretty excited by the dizzying effect of the giant, six-story-high wrap-around screen and the monster sound system. Afterward, as they wandered among some of the aircraft displayed outdoors, Burke noticed that Alex's interest in the museum was fading. He seemed pensive. Burke was about to ask him if he'd seen enough, when Alex stopped and looked at him.

"Cap, do you think you could show me where my dad died?"

Burke was not completely surprised by the question, in fact, he'd half expected it at some point.

"Sure," said Burke. "It's not far from here."

They got back into the Camaro, and just before turning out of the museum entrance, Burke stopped and pointed off to the left, down Springfield Street.

"That's the hotel your dad was booked into," he told Alex. "Right down there. Do you want to see it?"

"No," said Alex, leaning forward and looking down the road. "That's okay."

Within minutes, Burke found the entrance to the dam facility that Scott Kaminsky, the Riverside Police chief, had directed him and Kevin to four years ago. It all seemed pretty much the same to Burke as he drove in through the woodlot, bearing right at what appeared to be a cluster of filtration silos, and out into the open area next to the Mad River. *The grass is a little greener than it was then*, Burke thought.

He parked the car, and together they walked down to the riverbank. Burke noticed that the water was higher now than it had been four years ago. The driftwood log that had caught Michael Johnson was long gone, but there were others now, stranded along the bank. Standing at the top of the bank, Burke pointed down.

"Right about here. He was hooked onto an old log. The dam's over there."

Burke watched the boy contemplate the spot where his father had probably died. Alex didn't climb down to the water's edge as Burke expected, but squatted on his heels and crossed his arms across his knees, like a TV Indian, and looked back and forth between the dam and the river bank in front of him.

"Take your time here," Burke said, knowingly. "I'm in no hurry."

He walked back to the car and left Alex alone with his thoughts. At one point Alex rested his forehead on his crossed arms, and Burke could tell that he was crying. He guessed that after four years of wondering, Alex must still be trying to imagine the last moments of his father's life – and his brutal, mysterious death. Eventually, Alex got up and walked back toward the car, wiping his nose with a cloth handkerchief that he pulled from a back pocket of his shorts. Burke remembered, from the case file he'd read the night before, that Michael

Johnson had also been carrying a cloth handkerchief. *Like father, like son.*

"Can we go up on the dam, Cap?" asked Alex, stuffing the handkerchief back in his pocket.

Burke drove out the way they'd come in, turned onto Rt. 444, and after just a few hundred yards, he turned left and pulled onto Marl Road.

"This is where the Riverside Police found your dad's rental car," said Burke, parking the car at the side of the road. "Right here."

They got out, and Alex followed Burke past a vehicle barricade and onto the bikeway that crossed over the dam. It was a short walk to the top of the dam causeway, a hundred yards at most. Together, they looked over the guardrail on the east side of the dam, and down at the concrete conduits, some fifty feet below the roadway. Water raced through the conduits from the small reservoir lake created by the dam and flowed west toward Dayton. Burke thought about all the time he'd spent around the dam as a boy. On many Sundays, his family – along with various aunts, uncles, and cousins – had picnicked there at Huffman Dam Park. They swam and fished the lake, and picked wild blackberries in the scrub along the railroad tracks just below the Wright Brothers Memorial on the south side of the dam. They hunted morel mushrooms – *sponges and spikes* – on the north side, along a wooded hillside above Lower Valley Pike.

Burke could only imagine what the young man was thinking. Alex peered down at the hard, unforgiving concrete, and the rushing water. Without talking, they crossed the roadway to the west side where the river water shot through the conduit on the other side of the damn. Burke watched Alex look down the river to the spot where his father's body was found. Alex stared for a long time, but there were no more tears.

"Okay," he said, finally. "I'm good now."

Burke patted Alex gently on the back, and rested his hand on the boy's shoulder for a brief moment.

"Thanks, Cap," Alex said. "Thanks for bringing me here."

That evening, Burke and Maggie took Alex out to Jay's, their favorite seafood restaurant down in the old Oregon district, just east of downtown Dayton. After that, they went back to the house and finished the Scrabble game they'd all started the night before. Maggie won the match, going out with *a-v-i-a-t-o-r-s*, hitting two triple word scores and using all seven letters. Alex was yawning, and they all decided to turn in. Maggie had an 8:08 tee time with some of her golfing girlfriends, and Burke planned to drop in at the squad room on the way to the airport for the 10:06 flight that he'd booked to Hattiesburg.

12

Private Dick

Burke was up early the next day. He scanned and copied some of the pages from the Michael Johnson file that he thought might be useful. "Not much here," he said to himself, shaking his head.

Maggie left with one of her golfing buddies, while Burke and Alex hurried through a breakfast of cold cereal, bananas, O.J. and coffee. It was a beautiful, summer morning as they drove into downtown Dayton, and Burke pulled the Camaro into the parking lot behind the Police Department. Alex was happy to wait in the car, and Burke trotted around the building to the front door, apologized to Smitty for being in such a hurry, and ran up the stairs.

"Whoa! Look who's here again," Tarisa exclaimed when Burke got up to the squad room. He greeted the squad members, then dropped the Michael Johnson file on Kevin's desk.

"Thanks, Kevin," he said. "Hope nobody missed it."

"No problem, Pop," Kevin said. "But here, I have something else for you." He opened a desk drawer and pulled out a yellow, business-size envelope, handing it to Burke.

"What's this?" Burke asked, looking at the envelope, and then up at Kevin's grinning face.

"An application for an Ohio private investigator's license," said Kevin, still grinning. "I downloaded it for you."

"Jesus, Kevin. What the hell do I want this for?" Burke said, shrugging.

"You want *this* so that the next time you come down here wanting to get into the files, I might actually – *legally* – be allowed to let you see them," Kevin said.

"Holy shit, Kevin. Are you serious?"

"Goddamn right, I'm serious," said Kevin. "Look, Pop. If you're going to be snooping around, you need to be legal. Hell, you know how this works."

"Yeah, but it's not like I'm going to be doing this every day. And I'm not charging anybody any money. I'm doing this on my own damn dime."

"Look, Pop, just do it," said Kevin. "There's nothing much to it. I called the licensing office and explained who you were, and they said they could *grandfather* you in on most of the application. You don't even have to take an exam or anything. Hell, I filled out most of it for you already. Just finish it up and sign the goddamn thing and I'll send it in for you. Do it for *me*, okay?"

Burke looked at Kevin, then down at the envelope, and sighed. Kevin knew he had him.

"Jesus, Kevin," Burke said, shaking his head. "Me? A private dick? They're nothing but a big pain in the ass."

"Yeah, Pop. Nothing like *you*." Kevin said, slapping his father on the back. "Did I mention that there's a fee for the license?"

Burke didn't tell Kevin much of anything except that he was flying to Hattiesburg with Alex, and that he would be gone for a couple of days. They bumped knuckles and Burke hurried out of the squad room, with the Ohio private investigator license application in hand.

* * *

"I've never flown before," Alex said, surprising Burke on the way to the airport. He was very excited throughout the trip, especially the take-offs and landings, showing no fear. "Oh, man!" he must have said a dozen times, looking down from his window seat.

The flight to Hattiesburg – with changes in Philadelphia and Atlanta – was uneventful, and Burke recalled that Michael Johnson had made the same changes four years ago when he flew to Dayton. As they touched down in Mississippi, the pilot welcomed them to Hattiesburg and informed them that the temperature was a very warm 98 degrees.

"Good lord, Alex," said Burke when they walked down the steps of the air-conditioned turbo-prop and into the late afternoon Mississippi sunshine. "It's too goddamn hot!"

Michelle Johnson had offered to pick them up at the airport, but Burke wanted to rent a car. She'd insisted that he stay with her and Alex at their house, and Burke was happy to agree. Alex directed Burke on the twenty-minute ride to the house on the east side of Hattiesburg, in a section of town known as The Avenues, near the Southern Miss campus. When Burke and Alex arrived, Michelle came out to the driveway and hugged her somewhat embarrassed son for a long time. From what Burke could remember, she looked about the same as when he'd met her four years ago.

"It's good to see you, too, Captain Burke," she said, ignoring Burke's outstretched hand and hugging him as well. "Thank you so much for bringing Alex home."

"My pleasure," Burke said, patting Alex's shoulder. "He's a fine young man. And please, call me John. I'm retired now."

Michelle set Burke up in a small guest room – which appeared to be the repository for much of Michael Johnson's aviation book collection. She made light of the books and explained that Alex wouldn't let her get rid of them.

"I got some nice shrimp for dinner. Alex told me on the phone that you liked seafood," Michelle said. "It won't be ready for a while if you'd like to take a walk."

"It's awful hot out there, but I'd love a walk," said Burke. "Airplane seats seem to keep getting smaller."

He changed into shorts and sneakers and started out at a brisk pace, breaking a sweat instantly in the thick heat. The thirty-minute walk seemed to clear both his mind and body from the day spent in airplanes and airports. Back at the house, he took a quick shower and spent a few minutes browsing through Michael Johnson's library.

Michelle asked Burke to open a bottle of cold dry Riesling –
allowing Alex one glass – and served a delicious Gulf shrimp and pasta
dinner. The three of them reminisced about Burke's earlier visit to
Hattiesburg. He explained to Michelle that even though he'd retired,
he still had an intense interest in the unsolved Michael Johnson case.
Alex showed his mother the old airline ticket he'd found, and at
Burke's urging, told her about the visit he'd made to Charles Robinson
– and about the ominous warning. Michelle sighed, and patted her
son's hand.

"Oh, Alex," she said, shaking her head.

There was a pause in the conversation, and Alex politely asked if
he could be excused from the table. When he was gone, Burke asked
Michelle what she knew about Charles Robinson.

"Not much," she said. "He's probably in his mid-sixties, maybe a
little older. He's always in a motorized wheelchair, and he drives one
of those special vans – gets in and out by himself. I've seen him do it
at the Winn-Dixie. I think he got hurt in a plane crash, at least I think
that's what Mike said about him."

"Have you ever talked to him?" asked Burke.

"Just said hello once or twice, in the store," Michelle said. "You
know, just being polite. I don't think he has any idea who I am. He's
kind of a recluse from what I hear."

"But you knew his father, Henry Robinson?" Burke asked.

"Oh yes – Mr. Robinson," she said. "He and Mike were extremely
close. Mike was very, very sad when Mr. Robinson died. Years ago, he
sort of sponsored Mike – you know, like a Big Brother. Mr. Robinson,
he'd been a Tuskegee Airman during World War Two, and Mike
idolized him. I think he was a lieutenant colonel in the Air Force a long
time ago."

"But Mike didn't know his son Charles very well?" asked Burke.

"Well, not back then anyway," Michelle said. "And I never kept
up with Mike's life much after we split – or his friends. As far as I
know, Charles never lived in Hattiesburg until after Mr. Robinson died
and he inherited his father's house. I believe he lived in New Orleans
before that."

"And I take it you still have no idea why Mike went to Dayton in the first place, or why Charles Robinson had planned to go with him?"

"No idea. "What do *you* think it was all about?"

"No idea," Burke said, shaking his head. "Absolutely none. But I'm going to try to pay Charles a surprise visit tomorrow. Alex wants to go with me, but I told him he should maybe check with you. I know you've been worried."

"I don't know." Michelle shrugged. "Do you think there's any real danger involved? I mean, what do you make of all that *warning* stuff?"

"I'm not sure what to make of it," Burke told her. "On one hand it sounds like Charles Robinson might be a paranoid nut job. On the other hand, your ex-husband is dead. And while it could have been an accident – or even a suicide – nobody in the Dayton Police Department thinks so. And apparently, Charles had planned to go to Dayton with Mike. I'd like to find out why he didn't."

"Well, John, if you think it's okay."

"Good," Burke said. "Don't worry – I'll take care of him. I think it will help to have him there. Maybe Charles will feel sorry for him. Maybe he'll open up. We'll see."

After dinner, Burke insisted on helping clean up, then he took another walk around the neighborhood, this time with Michelle. It was cooler now, and some of the neighbors were relaxing on their porches or watering plants in the yards. He noticed that the neighbors were pretty well mixed, Black and white. Michelle seemed to know everyone, and Burke was amused when she introduced him – without missing a beat – as one of her old professors, back in town visiting.

"Nobody needs to know you have anything to do with Mike's death," she whispered conspiratorially.

When they returned to the house, Michelle fixed them each a tall glass of ice water and they sat out on the front stoop. She told Burke about her life with Mike, and how they'd simply grown apart and eventually divorced.

"I didn't want him to quit school, and then I didn't want him to be a cop. It just didn't work out. He changed, *I* changed. We stayed together for a while after I had Alex, but you know, it just didn't work out," Michelle said. "Speaking of school, did Alex tell you that he was the class valedictorian at Hattiesburg High this past year?"

"No!" said Burke, snapping to attention. "Wow! No, he hasn't really told me a whole lot about himself. That's pretty impressive."

"He was accepted at Cornell University, up in New York," Michelle said. "They offered him a pretty good package, too, but it still would have cost me a bundle. I would have come up with the money somehow, but Alex insisted on staying here and going to Southern Miss. He said he wanted to be able to keep an eye on *me*."

They chatted a while longer, then decided it was time to turn in for the night. The air conditioning was on, and Burke's room was comfortably cool when he got into bed. He'd stashed the envelope that Kevin had given him into his carry-on bag, and now he pulled it out and looked through the private investigator license application. *What a pain in the ass*, Burke thought, but he knew Kevin was right – this was indeed how it worked.

13

Chuck

Burke slept soundly that night. It was still plenty hot the next morning, and after breakfast, he and Alex decided to wait until ten o'clock before they descended, unannounced, on Charles Robinson.

Alex directed Burke to the house on Adeline Street, and as they pulled into the driveway to park, Burke noticed a small movement of the curtain at one front window.

"Well, looks like *somebody's* home," he said to Alex.

Together they walked up the wheelchair ramp to the shaded porch, and Burke was about to knock when the door opened. Charles Robinson sat in a motorized wheelchair, with a newspaper folded on his lap. He looked briefly at Burke through the screen door, and then fixed Alex with a scowl that lasted for several seconds. Burke could see that Charles was probably about his own age, maybe a little older, with a full head of gray hair. His upper body looked strong, but his legs were very thin. Burke had a vague notion that he'd seen Charles somewhere before, but quickly dismissed the thought.

Motoring forward, Charles pushed the screen door open. "Hello, Alex," he said sternly, all the while looking up at Burke.

"Hello, Mr. Robinson," Alex said, offering his hand in greeting. "This is Captain John Burke, from Dayton, Ohio. Cap, this is Mr. Charles Robinson."

Burke was struck once again by Alex's polite manner, now referring to Charles as Mr. Robinson.

"*Dayton*? Captain of *what*, exactly?" Robinson asked, shaking Alex's hand and then Burke's.

"Actually, nothing anymore," Burke said with a grin. "I'm retired."

"From the service?" Charles looked intently at Burke and gripped his hand tightly.

"No, no. I used to be head of the homicide division at the Dayton Police Department. Just call me John."

Charles let go of Burke's hand and motored forward onto the porch, edging them out of the way. "Excuse me," he said. Reaching around behind him, he grabbed the door handle and pulled the door shut. *Is there someone else inside?* Burke wondered.

Now they were all on the porch and Charles let the screen door bang shut behind him. He studied Burke's face again closely for several moments, and then looked at Alex.

"Well," he said, "I can't say that I'm happy to see you gentlemen. As a matter of fact, I think it's probably a very bad idea, you coming here."

"We're sorry to bother you, Charles," Burke said, "but Alex has asked me to help him figure out what happened to his father. I investigated Mike's death four years ago and pretty much came up empty-handed. I'm assuming you know what I'm talking about."

"Of course, I know," Charles said, clenching his jaw.

"I came down here to Hattiesburg back then, as part of my investigation, but your name never came up. Alex contacted me after he visited you last month – when he found your unused airline ticket. He said you tried to warn him off. Is that right?"

Charles sighed. He pulled a handkerchief from a pocket at the side of the wheelchair, wiped his brow, and pointed to a pair of padded deck chairs. "Why don't you guys sit down," he said. "It's too goddamn hot out here to be standing up."

"Should we go inside maybe?" asked Alex.

"No, it's safer to talk out here I think," said Charles.

He is a paranoid nut bag, Burke thought, as he and Alex sat down side by side. Charles wheeled over to face them, and Burke was glad they were now on the same level. Again, Charles seemed to be looking hard at Burke's face.

Charles hesitated, seeming to choose his words carefully. "First of all," he said at last, leaning forward, "I've never spoken about this with anyone. And I think you should both know that anyone who gets involved could be at risk."

He let that sink in as both Burke and Alex nodded. "I think whoever was responsible for Michael's death may be keeping track of me, too." He glanced at Alex. "Maybe you shouldn't get involved, son."

Alex's eyes were open wide as his gaze went from Charles to Burke, and then back to Charles.

"I'm not afraid," he said, sitting up, ramrod straight. "I want to find out who killed my dad."

Burke thought about what he'd said to Michelle – about keeping an eye on Alex. He wasn't sure where all this was going, but at this point, he still had his doubts about Charles Robinson's sanity.

"It's okay," Burke said to Charles. "I think Alex should know everything."

"Okay then," said Charles, again staring hard at Burke's face, actually squinting a bit, as if to get a better look.

"You know what, John, I think we know each other," he said. "From Riverside. Did you live in Riverside?"

"Good lord!" Burke sat forward in his chair. "I grew up there! Did *you* live in Riverside?"

"Yeah," said Charles. "Page Manor – base housing. My old man was a Major at Wright-Patt back then. You had a sister, am I right? Mary Burke?"

Page Manor was a vast mix of civilian and base housing, just across Airway Road from Wright Field, the original part of Wright-Patterson AFB that now was home to the Air Force Museum. The neighborhood that Burke grew up in was a ten-minute walk from Page Manor.

"Jesus," Burke said. "You knew Mary?"

"Hell, John," said Charles, "I knew *you*!"

Burke was racking his brain, trying to figure out how this could be. For many years, he'd repressed a lot of memories from that part of his life – another one of his issues – and he often had trouble recalling things. He knew he didn't know a whole lot of Black people back then – there sure hadn't been any in *his* neighborhood. Almost all the Black kids around there were Air Force kids from base housing.

"Jesus!" Burke exclaimed suddenly, almost coming out of the chair. "*Chuck Robinson*! You're Chuck Robinson!"

Charles was laughing as Burke grabbed his hand and shook it with both of his own. Alex sat there grinning at this new development. The tension that had existed just moments before dissolved instantly.

"I hope you don't mind my saying so," Charles admitted, "but I had the *hots* for your big sister. I really thought she was something. But hell, you know how it was back then. She was white. I was Black. That just was *not* going to happen."

Back in the mid-1960s, Mary had attended a Catholic high school while Charles went to Riverside High, the same school where Burke went after he finished grade school at St. Nicks. Burke and Charles had even been on the Riverside High wrestling team together for one year – Charles as a senior, Burke as a freshman. Mary and some of her Catholic friends sometimes hung out with the Riverside kids, including Chuck. Burke recalled the time when he watched Chuck back down a big, mean white kid from the neighborhood. The boy had been picking on a younger, smaller, white friend of Chuck's, and Chuck called him out. There was going to be a fight in the alley behind the Page Manor shopping center, but the mean kid never showed up.

"Mary and I even went on a date once. Well, sort of a date. I don't think either one of us ever called it that," Charles said. "We went out to Yellow Springs – in my dad's car – and we walked around town. Then we had a picnic in Glen Helen. And you know what? Nobody gave us any shit."

Glen Helen was a little nature preserve that belonged to Antioch College. Yellow Springs had long been a bastion for liberal causes – especially civil rights – ever since the days of the Underground

Railroad. There were quite a few "salt n' pepper" couples living there already in the early 1960s.

"Jesus, Chuck, you were always nice to me," Burke said. "A lot of Mary's friends just ignored me."

"Please, call me Charles. I haven't been Chuck since college."

"Goddamn," said Burke. "I had this funny feeling when I first saw you, but now I can really see it. You still look the same in a lot of ways."

"Same with you, John – I guess we're okay for a couple of old farts," Charles said, laughing.

Alex was clearly amused at the direction the conversation had taken. He couldn't wait to tell his mom.

"So – *Charles*," said Burke, "do you mind if I ask what the hell happened to your legs?"

"Not at all," Charles replied, looking down and patting his withered thighs. "I was in a mid-air jet collision."

"Holy shit!" said Burke.

"Yeah, holy shit is right. After Riverside I went to Ohio State. I got into the Air Force ROTC program, and when I graduated, I got accepted into flight school. The war was still going full tilt in Vietnam and they were training a lot of pilots. I was stationed at Reese Air Force Base, over near Lubbock, Texas." He fell silent for a moment, remembering.

"Anyway, I was in the back seat of a T-38, behind my instructor, and we clipped the wing of another T-38. *In mid-fucking-air!*" Charles actually grimaced at the thought.

"Oh my god!" Alex blurted.

"We had to punch out. Apparently, the canopy didn't quite open all the way when we ejected, and I got knocked cold. When I woke up, I was strapped down in an ambulance with a broken spine – probably happened when I landed." Charles shook his head. "The other thirty-eight bailed out too, but nobody else got hurt – and they never, *ever*, told me what exactly the fuck went wrong."

"Jesus, Charles," Burke said. "That's horrible."

"Yeah," said Charles, nodding his head, "tell me about it. Anyway, after that I came to Hattiesburg and lived with my folks. Mom was from here, so they moved back down when Dad retired from the Air Force. I went back to school at Southern Miss and majored in history. Eventually, I got into a PhD program at Tulane and moved to New Orleans. They hired me at Xavier University and I've been teaching there for thirty-five years. Just one class a week now, just for something to do."

"Your parents moved back down here from Dayton?" asked Burke.

"No, no," Charles said, shaking his head. "From Washington. Right after the Air Force closed down Blue Book, they moved Dad to the Pentagon so they could keep an eye on him. He quit the Air Force pretty soon after that and they moved down here and bought this house. Dad did some consulting for a while, for a couple of different defense contractors, and then he took up golf and started fooling around in the stock market. Turns out he was pretty good at it – not at golf, but the stock market. Mom died from breast cancer in 2002, two years before Dad. She'd always wanted to visit China, so Dad took her there the year before she died."

Burke listened, but he fixated on something Charles had said, something that sounded vaguely familiar.

"What the hell is *Blue Book*?" he asked.

14

Whipping Boy

"*Blue Book?*" Charles sat back in his wheelchair. "Hell, John – Project Blue Book! That's what started this whole goddamn mess."

"*What* mess?" Burke asked. "You mean Michael Johnson's death?"

"Yes." Charles nodded. "*And* my father's death."

He looked at Alex. "I'm afraid I'm the one who got your dad involved – and I'm very, very sorry about that. I hope you can forgive me. It never crossed my mind that such an awful thing would happen, and I can only guess, now, *why* it happened."

"Well, yeah, I forgive you . . . I guess," said Alex with a shrug. "But what *did* happen?"

"Well, unfortunately, I can't tell you that for sure. Again, I can only speculate."

"But what's Project Blue Book got to do with all of this?" asked a confused Burke. "I thought it had something to do with UFOs. Hell, there's even a silly little display about it in the Air Force Museum. It's like the Air Force is making fun of that whole thing."

"Exactly," Charles said. "Just what the CIA wants you to think. And they made my poor dad the butt of the joke. Let me tell you about it . . ."

Like the historian he was, Charles started at the beginning, with his father. Henry Robinson was from a small town in North Carolina, and his parents had scrimped and saved to send him to college. He'd always been a good student, and in 1939 he was accepted at Hampton

Institute – now Hampton University, a historically Black college in Hampton, Virginia. "That's where he met my mom – Lorraine."

When World War II began, Henry was not very interested in joining the war effort until a friend of his told him about a program that the Army Air Force was starting at Tuskegee Institute in Alabama – another historically Black school – for training a squadron of Black fighter pilots. "Dad wasn't particularly patriotic back then, I'm pretty sure," Charles said. "I think he just liked the idea of flying."

"The Tuskegee Airmen," he continued, proudly. "The 99th Pursuit Squadron – declared combat ready in 1943. Dad flew a lot of combat missions over Northern Africa and Sicily, and by the end of the war, he was one of the squadron's most highly decorated pilots. "The krauts called him the Black Jack. *Schwartz Bube,* I think it was. Something like that." Charles snickered. "His buddies called him 'the Black Booby'."

"Black Booby!" Alex repeated, grinning. "Excellent."

"After the war, Dad left the military, mostly over the issue of the segregation policy. He went back to finish his degree at Hampton, married Mom, and then . . ." Charles poked his chest with a thumb. "Moi."

Burke smiled. Alex laughed. "Then what?" he asked.

"Well, Dad went on to earn a master's degree in physics at the University of Chicago, and then a PhD at Cornell University. The Cornell physics department at that time included Hans Bethe . . . Bobby Wilson . . . Richard Feynman. They all worked on the Manhattan Project – the first atomic bomb. The bomb boys. That's what Dad and his friend, Martin, always called them."

Burke held up a hand, interrupting and turning to Alex. "By the way – your mom told me you were accepted at Cornell."

"Wow!" Charles was genuinely impressed, and he high-fived Alex. "Congratulations!"

"Thanks, Mr. Robinson," Alex said, somewhat wistfully. "But I'll stay here and go to Southern Miss – it's a lot cheaper for Mom."

Charles nodded sympathetically. Alex urged him to continue with Henry Robinson's story.

"Well, by that time, Harry Truman put an end to segregation in the military, and a new, separate branch was established – the United States Air Force. Dad decided he wanted to fly again, and despite being thirty-one years old they welcomed him into the Air Force. He joined at the lowest officer's rank – Second Lieutenant. Before long, he was the oldest First Lieutenant in the Air Force. He flew a handful of combat and support missions over Korea in a P-51 Mustang, left over from World War Two. Then he retrained in the F-86 Sabre jet."

"We saw both of those at the museum," Alex reminded Burke. They bumped knuckles.

"Well, Dad didn't much care for the jets," Charles said. "But he eventually shot down three Russian Migs, and that was one more than Buzz Aldrin shot down. They were good buddies. I remember Dad getting pretty emotional when Buzz walked on the moon."

Charles smiled to himself, remembering.

"After Korea, Dad was promoted to Captain, and throughout the early part of the Cold War he was stationed at various bases around the U.S. and in Europe, and then Southeast Asia. At first, he was a pilot instructor, but then it was mostly administrative positions. By the time the U.S. got involved in Vietnam in the early 1960s, Dad was a Major, and he was offered several positions there. But he turned them all down. He thought U.S. policy there was seriously flawed."

"And he was right," Burke said with a nod. "What a mess that was."

"Yeah," Charles agreed. "And that brings us to Project Blue Book. The Air Force always said that Dad's physics background was the reason why they made him the director of the project." Charles, frowned, and shook his head. "But he knew it was a thankless job. The Air Force was sticking it to him for not accepting a position in Vietnam. So, he took over Blue Book in 1963, and ran it until it was shut down in 1969."

"But it must have been pretty interesting," said Burke.

"No, it was a joke. He hated it from the start," Charles said angrily. "He never bitched to me about it, but I overheard him talking to my mother, and to Martin. He knew the entire program was merely a front run by the CIA, and had been from the beginning back in 1952. His main job was to debunk *everything* – every UFO report, every sighting, and every claim – and a lot of those reports were very serious and made by some *extremely* credible witnesses. A lot of hard evidence was generated, but the CIA was calling all the shots."

"So, did he get to see any real UFO evidence?" a wide-eyed Alex asked.

"I never really knew what all he saw," Charles said, patting his sweaty neck with a handkerchief. "Probably more than he ever told anybody. Martin, maybe. He could have told him, I suppose."

"So, who's Martin?" asked Burke. The name had come up several times.

"Martin Novak," Charles replied. "Dad's best friend. He was a nuclear chemist who taught at the Air Force Institute of Technology at Wright-Patt. They met when they were both working on advanced degrees at Cornell, back in the forties."

"Did he work with your dad on the UFO program?" Burke wished he had a notebook. *But it's probably better to keep this informal for now,* he thought. He would write something up later.

"Some, I think. I have no idea what all he knows. Not as much as Dad." Charles shrugged. "Martin did tell me once that even as the director of Blue Book, Dad had been denied access to some of the information that came into the program. There were several highly secure areas and buildings on the base that he'd never been allowed to enter. And guess who guarded those areas?"

"The CIA?" guessed Alex, his eyebrows arching.

Charles nodded. "Private security contractors *employed* by the CIA. Nasty fellows."

He wiped his brow and continued. "But Martin told me that as scientists, they'd both been asked to work with materials that he could only describe as 'otherworldly.' Occasionally, I think Dad was given access to material that he wouldn't talk about at all, with *anyone*, not even Martin."

"Wow!" Alex was bug-eyed.

Charles furrowed his brow and his eyes hardened. "Sometimes he'd be so upset that he couldn't eat or sleep for days. We'd know something was going on, but he wouldn't talk about it. To be honest, I think there were several times when he somehow breached security – maybe by accident, maybe on purpose – and saw something that he shouldn't have seen."

"But he debunked it all?" Burke asked. "Said it was all nonsense?"

"Well, yeah," said Charles. "He had to. Supposedly, Blue Book had two main missions. One was to determine if UFOs were a threat to national security, the other was to study the scientific data that was generated. The work was being done, but the public was never told the truth. Dad was forced to lie, and it was killing him."

"What if he'd told the truth?" asked Alex.

"Shit!" Charles exclaimed. "The Air Force would've crucified him. But, hell, by the mid '60s there were a lot of highly regarded scientists, and even some top brass that thought the whole project was illogical, unscientific – a travesty. Poor Dad, he was just the whipping boy."

"Jesus, Charles," said Burke. "How did he take being hushed up like that?"

"I don't know *how* he hung in there," Charles said, shaking his head. "I think he decided he wasn't going to let them win. He thought they wanted to get rid of him, and *they* most likely thought that he would quit the Air Force."

"He should have quit," said Alex.

"I agree completely," Charles replied. "Toward the end, the Air Force – actually, the CIA according to Dad – funded an 'independent' study of Blue Book. It was called the *Condon Report,* and it was short and sweet, very low-budget. When it wrapped up 1968, it concluded that not a single UFO report that had been investigated or evaluated by the Air Force had ever posed a threat to national security. It said something like, 'None of the evidence represented technological advancements or principles beyond the range of present-day scientific knowledge.' What a joke!"

"I'll bet your dad didn't think it was so funny," Burke said.

"Didn't matter what he thought," growled Charles. The report was generally accepted by the American scientific community, and that put an end to almost all serious academic interest in UFOs ever since. Blue Book was shut down in 1969. Good riddance!"

"Your dad must have been relieved," said Alex.

"I'm sure he was. But he was ordered to write his own summation on the project that would be made available to the general public. It was supposed to match the *Condon Report*, which it mostly did. He debunked over 12,500 UFO reports as . . . 'misidentifications of natural phenomena' I think he wrote. 'Clouds and stars.' 'Conventional aircraft.' He did note that around 700 sightings were classified as *unexplained*, but there was no evidence of 'extraterrestrial vehicles'. But Dad got in a parting shot, though – sort of. He *tried*, anyway."

"Like what?" Burke asked.

"Well, in a little paragraph at the end of his report, Dad stated that personally, he believed it was arrogant to think that human beings represented the only intelligent life in the universe, and that it was 'highly likely' that life did exist beyond earth, even though Project Blue Book had found no evidence of 'extraterrestrial visitation.'" Charles mimed air quotes.

"Good for him!" Alex grinned.

"I totally agree." Said Charles. "Dad's superiors ordered him to remove the paragraph from the report, but Dad refused. When the Air Force published the report, the paragraph was deleted anyway."

"That sucks!" exclaimed Alex.

"After that," Charles said, "Dad was 'promoted' to lieutenant colonel and assigned to the Pentagon. I guess they made it pretty clear there would be no further advancement in his military career. Within a year he quit the Air Force. He'd lost the battle."

15
Polonium-210

"Dad never actually told me how he felt, but I knew he was very angry about how he'd been treated. And he was bitter about what happened to me – my accident." Charles patted the arms of his wheel chair. "He'd tried to talk me out of joining the Air Force in the first place. But you know how it is, I wanted to spread my own wings, so to speak. Anyway, once he retired, he pretty much distanced himself from the Air Force. He was happy to help out at the little military museum here in town, but that was about it. I think his bitterness may have inadvertently led to Mike's death."

"Do you think *my* dad knew all this?" Alex asked. "I mean, you know, about how bitter your father was?"

"Probably just from what I told him," said Charles. "Dad didn't like to talk about it. But Mike and I talked about it a lot after Dad died. Once I'd figured out that he'd been murdered, I asked Mike to help me look into Dad's death."

"*Jesus Christ!*" Burke sat up. "Your dad was *murdered?*"

"I think so," said Charles calmly. "I'm almost certain."

"How?" asked Burke. "Who do you think did it?"

"Well, that's what Mike and I were trying to figure out," Charles said. "But I'm fairly certain Dad was poisoned."

"*Poisoned?*" Burke and Alex exclaimed in unison.

"Yeah. Do you remember, about six years ago, there was a Russian journalist who died in London, a former KGB agent. The Brits figured out he'd been poisoned with a radioactive substance called *polonium-*

210. All it took was a tiny amount, and everyone was pretty sure he'd been assassinated by the KGB. He'd sought asylum in England and was doing some work with MI6, the British secret service."

"I *do* remember that story," said Burke. "In fact, I was just thinking about it a few days ago. I read that the Palestinians think that's the same stuff that killed Yasser Arafat. They want to dig him up."

Alex glanced back and forth at the two men, puzzled.

"Exactly," said Charles. "Anyway, Dad died mysteriously. He'd been healthy as a horse and his death came right out of the blue. Nobody could figure it out. The doctors did every test they could think of here in Hattiesburg, and then more up at the U. of M. hospital in Jackson. They even tested for all the common poisons, but there was no explanation for the symptoms. Dizziness – vomiting – swelling of the stomach – loss of hair. There was nerve damage throughout his body. And then his heart failed. That's what was listed on his death certificate – *heart failure*. But he died the same way the Russian died."

"And you think the stuff that killed the KGB guy is the same thing that killed your dad?" Burke asked.

"I pretty much *know* it is," said Charles. He turned to Alex. "Do me a favor, will you, son? Go in the house – my office is just off the living room, to the right, you'll see it. There's a bookcase on the wall next to the desk. On the second shelf down there's a book called *Modern Nuclear Chemistry*. Could you please find it and bring it out here?"

Alex hopped up eagerly and went into the house. Burke looked at Charles and shook his head, thinking about everything the man had been telling them. He was beginning to think that Charles' paranoia was actually – *maybe* – justified.

Alex came back to the porch, and handed the book to Charles.

"Thanks, Alex." Charles opened the book and removed several letters that were pressed between the pages.

"So, way back when that Russian agent died," he said, "I read about it and saw it on the news – about the symptoms and how he died. And a big ol' light went on in my head. I went online and found everything I could about polonium-210 and radiation poisoning. And whaddya know? It *all* matched up with Dad's death. I also found out that the substance was extremely rare. Only about three ounces of the stuff is produced in a year – *worldwide* – and it is *very* highly regulated. The only countries in the world that would likely have access to polonium-210 are countries with nuclear programs. I had to share my thoughts with someone, so I wrote a letter to Martin Novak about it."

Charles held up a letter. "This was his reply."

He handed the letter to Burke. It was the same letter Charles had dug out and read himself just a few days earlier. Burke and Alex put their heads together and started to read what Martin Novak had written six years ago. The letter was on AFIT stationary and full of chemical calculations.

"You may want to skip to the end, after all the science," Charles suggested. He pulled out his handkerchief and patted at the beads of sweat that had formed on his face.

"Man! That is awesome!" Alex said, looking up when he'd finished reading. Burke agreed.

"So, did you have any of your dad's personal belongings anymore?" Burke asked. "To send to the lab in Switzerland?"

"Plenty," Charles said, stuffing the handkerchief back into a pocket of the wheelchair. "I inherited the house after he died, and I boxed up a lot of Dad's stuff and put it in the garage out back. Anyway, I found his Dopp kit – toothbrush, hair brush, razor – it was all in there. He had it in the hospital, and I ended up with it after he died. I had his wristwatch and a couple of his sweat-stained golf hats – lots of stuff. I wrote to Martin again, and here's the letter he sent me." He handed Burke another envelope. "It's the contact information at the Swiss lab."

Alex and Burke read the second letter together. This one was written on plain white stationary.

January 7, 2007

Dear Charles,

Here is my contact - a former colleague - in Lausanne. Be sure to mention my name in your inquiry. I expect he will be happy to help you out, but expect to pay a sizable fee.

Dr. Jürg Bütler
Swiss Institute of Radiation Physics
University Hospital of Lausanne
Rue du Bugnon 46
1011 Lausanne, Switzerland

Again, I urge caution. There are some circumstances involving Henry's trip to China in 2001 that you should be made aware of. I'd rather not discuss this matter in a letter. At some point we need to sit down together, face to face.

All the best,
Martin

"So, did you contact the lab?" Burke asked, handing the letter back.

"I did," said Charles, "And I sent them all of Dad's personal items. I waited quite a while, but then this letter finally came."

He took the last envelope from the open book on his lap and gave it to Alex. Burke and Alex read the letter from Dr. Jürg Bütler, written in English, verifying that Charles suspicions had been correct – unusually high traces of polonium-210 were found on many of Henry's items. Dr. Bütler pointed out that testing tissue taken from Henry Robinson's body was the only way to positively verify that polonium poisoning was indeed the cause of his death. A detailed report on the lab's findings was included with the letter. Alex folded it all, put it back in the envelope, and handed it back to Charles.

"Did you have your father's body exhumed?" Burke asked him.

"I didn't," Charles said. "You read Martin's letter. He'd counseled against it from the start, and I think he was right. I wanted to keep this quiet. And personally, I didn't need any more proof."

"Man," Burke said, leaning back and wiping his brow with his arm. He was more than a little spooked by the letters. "That part in Martin's first letter, cautioning you not to call or email him – what was that all about? Are you being watched, Charles?"

"Well, it's funny," Charles said. "After Mom and Dad got back from China, in 2001, Dad seemed to change. He'd grown sort of surly and quiet. Mom and I both noticed it. When Mom asked him about it, he said it was just old age. Said he was worried about her declining health. He spent a lot of time writing in his office, and he wouldn't tell us what he was writing, just that we would find out when he was finished. He wrote by hand – they didn't even own a computer, if you can believe it. After Mom died, all he *did* was write. Whatever it was he was writing he kept in a binder – a blue binder – locked in the top drawer of his desk. It's the same desk I use now."

"Did you ever get to read what he was writing?" asked Alex.

"Never," Charles said with a shrug. "After his death I wanted to get a look at the binder, but I couldn't find a key to the drawer. I had to have a locksmith come and open it. When he opened the drawer, the binder was gone."

"*Gone?*" exclaimed Burke.

"Gone," Charles said. "Without a trace. I never found it."

"Jesus," said Burke.

"I believe someone took it," said Charles. "I think someone came in here and found the key – or picked the lock – and stole it."

"And you think whoever took the binder is spying on you?" asked Burke. "Is that why you didn't want Martin to call or email?"

"Well, I think they were spying on *Dad*," Charles said. "After he died and I moved in here, I kept his land line phone – same number – and I noticed some weird clicking on the line once in a while.

70

Sometimes when I'd be talking to someone, there would be dead air for a second. I think the phone is bugged, or *was* – maybe still is. Hell, I think the house may be bugged."

"And you think it has something to do with the binder?" Burke asked.

"Yes. I do," said Charles. "I think someone was very interested in what Dad was writing. I never got a look at that binder, but my guess is that it had something to do with Blue Book. My gut tells me that Dad was writing down what he *really* knew about the project – information that was very top secret that he'd always been forced to publicly deny. He'd talked about doing it for years. I think he may have been planning to publish his findings."

"But who do you believe was interested in them?" Burke wondered. "The CIA?"

"That would be my guess," said Charles.

16

National Security

"What's that bit about China that Martin mentioned in the second letter?" asked Burke. "What's that all about?"

"I've never had the chance to find out," Charles said, regretfully. "We never met face to face the way Martin wanted to."

"Why?" Alex asked. "Is Martin dead too?"

"No, no," said Charles, shaking his head. "He's very much alive, as far as I know. Mike and I were planning to go up to Dayton to talk to him. Back when Dad got sick, toward the end, he kept asking for Martin, saying he had to talk to him. But that never happened."

"So, wait a sec," Alex said, holding up his hand. "What did *my* dad have to do with all this?"

"Well, nothing really," said Charles, shrugging. "It's *my* fault Mike got involved. After I got the lab results back from Switzerland, I wasn't sure what to do next. I wrote to Martin, but it turned out he was in Europe with his wife. I needed to talk to someone, and I reached out to Mike. He was very close to my dad, and I knew he took Dad's death pretty hard. So, I told him everything that was going on – *everything* – and I showed him these letters. He was pretty pissed off about the way the Air Force and the CIA had treated my dad, and wanted to help me find out what was going on. We figured I needed to talk to Martin, and Mike insisted on going up to Dayton with me."

Charles reached out and patted Alex's knee.

"I'm really sorry for what happened to your father, Alex," he said. "I'm sorry I got him mixed up in this mess."

Alex looked away from Charles for a few moments. "Me too," he said quietly, looking back. "But that's okay."

They were all quiet after that, and Burke found that his mind kept returning to one word – China.

"So, Charles, you have no idea what Martin was referring to about the China trip?" Burke asked, breaking the silence.

"Not really," said Charles, with a shrug. "That's why Mike and I decided I needed to talk to him. Martin finally wrote me when he got back from Europe, and I wrote him back and asked if he could come down, but he said he didn't want to fly anymore. Said I would have to come to Dayton. Apparently, he'd had a fairly serious blood clot problem on the flight home from Europe. So, Mike and I were going to fly up to Dayton."

"Which brings us to the unused ticket," said Burke.

"Exactly. We were all set to go. Mike had some vacation time, and I was *very* grateful that he wanted to come – flying ain't much fun in *this* goddamn thing," Charles said, patting the arms of the wheelchair.

"So why didn't you go?" asked Alex.

"Well, a day or two before we were supposed to fly, I got a *whopper* of a bladder infection – sort of comes with the territory, if you know what I mean." Charles frowned and patted the wheelchair again.

"So, my dad went by himself," Alex surmised, leaning back.

"Yep," said Charles. "He insisted on going anyway. He'd already bought the tickets and said he would go and talk to Martin about China, and find out if he knew anything about what was going on. Mike said he would be my ears. Plus, he *really* wanted to see the Air Force Museum. We'd arranged to stay at Martin's house, but Mike said he felt a little funny about it if I wasn't going to be there. I think he booked a room in a hotel right across the street from the museum."

"Yeah," said Burke. "He did."

Again, they were all quiet for a long moment. Burke imagined that Alex's mind, like his own, must have been racing through the pile of information they'd been fed.

"What about the binder," Burke asked, looking at Charles. "What makes you think it was stolen? Maybe your father hid it somewhere?"

"I suppose he could have," said Charles, "but I never found it in the house."

"Could it have been taken *before* he died?" Burke asked. "What if someone found out what he was writing and didn't like it? Could that have happened?"

"Well, I suppose," said Charles. "Unfortunately, I don't know *when* it disappeared."

Burke slouched back into the deck chair, and sighed. *UFOs?! Could this really have something to do with UFOs?* It just seemed so absurd. The whole thing was like some bizarre conspiracy theory, something you'd find on the internet that just made you shake your head and laugh. But at the same time, *two people were dead!*

Burke was suddenly struck by a thought. "So, Charles," he said, "you never talked to Martin Novak about what happened in China after Mike died? You never got back in touch with him, is that right?"

"Never," Charles said.

"Why not?"

Charles gripped the arms of the wheelchair, set his jaw, pursed his lips, leaned forward slowly, and looked Burke right in the eye.

"I got a phone call," he said. "Probably even before you found Mike in the river. It was short and very much to the point. The caller said that Michael Johnson was dead – that it was a matter of national security. He told me that if I was smart, that would be the end of the matter. That's all he said."

Charles sat back in the wheelchair and looked at Alex, then at Burke, waiting for their reactions. He could tell from the expressions on their faces that they were impressed by what he'd just told them.

"I don't even know if poor Mike ever got a chance to talk to Martin before he was killed," Charles said. "But *somebody* knew what we were up to, and *somebody* decided it had to stop. I'm guessing Martin may have received a similar phone call. He's never tried to contact me since. I sure as hell have never tried to contact him."

"Jesus! No wonder you're paranoid," Burke exclaimed. Realizing immediately that he was thinking out loud, he added, "Sorry, Charles."

"That's okay. I *am* fucking paranoid! And now you see why I didn't want to get anyone else involved."

Burke thought again of the promise he'd made to Michelle Johnson about taking care of her son, and he and Charles both looked at Alex. He appeared to be slightly stunned. When Alex noticed them watching him, he snapped out of it.

"I'm okay," he said. "Really. I'm glad I know all this."

Burke turned to Charles. "Why do you think someone killed Mike and not you – or Martin?"

"I've given that a lot of thought," Charles replied. "I think they figured killing Mike would scare us off – and they were right. Hell, I'm crippled, and Martin's an old man. We were low risk. I think the circumstances were right, and they just calculated their risks."

"But why weren't they afraid an investigation into Mike's death would lead to you or Martin?" asked Burke.

"Again, calculated risk," said Charles. "I think they're pretty good at what they do. Hell, John, they were probably shadowing *your* investigation! If you'd gotten too close, maybe they *would* have killed us. Maybe they would have killed *you*."

"I doubt that," Burke said, dismissively. But a cold wave of fear and anger – mostly anger – washed over him. *How nice of them*, Burke thought, *they'll only kill me if I get close.* He quickly pushed any serious thought of his own death out of his head.

"So that's about it," Charles said. "Now you know everything. Everything *I* know anyway. Martin may have something to add. But now it's not just me and Martin anymore – now it's you guys, too. And I've got to say that for *me*, it feels good to tell this shit to someone else. I've been looking over my shoulder and around corners for the last four years, and it's starting to get to me."

Charles reached into a deep leather pocket at the side of his wheelchair and pulled out a handgun. Burke immediately identified it as a 9-millimeter Beretta, similar in some ways to the 9 milli Glock 17 service pistol that was currently wrapped in a towel and hidden inside a shoebox on the upper shelf in Burke's bedroom closet back in Dayton. The DPD had let him keep it when he retired from the force.

In almost forty years as a police officer, the only time Burke had ever fired a gun in the line of duty had been a warning shot.

"I bought this not long after I got that phone call," Charles said, hefting the gun. "I felt vulnerable, stuck in this goddamn chair all the time. And poor Martin, he's just an old man – he must have been scared shitless. But hell, maybe that guy on the phone is good for his word – you know, that the matter *is* over as long as I behave myself. Maybe I didn't really need this. But *now* what?"

The three of them looked at each other. *Yeah, now what?* Burke thought. *Look the other way? Drop the whole goddamn thing like it was a red-hot flaming bag of shit?* That's certainly what his head was saying, but his heart had something else to say about the fact that two men may have been murdered – *targeted* – and justice was not being served. *Alex deserves to know what happened to his father.*

Burke discussed with Charles and Alex the idea of going to a federal authority with the story – but which one? *Who could they trust?* Certainly not the Air Force or the CIA or the NSA. Those agencies are all so connected through the Department of Defense that it didn't matter. "Maybe we should talk to the FBI," Burke suggested. "At least they're in the Department of Justice." He'd worked on a case or two with some of the FBI agents out of Cincinnati, and it was well known that the CIA and the FBI could rub each other the wrong way. But, Burke knew, they could also collaborate.

Lingering in the back of his mind was the strange mix of absurdity and reality that he couldn't shake. Was Project Blue Book a whole lot more than the joke that the CIA had turned it into? Were there elements of the project that were still so top secret that two men – *who knew too much* – may have been killed in order to maintain that secrecy?

Suppose Henry Robinson *had* actually been spied upon – and robbed – and *poisoned?* What if Charles was *still* being spied upon? Was his house bugged? *Was this goddamn front porch bugged?* Burke couldn't believe that he'd gotten involved in something so insane. When he suggested that they should wait for now, Charles and Alex agreed. Burke would return to Dayton and talk to Martin Novak. Charles supplied him with what he thought was a current phone number and address.

"Oh, wait a minute," Charles said. He reached into the same pocket of the wheelchair where he kept his handkerchief, and pulled out a ring full of keys. He carefully separated a small pocket knife from the ring. "Here," he said, handing the knife to Burke. "Martin gave me this when I was a kid, twelve or thirteen maybe. Martin and Sylvia had come for dinner – but they didn't know it was my birthday. When they found out, Martin felt bad they didn't have a present, so he pulled this knife out of his pocket and gave it to me. Just show him that – he'll know you talked to me."

Burke looked closely at the knife, opening and closing the blade. On one side, a small engraving of a spreading tree was imbedded in the bone handle. On the other side, a small swastika.

"Martin said a friend of his gave it to him after the war," said Charles. "He said the guy was in the 3rd Infantry in 1945, and when they got to the Berghof, the Brits had already bombed it. That was Hitler's summer house. Anyway, he told Martin he found the knife in the rubble. Martin always called it *Hitler's knife.*"

"Cool," said Alex as Burke passed him the knife. He inspected it closely and handed it back to Burke.

They discussed what level of caution was needed from here on out. Charles admitted that his paranoia was possibly unfounded – that perhaps he was no longer being monitored, if he had been at all. And maybe Martin Novak wasn't being watched. It was the best they could hope for, and they would keep all this to themselves for now. Burke would talk to Alex's mother and try his best to relieve her anxiety without telling her too much. He would do the same with his own family, Maggie and Kevin. For now, they decided, they would keep any communication between them to a minimum. Burke realized that despite how absurd it all seemed, some of Charles' paranoia was creeping into his *own* mind.

Charles insisted on taking Burke and Alex to lunch and suggested they all pile into his handi-van and drive out to Leatha's Bar-B-Que Inn. "Best barbecue in Mississippi!" Charles declared.

"What about seafood?" Burke asked, hopefully.

"Hell, that's easy" Charles said. "Right around the corner at the Triangle."

Charles led the way in his wheelchair, down the street and around the corner to E & L's Triangle Seafood. It was a blue-collar lunch spot, and Burke noticed quite a few cops in the restaurant. On Charles' recommendation, Burke ordered a shrimp po-boy and a cup of seafood gumbo. He was not disappointed. After lunch, they paraded back to Adeline Street and said their goodbyes. Burke told Charles that he and Alex were going to stop in at the Hattiesburg Police Department – Burke wanted to say hello to Chief Luther Banks. Banks had been very helpful during Burke's investigation four years earlier, and the two men had gotten along well.

"He's a good man," Charles said. "I see him at the pistol range occasionally. Please give him my regards if you think of it."

It was just a short drive to the police station on James Street, and not only did Luther Banks remember Burke, he seemed genuinely pleased to see him again. Banks was surprised to find out that the young man with Burke was Michael Johnson's son ". . . all grown up." Burke explained that although he was now retired from the DPD, Alex had asked him to look into some new information that had come up regarding his father's death. Banks didn't pry, and playfully chided Burke about being a private investigator.

"But if you need any help on this," he assured Burke, high-fiving, "I'm your man."

That evening, Burke took Alex and his mother out for dinner to yet another seafood place – the Crescent City Grill. Burke started with a dozen fresh Gulf oysters, then ordered the catch of the day, flounder. They talked about Charles and Mr. Robinson, and Burke very tactfully told Michelle that Charles had given him some new leads. He explained that he and Alex had promised Charles they would keep the information just between them for the time being. He said – *and hoped and prayed* – that none of them were in any sort of danger. Burke said this for Alex's benefit as much as for his mother's. Whether Alex believed it or not, the young man didn't seem too worried.

Burke slept fitfully that night. He couldn't shake the image of Charles Robinson trapped in his wheelchair and holding the Beretta in his hand. In the morning, he ate a piece of toast and drank some coffee, said goodbye to Alex and Michelle, and drove himself to the airport. As he waited to board the plane for the first leg of his flight to Dayton, Burke found himself looking around at the others waiting in the boarding area, checking to see whether anyone was looking at *him*.

17

Brian Lopez

That afternoon, as Burke was flying home from Hattiesburg, Brian Lopez drove to the service alley of the building in North Dayton where Sarah Sheldrake had lived – and died. It had been just over ten months since her death. Brian poked a bouquet of yellow roses into a chain link fence next to the dumpster at the very spot where Sarah had landed after falling from a seventh-floor window of her apartment. Yellow roses were her favorite, and sometimes the withered bouquet from his last visit was still stuck there in the fence, brown and shrunken. Other times, the previous bouquet was gone, probably plucked out by a maintenance man and tossed into the dumpster.

Brian allowed himself to cry as he leaned against the fence, staring up at the window from which Sarah had fallen. *Pushed.* He knew that now. He'd only suspected, but now he knew. His employer – BlackSnake Security – had most likely been involved.

From the start, Brian had tried his best to keep his relationship with Sarah a secret. He knew that any romantic relationship beyond a dalliance was frowned upon by BlackSnake. He may have crossed a line by ignoring one of the company's unwritten rules, but still, he couldn't believe that Sarah's death had been the result. Was BlackSnake really *that* ruthless?

But if BlackSnake hadn't known about Sarah *before* she died, they certainly knew about the relationship afterword. When the Dayton Police Department discovered that Brian was Sarah's boyfriend, he'd been questioned about the incident, which was eventually determined to be an accident. Following the strict procedural guidelines designed by BlackSnake for that type of situation, Brian had put the DPD in touch with BlackSnake through a liaison officer at the WPAFB headquarters. Brian's handlers had confirmed that he had been on the base at the time of Sarah's death, and that had been that. BlackSnake had not rebuked Brian for his indiscretion, and Sarah's death had never been mentioned again – until yesterday, when an envelope had arrived in Brian's mail.

It was a yellow padded CD mailer with no return address, postmarked Dayton, Ohio. When Brian opened it, he found a single DVD data disc with no markings on the front. Curious, he immediately loaded the disc into his computer. When he sat down and opened the file, he could barely believe what he was seeing. Someone had scanned nearly fifty documents – some hand written on stationary, the rest mostly typed letters and emails. All had been heavily redacted, including the letterheads, email addresses, and names – all except for one name. Sarah Sheldrake.

Despite the redacting, Brian had seen enough BlackSnake, CIA, and NSA documents to recognize what he was looking at, and as he read, he discovered the twisted truth about his beautiful, beloved Sarah.

She had been a Chinese agent, and her relationship with the Chinese Ministry of State Security had already been known when she had stepped off a Chinese Airline flight at Kennedy International Airport in New York City in October, 2010. Her intentions were unknown, however, and the agencies involved decided to watch and wait. She'd been tracked the entire time she was in the country, and when she became involved with Brian – an independent security operative working in a highly restricted facility on a USAF base – there had been a long exchange about how to deal with her.

Rather than confront the Chinese government with the situation and risk any embarrassing – or possibly dangerous – diplomatic fallout, it had been decided that the *prudent* course of action would be to simply neutralize Sarah Sheldrake. It was a *proven* course of action, engaged in and understood by both governments. There was little information on the disc regarding Sarah's actual death, only that the action taken had been successful.

By the time Brian finished scrolling through the documents, he felt as though he'd been kicked in the balls. Sarah Sheldrake had been an enemy of the state. She had been a targeted kill. Brian had no idea who'd sent the CD – but his best guess was maybe a sympathetic co-worker who'd somehow hacked the information and sent it to him as consolation. But Brian was not consoled. He was shocked by what he'd learned, and it didn't change how he felt about Sarah. He could not accept that she hadn't loved him as deeply as he had loved her. His name had been redacted from the documents, but he understood how his relationship with Sarah had been perceived by the writers. Certain terms, referring to Brian, struck him especially hard – *duped* – *false obsession* – *professionally deceived* – but he would never believe it. They were wrong.

Sarah had made him feel something he'd never felt with anyone. But even before Brian had met Sarah and fallen in love, he'd been thinking of quitting BlackSnake. He'd struggled with certain aspects of the job, questioning the way it often seemed to veer away from honorable and patriotic, sometimes even bordering on criminal. When Sarah came into his life, he knew that it was time to move on, to put BlackSnake behind him. Sarah talked about quitting her occupation as an "exotic dancer" as well. They talked about getting married, and about moving to the West Coast to be near her father, maybe even starting a family. Brian knew he would never believe that it was all a lie.

And another thing he knew – you didn't just *quit* BlackSnake.

18

Barry Goldwater

Burke's connecting flight from Philadelphia landed in Dayton mid-afternoon. After retrieving his checked-through backpack from the luggage carousel – Burke had realized at the last minute that he would not have been able to get *Hitler's knife* past the TSA agents in the boarding area – he drove directly to the Dayton Police headquarters downtown, happy to be back in his Camaro. He'd finished filling out the private investigator license application and wanted to drop it off to Kevin.

"How'd it go in Hattiesburg, Pops?" Kevin asked him, hugging his dad.

"Very interesting," said Burke. "Bordering on bizarre. I got some new information that may be related to Michael Johnson's death. I need to check it out."

"Anything you'd care to share with the Dayton Police Department?" asked Kevin, arching his eyebrows. "After all – last time I looked – we *were* the legal authority covering that investigation."

"I'll let you know," said a grinning Burke. "What's the fee for the license?"

"Three hundred seventy-five bucks," Kevin said. "They're letting you skip the exam. I'll scan the application and send it in for you, and if you give me your credit card info, I can send that, too. It'll be a done deal within a day, they said. You'll get an ID card for your wallet and a copy of the license to hang your wall."

"Yeah, right," Burke said with a smirk. "I'll hang it on my wall. Maggie will love it."

Burke was looking forward to being back home with Maggie, and he headed north out of downtown on Keowee Street. But at the last minute, just after he crossed over the Mad River, he turned right onto Valley Street and connected to Route 4, going east. He wanted to check out the Project Blue Book exhibit at the Air Force Museum. He'd never paid much attention to it, and he wanted to see if his memory of the display was correct.

He turned on to Bong Street – named after Dick Bong, America's top flying ace in World War II – parked in the museum lot and hurried into the museum. He headed straight to where he remembered the Project Blue Book exhibit to be, near the cafeteria. The entire display was as he remembered it, consisting of a few photos, four or five printed placards debunking the UFO phenomenon, some "supposed" UFO-related artifacts, including pieces of a buckwheat pancake that had reportedly been served by a friendly alien to a man in Wisconsin, and a copy of the Condon Committee report from 1969. That was it.

That was it?

Burke left the museum literally shaking his head, having heard a much different story in Hattiesburg from Charles Robinson about Project Blue Book. He put the top down on the Camaro and headed for home. When he turned on the radio, tuned to an oldies station, the first song he heard was *The Purple People Eater*, a novelty song from 1958 sung by Sheb Wooley, about an alien coming to earth to join a rock-and-roll band. Burke had to laugh, and silly as it was, he sang along –

It was a one-eyed, one-horn flyin' purple people eater
One-eyed, one-horned flyin' purple people eater
One-eyed one-horned flyin' purple people eater
Sure looks strange to me...

* * *

Maggie cooked a "welcome home" dinner for Burke, and while they ate, he told her as much as he felt comfortable revealing, about his trip south. After that, they watched the evening news and started a Scrabble game. The Cincinnati Reds had the night off, but the local PBS station was showing a BBC show on *Masterpiece Mystery,* starring Kenneth Branagh as Kurt Wallander, the Swedish detective created by novelist Henning Mankel. Burke had read all ten or eleven of the books in the series, and he identified a bit with the Wallander character. They each had only one child – a daughter, in the Swedish cop's case, who was also a cop – and a troubled relationship with his wife. But now, Burke reflected happily, he and Maggie had been steadily moving beyond their troubles.

The Scrabble game suffered from their attention to Wallander, and when the show ended, Maggie went to bed. Burke fixed himself a Jack Daniel's on the rocks, booted up Maggie's computer (he insisted that he didn't want one of his own, not even a laptop) and started Googling. He began with the Wikipedia entries for Lt. Col. Henry Robinson and Project Blue Book, which led to the fabled Roswell incident, and before long Burke realized that there were hundreds – maybe thousands – of websites and blogs devoted to UFOs and UFO conspiracies. He was surprised at how many of them pointed a finger at the CIA and its patsy – Project Blue Book – for their part in debunking the UFO issue. By hiding information about their operatives, lying about their participation in UFO related investigations and even dispensing false information, it appeared that from the very beginning, in 1947, the CIA's general intention was to create a smoke and mirrors atmosphere around the entire UFO problem. Most ufologists believed that during his tenure as director of Blue Book, Henry Robinson had been under direct orders to debunk every UFO incident or report that crossed his desk.

Burke decided to go straight to the government agency websites to see what they had to say. He was astonished to find a long, candid essay – on the CIA's own website – admitting to the many lies and cover-ups that had indeed misled the public and the politicians, even top members of the military brass, for decades. *Decades.* Burke thought the essay must have been written to rebut the massive amount of damning information being published on the internet by ufologists and conspiracy theorists about the CIA's involvement in Blue Book.

According to the essay on their website, one of the two main admitted goals of the CIA's covert nature was to keep the general public from mass hysteria and panic over the possible existence of alien intelligence. The CIA felt obligated to debunk every report and incident and to do it without admitting their participation. They figured that if the public knew the CIA was interested, the public would think there must be something valid about the reports.

The essay went on to reveal the CIA's other covert goal. Starting in the mid-1950's, it became necessary to hide the existence of their latest project – the top secret, high altitude, experimental, reconnaissance aircraft known as the U-2. At the time, most commercial airliners flew between 10,000 and 20,000 feet, and once the U-2 started test flights – at up to 60,000 feet – commercial pilots and air traffic controllers were responsible for a big spike in UFO sightings. The CIA was loath to disclose the project, and Blue Book was forced to debunk the sightings in any way they could. In 1960, the U-2 project was accidentally disclosed to the entire world – *oops* – when a U-2 spy plane piloted by CIA pilot Francis Gary Powers was shot down by the Russians. Powers had been conducting photographic surveillance in Russian airspace. It was a highly embarrassing moment for the CIA, and a most humiliating – and dangerous – incident for President Eisenhower and the U.S. government. Other than the Cuban Missile Crisis during the Kennedy administration, the shooting down of the U-2 may have been the most dangerous incident of the entire Cold War for the U.S. government.

After reading the essay, it was clear to Burke that ever since Project Blue Book was shuttered in 1969, CIA policies had managed to squash any real scientific or political interest in the UFO issue. Since then, the only ones interested in UFOs seemed to be amateur ufologists and conspiracy theorists.

But to Burke, the most interesting aspect of the CIA essay was not what was stated, but what was left out. Although Henry Robinson had directed Blue Book from 1963 until it folded in 1969, there was not a single mention of his name in the CIA essay. Curiously, Burke went to the official website of the USAF and typed Henry Robinson's name into the "Search" feature. No results were found. He did the same on the WPAFB website and again, *no results*. Burke tried once more on the Museum of the USAF site. *Nothing*. It seemed to Burke that the CIA and the Air Force were saying only one thing to Henry Robinson – *you never existed*.

Burke dug deeper on the Roswell Incident, perhaps the most well-known UFO incident of them all. In the summer of 1947, something crashed into the desert near Roswell, New Mexico. A public information officer from the nearby Roswell Army Air Field issued a press release saying a "flying disc" had crashed. Later that day, the commanding general issued another statement saying that the debris was from a weather balloon. A newly formed government agency – the CIA – managed to see that the incident was ignored and forgotten for the next thirty years.

In 1978, long after Project Blue Book was closed, new details about the crash in Roswell began to emerge, including eye-witness accounts and reports of witness intimidation. According to both military and civilian witnesses, there had been a huge military operation at the time aimed at recovering the debris – including several alien corpses. The material and the bodies had been transported to WPAFB in Dayton, Ohio.

Ufologists believe that the material remained at WPAFB for many years, under armed guard in Area B, in a highly restricted building known as Hangar 18. Many think that the Roswell material was eventually moved to an even more restricted, top-secret facility in what is known as Area 51, at a remote section of Edwards AFB in southern Nevada. Be it in Hangar 18 or Area 51, *reverse engineering* of the highly sophisticated crash debris is thought to have been the military's main goal in the top-secret program. Government scientists wanted to analyze the debris, to see what it was and how it worked. They wanted to duplicate it.

Year after year, rumors about the incident swirled throughout civilian, scientific, and military circles. After U.S. congressional inquiries were made in the early 1990's, the U.S. Secretary of the Air Force was asked to conduct an internal investigation. The first results were released in 1995, its conclusion being that the material recovered in 1947 was likely related to an old, top-secret Cold War program called Project Mogul. Mogul was conducted by the U.S. Army Air Force and involved sending microphones aloft in high altitude balloons that could detect sound waves generated from Soviet nuclear bomb tests.

A second report released in 1997 concluded that reports of recovered "alien" corpses were likely just witnesses innocent, *transformed memories* of actual military plane crashes or test crashes, possibly involving anthropomorphic crash dummies – or simply hoaxes perpetrated by false witnesses or UFO proponents.

However, UFO conspiracy theorists claim that a top-secret group, supposedly code-named Majestic 12, or MJ-12, was formed in 1947, after the Roswell incident. The group was formed by executive order from then President Harry Truman and included scientists, military leaders, and government officials. The purpose of the group was to investigate the recovery of the UFO in Roswell. A letter concerning the group, written to Secretary of State James Forrestal and signed by Truman, along with other documentation about MJ-12, has all been proven to be a hoax– at least according to the CIA, the State Department, and the Department of Defense.

Burke searched the website of the *National Archives*, which now has in its custody the entire collection of records from Project Blue Book, records from the Truman and Eisenhower administrations, and records from the USAF and Joint Chiefs of Staff and the National Security Council. Burke found that several Freedom of Information Act requests for documents pertaining to MJ-12 had all turned up negative, except for one inconclusive memorandum dated 1954.The Archives had also failed to turn up a single document in the Blue Book records mentioning the Roswell incident.

As Burke continued Googling, several incidents involving former Arizona Senator Barry Goldwater kept popping up. Goldwater had been the Republican presidential candidate in 1964. He'd been a

USAAF pilot during WWII, and after the war he rose to the rank of major general as a command pilot in the Air Force Reserve. At the beginning of the war, Goldwater had even been one of the flight instructors for Dick Bong – the future fighter pilot ace.

Burke found an article from the *The New Yorker*, written in 1988, in which Goldwater said he believed there had been a cover up regarding the Roswell incident, and he made the same claim six years later in 1994, during a Larry King interview.

Was this guy nuts? Burke didn't know what to make of it all. As far as he could tell, the government had been extremely successful in their debunking of the entire UFO issue. As far as they were concerned, it was dead. The ufologists and the conspiracy theorists were not about to let it die, however, and much of the evidence was compelling.

Burke thought back to a day long ago when he was maybe twelve years old. He and his father had personally witnessed something that they could only explain as an unidentified flying object. They'd been hunting for morel mushrooms in the woods outside of Spring Valley, a small village east of Dayton. Walking back along the railroad tracks, they'd just reached their car parked on Main Street, when something caused them both to look up at the same moment. They watched as a triangular-shaped craft crossed the sky overhead. It had emerged from the east horizon, above the old Indian mound in the center of town, and within four or five seconds it had disappeared at the west horizon, over the trees lining the bank of the Little Miami River. There had been absolutely no sound.

In the car on the way home they decided that they had indeed seen a UFO. *What could go that fast – and not make any sound?* Talking later, they found it odd that neither of them could really describe how large the craft was, or how high it had flown. Because of nearby WPAFB, they were used to seeing strange, experimental aircraft in the sky all the time, but this – this was something they had never seen before. They eagerly looked in the newspaper the next day to see if there were any stories about other reported sightings, but none appeared. When they told others about the sighting, no one got too excited, including

Burke's own mother and sister. Not even Burke's buddies. *Yeah, right – you dipshit.*

Burke shut off the computer, brushed his teeth, and crawled into bed next to Maggie. He smiled in the dark, thinking of his old childhood friends. But the smile quickly faded as he reminded himself again that two men were dead – murdered most likely – and tomorrow he would dig deeper into those deaths. He would try to arrange a visit with Martin Novak.

19

Martin Novak

The next morning was Friday, and Maggie asked Burke if he was interested in playing golf. Without offering a name, Burke told her that he was going to try to meet with someone who might be able to help in his investigation of Michael Johnson's death. *His investigation.* Maggie gave Burke a funny look.

"Kevin tells me you're planning to apply for a private investigator license," she said. "Is that correct?"

"That is correct, your honor," Burke said with a grin. "I was going to tell you. Kevin already sent in the paperwork."

Maggie sighed. "I thought you retired, Johnny."

"Don't worry, honey," said Burke. "It's just for this one case. I want to help Alex. Kevin thought I should apply for the license so that *he* can feel better about giving me access to police information."

They decided they would play golf the next day. Maggie said she would call Jim McGowan and his wife, Kathy, to see if they wanted to join them at Community. Community was Burke's favorite among the city's public courses. McGowan was a retired Air Force general, and he and Burke had known each other when they were kids going to school at St. Nick's. They'd gotten re-acquainted the previous summer during Burke's final case as a homicide detective, the case involving the abusive priest from their old parish.

After breakfast, Burke found the address and phone number that Charles had supplied for Martin Novak. He'd been thinking about just showing up at Martin's unannounced, afraid that if he called first,

Martin might refuse to talk to him. He didn't know if the old man was going to be as paranoid as Charles had been. On the other hand, Burke couldn't be sure that the address was current, or even the phone number for that matter. He looked in the phone book and searched online with no luck. In the end, Burke decided the polite thing to do was to call the number he had, and he waited until ten o'clock before he dialed. After three or four rings, a male voice answered.

"Is this Dr. Martin Novak?" Burke asked.

"This is Martin."

"Hi, Martin. My name is John Burke, and I used to be the head of the homicide division for the Dayton Police Department." He paused, waiting for a response. When none came, he continued.

"I'm no longer with the department," he explained. "Now, I'm a private investigator, and I've been looking into the death of a man named Michael Johnson. He died here in Dayton about four years ago." He waited again, but there was no response. Burke expected Martin to hang up at any second.

"Martin?" he said. "Are you there?"

"I'm here," Martin said. "I remember you from the newspaper. Captain John Burke."

"That's me," Burke said. "Anyway, I'm sorry to be bothering you, but I was given your name and phone number by an old friend of yours – Charles Robinson, from Hattiesburg, Mississippi."

"Oh, good lord," said Martin. There was a long pause. "Yes . . . yes, Charles Robinson is indeed a friend of mine. We haven't been in touch for several years, however."

"That's what Charles told me. But he thought I should talk to you about Michael Johnson. He thinks you could have been one of the last people to see Johnson before he died."

Burke waited again for several moments. "What else did Charles tell you, Captain Burke?" Martin finally asked. Burke could tell he was suspicious.

"Well," said Burke, "quite a bit actually. That's why I'm calling. I was hoping we could sit down and talk about it. Is that possible, Martin? Sometime today maybe?"

Another long pause. Burke knew that Martin had been caught off guard by the revival of an unpleasant, possibly dangerous episode from his past. Charles Robinson had said that Martin may have also received a warning after Michael Johnson's death.

"If you must, Captain Burke," Martin said at last. "You can come to my house. My wife left early this morning for a bridge tournament in Cleveland. She'll be gone all weekend."

"Great," said Burke. "And please, call me John. Are you still at 567 Bobtail Court in Riverside?"

"That's right. Can you come this morning?"

"I can be there in half an hour. Is that all right?"

"I'll be here," said Martin.

Burke could only imagine what was going through the old man's mind as he washed up the breakfast dishes. With the top down on the Camaro, he drove through downtown Dayton and headed east on Fifth Street, angling off onto Belfair Avenue toward the suburbs where he grew up. He passed St. Nicks, his old parish church, and drove to Martin's neighborhood at the eastern edge of Riverside.

As he slowed and turned onto Buckhorn Drive, Burke noticed a black GMC SUV parked at the side of the road. As a cop, he'd learned to pay attention to license plates – a habit he knew he would probably never break. This time, it was the U.S. Government license plate that had drawn his eye to the SUV. He didn't get the plate number, but noticed that the windows of the SUV were heavily – probably illegally – tinted. Because of Wright-Patt, there were plenty of vehicles with government plates driving around in the Dayton area, but this one caught his attention.

He found Bobtail Court right where Google Maps indicated it would be. Martin's house was located dead center at the back of the court. The development had been carved out of an old woodlot, and the somewhat ostentatious, two-story houses were shaded by tall, mature oaks and maples. He pulled into the driveway and got out. When he looked back toward Buckhorn Drive, the black SUV was not in sight.

Martin Novak answered the door and shook Burke's hand, inviting him in. He was a small man and appeared to be in good health, wiry and tan, and not at all stooped. They were standing on a tiled floor in a two-story open foyer that opened into a living room on one side and a short hallway on the other, with stairs curving up to an open second floor hall. The newel post, handrail, and spindles were probably oak. A cut-glass chandelier hung high above them from the cathedral ceiling. Although there was plenty of natural light in the room, the chandelier was lit. A round, frameless mirror hung on the wall above a small table. An umbrella stand held three umbrellas. There was a small pile of mail, a ceramic bowl containing a set of keys and a few pens and markers, and an unopened box of teardrop-shaped chandelier bulbs on the table. Burke looked up again at the chandelier and noticed several burned out bulbs. He was amused to find that his detective's attention to detail was still intact.

"I have something for you – from Charles Robinson," Burke said, reaching into his pants pocket. He pulled out the swastika-adorned pocketknife that Charles had given him, and handed it to Martin. For several seconds Martin stared at the knife, turning it front to back in his open palm.

"Hitler's knife," he said finally, looking up at Burke. The tension seemed to drain from his face, and he smiled.

"How is Charles?" he asked.

"He's fine – appears to be quite healthy," said Burke. "It turns out Charles and I knew each other when we were kids, back when he was just Chuck, from Page Manor. Anyway, he asked me to extend his apology to you, for dredging up this business. He wanted me to tell you that he thinks it's time something was done about it, and he hoped you would understand – and be willing to cooperate."

Martin grimaced. "Well, he's probably right. And when the time comes, I suppose I'd rather die with a clear conscience," he said ominously. "Let's go out in the yard."

He led the way out through the house to a shaded brick terrace, and they sat down across from each other on teak chairs. Burke got right down to business and laid it out for Martin, starting with Alex finding the unused airline ticket, and the boy's bus trip to Dayton in search of Burke. He explained his earlier investigation into Michael Johnson's death four years ago and how he and the DPD had come up empty-handed. He repeated everything Charles had told him about Henry Robinson's death from polonium poisoning, and about Project Blue Book and Henry's distaste for the project – how Henry had seen himself as a pawn – the humiliation he'd felt, and his distrust of the CIA. Martin listened, slouching in the chair, often nodding in agreement as Burke went on.

Burke told Martin about Charles' belief that the CIA may have had national security concerns regarding the writing that Henry had been doing secretly, and how the blue binder had mysteriously disappeared.

"Charles said his dad kept asking to see you, when he was sick," said Burke.

Martin put his head in his hand, but said nothing. Burke continued.

"Charles said he doesn't know who took the binder or exactly when it disappeared. He thinks his father had been writing down what he *really* knew about Blue Book."

Burke thought Martin was about to say something, but the old man simply motioned for him to continue.

"He regrets that he never talked to you about his parents' trip to China. Something important apparently happened there, and he thinks you know about it. That's why he and Michael Johnson were going to come up here, to talk to you about the trip."

Martin looked up through the trees.

"We crucify ourselves between two thieves – regret for the past and fear of the future," he said, shaking his head. "I forget who said that, John, but I've always remembered it."

Burke let the quote sink in. "Charles thinks he's being watched. He got a threatening phone call shortly after Michael Johnson died, and he figures you must have gotten a similar call."

Martin actually shivered. "I did," he admitted. "And I was quite frightened. I've never talked about Michael's death again, with anyone.

Especially with Charles. In fact, I probably shouldn't be talking to you right now. The last time I talked about Henry Robinson, it may have cost Michael Johnson his life."

"Look, Martin," Burke said, moving to the edge of his chair. "I can't force you to talk about this, but here's the deal. I told you I wasn't a cop anymore, but as a licensed private investigator I'll *eventually* have to pass on any evidence I discover about this case to the DPD. Right now, I know more than they do. As far as the DPD is concerned, Michael Johnson's death has never been explained in a satisfactory manner, and the case is still open. Cold maybe, but not closed. I retired last year, but this is the one case that still haunts me, and now I have some new information. Alex Johnson found that airline ticket, and you and Charles have been connected to the case. I want to close this case, and if you don't talk to me, you'll have to talk to the DPD."

Burke sat back with a sigh. He'd come across more hard-assed than he'd meant to. *Martin's just a scared old man,* he thought. Burke knew that he was letting himself become obsessed with the case, and that some of his motivation came from the fact that Michael Johnson had been a fellow cop. This case really pissed him off, and had for four long years. But there was more to it than that.

And then it hit him. It was that last thing Martin had said. *"It may have cost Michael Johnson his life."* Charles had said the same thing in Hattiesburg. Now, sitting across from this scared, little old man, Burke knew what it was.

It was his *own* fear.

Martin must have sensed what Burke was thinking. "You have to realize something, John," he said. "You could be getting in way over your head here."

"I believe I understand that," said Burke, grimacing.

"Then I'll tell you what I know," Martin said, sighing. "I'm an old man now. What does it matter?"

"Tell me about Michael Johnson. Did you two meet when he came to Dayton?"

"Yes. He came here to the house. I was a little taken aback when he showed up without Charles, but Mike explained the whole situation. I remember it was very hot that day and we talked inside, in the air conditioning. Charles and I had arranged that he and Michael were going to stay here with me. I'd planned it so they would come when Sylvia – my wife – was in California visiting her sister. She didn't know a thing about any of it. Later, she was oblivious when Michael's death was mentioned in the newspaper."

"But he didn't stay here, did he?"

"No," said Martin. "I think he probably felt uncomfortable staying here without Charles. He booked a room at a hotel near the Air Force Museum and was planning to spend some time there before he went back to Mississippi. I got the feeling he was quite the airplane buff."

"Did he ask you about China?" said Burke. "About whatever it was that happened to Henry Robinson when he was over there?"

Martin considered the question for several moments, wrinkling his brow and rubbing his forehead. "He did. And now I will tell *you*," Martin said. "Then you and I, and some fellows in China, will be the only people on this planet who will know. Henry Robinson and Michael knew, and now they are both dead."

Burke thought about that. "Do you suppose that whoever is responsible for their deaths might also know?" Burke said.

"Well, if it isn't the Chinese, then yes," said Martin, "I suppose they might."

20

Beijing, China: April, 2001

It was just after three o'clock in the afternoon when Henry Robinson gave his wife a kiss and headed for the hotel elevator. Lorraine was tired and wanted to lie down for a nap, so Henry decided to go for a walk in nearby Tiananmen Square while she slept. They'd been in their room at the Grand Hyatt Beijing for three days now, and the sightseeing and museum visits had begun to take their toll on Lorraine. She'd finished a round of chemotherapy treatments for breast cancer only a month before, but had always wanted to see Beijing before she died, and Henry arranged the trip.

He left the hotel through the front entrance and began walking west on Chang An Avenue. He hadn't gone far when a black Mercedes exited the curb lane and pulled up over the curb, just in front of him. Two young Chinese men wearing black suits and ties exited the car and approached him, smiling.

"You must come with us, Mr. Robinson," one of them said in perfect, unaccented English, and before Henry could protest, he was quickly ushered into the back seat of the car where the man joined him. The other man closed the door and got in front where a third man sat at the wheel. Henry had been taken by surprise, but he did not feel particularly frightened. There had been other pedestrians near Henry on the sidewalk, but when he looked out, no one seemed to be taking any interest in his abduction.

"There must be some mistake," Henry said as the car pulled away from the curb and merged into the six crowded lanes of westbound traffic.

"There has been no mistake, Mr. Robinson," said the young man. "And I can assure you that you are in no danger whatsoever. Our superiors merely wish to speak with you, and afterward you will be returned immediately to your hotel."

"May I ask who your superiors are," said Henry, "and what it is they wish to speak with me about?"

"I'm afraid I've shared with you all that I can," the man said, still smiling. He turned his face away from Henry and looked out at the traffic. The driver expertly guided the Mercedes through the lanes, weaving in and out to pass slower vehicles. After several turns, the young man sitting next to Henry reached into the inside pocket of his jacket and produced a thick, black cloth bag.

"I'm sorry, Mr. Robinson, but I'm afraid I have to ask you to put this over your head for the moment," he said, handing Henry the bag. "May I help you with it?"

Henry looked at the bag, and then at the young man. He was about to protest, to tell the man that it wasn't necessary, that he was already lost. Instead, he decided that he would not speak another word, took the bag, and placed it over his head.

"Thank you for your cooperation," the man said.

After another five or six minutes, two right turns and two lefts, the car slowed and stopped. Henry was helped out of the car and escorted by two of the men, one at each elbow. They walked maybe twenty steps and then down a short flight of stairs, into a building and onto an elevator. Henry had counted seven electronic beeps when the elevator stopped. He was led down a quiet hall and into a room. He heard the door close behind him, and the bag was quickly and gently removed. When his eyes adjusted to the light, Henry could see that the room was windowless. It was simply furnished, with a table and several chairs. An overhead light fixture lit the center of the room only. Henry was asked to sit down at the table, and when he had taken a seat, three men emerged from an unlit portion of the room. The young men who had escorted Henry left through the door.

Two of the men remaining in the room appeared to be Chinese and middle-aged. One was fat, one was thin. The third man was Caucasian, maybe sixty years old. Henry didn't recognize any of them. The Chinese men were dressed in similar olive-green suits, buttoned at the throat over white collared shirts. There were no military markings of any kind, but to Henry, they somehow appeared to be military men. They sat down side by side across from Henry, and the Caucasian man, wearing a sport coat and tie, remained standing just behind them. Henry was more angry than frightened, and he spoke first.

"What the hell is this all about?" he asked, looking over the heads of the seated Chinese and staring straight at the Caucasian.

"We assure you that you are in no danger, Mr. Robinson," offered the thin Chinese man in accented English. "We apologize for bringing you in this way."

"Who the hell are you?" Henry sneered, looking at the man who had spoken.

"I'm not at liberty to tell you that. But I *can* tell you that we represent a faction of the Chinese government. We are prepared to make you a generous offer."

"Offer my ass!" shouted Henry. He looked up at the Caucasian. "And who the hell are *you*?"

"Can't tell you that," the man said, half smiling. He was an American as far as Henry could tell, but with no discernable regional accent, and he also struck Henry as being military in his bearing.

"We know quite a bit about you and your *family*, Mr. Robinson," snapped the fat Chinese man, also in accented English. "And we know about your participation in the American Air Force study of unidentified, extraterrestrial flight known as Project Blue Book."

Henry could not believe what he was hearing. He looked hard at the American but was sure he had never met this man before. *He's a traitor*, Henry thought.

"We know, as do certain elements of your American government, that the issue of these – these UFOs as they are called – is still very relevant, despite what the public has been led to believe. We know that the technology gained from the ongoing study of this issue has advanced your country well beyond what has been achieved by the rest of the world. We are simply interested in *leveling the playing field*, as you say in your country. Our friend here has provided us with a great deal of information, and he recommended that you might be able to further help us." Henry looked again at the American. The American looked back at him with the same half smile.

The seated man continued. "According to our information, your relationship with the U.S. Air Force ended . . . on a sour note, shall we say? We thought that perhaps you would not be averse to the idea of sharing your knowledge of Project Blue Book . . . with *us*. If you could be persuaded, we are prepared to pay you whatever you wish for this information, within reason of course. The money would be available to you through an untraceable account."

Someone had done their homework, Henry thought, but did these people really think he would betray his country's secrets just because he had been screwed by the Air Force? At the same time, he had to admit that the idea had crossed his mind before – not betraying his country, but the idea of publishing what he had learned during his tenure as the director of Blue Book. He'd been sworn to secrecy in 1963, but keeping his mouth shut for all these years had been hard on him. From the beginning, he had watched with distaste as the CIA and the Air Force continued to hide the truth from the public. And no one – *absolutely no one* – of his stature had ever stepped into the UFO fray with the quality and quantity of information that he possessed. The closer Henry came to the natural end of his life, the more he'd thought about it. But this would be treason.

"You can kiss my ass," Henry said scornfully, glaring up at the American.

All three men on the other side of the table grinned at this. "*Exactly* the response our friend here had anticipated," the fat Chinese man said.

"We understand your response, Mr. Robinson," said the thin man as he stood up. "All that we ask now is that you consider the offer. As

I said before, we know quite a bit about your family. We recommend that this meeting remain confidential – that you tell no one about what we have asked of you. Should you ever decide to cooperate with our request, there will be no way for you to contact us. Instead, we will be contacting you periodically."

"Thank you, Mr. Robinson, and again we apologize for bringing you in this way," said the fat man, offering a quick bow. "You will now be returned to your hotel."

Henry recognized the barely veiled threat to his family. He looked at the American who said nothing. The young men came back into the room and one of them handed Henry the black bag and asked him to put it back on. He was led out and driven back to the Grand Hyatt. Part way there he was told that he could remove the bag. All the time they were driving, Henry had been thinking about the threat. He wondered if his abductors knew that Lorraine was probably not long for this world, barring a miracle. But his paraplegic son, Charles, was vulnerable. Henry thought about what had been said, and concluded that if he did nothing to cooperate with the Chinese, there would be no repercussion. The threat was simply to keep him from going to the American authorities and informing them of the offer.

Lorraine was asleep when Henry returned to their room. He got into the other bed, feeling exhausted himself now. Lying on his back, he stared at the ceiling. It was as if he had just dreamed the last hour. He took several deep breaths and tried to relax. An old military acronym that he hadn't thought of in years – *snafu* – popped into his head.

"*Situation normal, all fucked up,*" he said softly.

21

Maybe, Maybe, Maybe

"So, that's what happened in China." Martin sighed, looking at Burke. "Henry came to visit me as soon as they got back to the States, and I remember him being pretty upset. I think he had to tell someone, and I guess I'm the only one he trusted. As far as I know, he never told Lorraine or Charles. He didn't want them to worry."

"So, you told this whole story to Michael Johnson when he came to Dayton?" Burke asked him.

"Yes," said Martin. "Michael was here on Charles' behalf, and Charles needed to know. And the next day poor Michael was dead. Murdered, I'm quite sure."

"And then you got the warning call," Burke said.

"Yes, that morning," said Martin. "Then I saw it on the news that night, about Michael being found in the river. I remember watching you being interviewed on TV. You said the police were treating Mike's death as an accident or a suicide, but you hadn't ruled out foul play and asked for the public's help." Martin sighed heavily. "I felt terrible, but did nothing. I was quite frightened."

"We never closed the book on it," Burke said. "Mike was a cop. We all figured he got whacked, but we had no idea why, and we never turned up a single goddamn clue."

"And now?" said Martin, "Now do you have any idea who did it?"

"Probably the same people who killed Henry Robinson," said Burke with a shrug. "The CIA? The Chinese? Who the hell knows? But I think whoever did it was most likely interested in whatever it was

103

that Henry was writing. Either they wanted it, or they didn't want someone else to get it."

"But why would the Chinese kill Henry?" Martin asked. "They were hoping he would tell them what he knew about Blue Book."

Burke shrugged, and Martin went on. "I can't imagine Henry *ever* betraying his country to the Chinese. I *can*, however, imagine him publishing what he knew about Blue Book in the U.S. I don't think he would have thought of that as traitorous. I think he felt that the public should know."

"But, Martin, what if Henry *did* take the Chinese up on their offer?" asked Burke. "Don't you think he might have been tempted? It could have been for a *lot* of money."

"He didn't need any money," Martin scoffed. "Henry was loaded. He was very smart, and he figured out how to buy and sell stocks. Back in the 90's, before the bubble burst, I let him play with some of my retirement money. He made us a small fortune – that's when we bought this damn McMansion." Martin pointed with his thumb, and both men looked over at the large house.

"No, I don't think Henry was too worried about the Chinese," Martin said. "He figured he would be okay as long as he never told anyone about the meeting in Beijing."

"Maybe the CIA knew about the meeting in China anyway, and they were afraid Henry was going to take the Chinese up on the offer," Burke said. "Maybe the CIA took the binder and then decided to kill Henry as well, to keep him from telling the world what he knew. Hell, maybe Henry was leading the Chinese on somehow, and he double-crossed them. Maybe he changed his mind and told the CIA about the meeting and the Chinese found out. Maybe the Chinese double-crossed Henry. Maybe *they* took the binder, and then killed him."

"Maybe, maybe, maybe" Martin murmured.

"Yeah," said Burke, slumping. "Maybe."

"Like I said, I don't think he ever made a deal with the Chinese," said Martin. "But he never told me what he *was* going to do with what he'd written. I think he was pretty conflicted about it. That's how it seemed anyway, the last time I saw him."

Burke sat up. "Wait . . . you saw him again? When?" he asked. "Did you know what Henry was writing?"

Martin glanced over at the house and leaned forward, forearms resting on his knees and hands clasped. He stared at the ground in front of him for a moment before looking up at Burke.

"John, there were actually *two* binders. And nobody stole them from Henry," he said quietly. "He drove up here about a month before he got sick. He told me he thought he was being watched. He gave them to me."

22

Brian Lopez

Brian Lopez had been sitting in the Black SUV, parked just off Belfair Avenue on Buckhorn Drive, when Burke's Camaro passed him, turning into Martin Novak's neighborhood. Using a secure cell phone, he'd called in Burke's position and then waited half a minute before following him to Bobtail Court. He already knew where Burke was headed. The assignment had been spur-of-the-moment, and Brian happened to be on duty at the base when the request was passed down.

Parked now on Buckhorn Drive near the entry of the cul-de-sac, he could see Burke's car parked in Martin Novak's driveway. He'd been instructed to keep his distance and to call in when the *rabbit* left the house. He hadn't been told who Burke was – only the make, model, color and license plate number of the car, and he'd admired the orange metallic Camaro when it had turned off Belfair Avenue. Whoever lived at 567 Bobtail Court was also unknown to Brian.

It was not completely out of the ordinary to be sent on assignment off the base. Usually, his shift was spent close to the center of Area B, in or near a building on Eighth Street, between G and K Streets. The building is windowless, and not numbered like most of the other buildings on the base. From the outside it looks to be three stories tall, but nine sprawling floors lay deep beneath, and several other buildings in Area B could be reached from inside the building through a vast, underground tunnel system. Ventilation, heating and air-conditioning conduits penetrate the surface at smaller mechanical buildings spread throughout the area. In his five years on the base, Brian had been granted access to only about twenty percent of the interior of the complex – known by everyone as *the box*.

Depending on his shift, Brian's time in Area B usually consisted of patrol and guard duty, surveillance, and other security-related tasks like monitoring camera feeds, or registering visitors and escorting them in and out, and around the building complex. He was often not privy to the identities of the visitors, and would be required to hand them off to someone with a higher clearance level. He and the other BlackSnake employees had heard idle chatter about what went on in the complex, but they'd been sworn to secrecy and were absolutely forbidden to repeat or disclose anything they heard or saw, or even to speculate among themselves. Special assignments – like shadowing Burke – could be mundane in nature. Occasionally, a task could be considered highly critical to the security of the country. Again, unless deemed necessary, the employees were not allowed to discuss or to speculate among themselves about the nature of their assigned special tasks. The left hand did not always know what the right hand was doing.

Brian knew that Wright-Patterson Air Force Base was one of the largest bases in the country, and arguably the most important. Area B is the heart of WPAFB, located within the confines of the base just to the east side of the original, triangle-shaped Wright Field runway system. The three large hangars of The National Museum of the USAF dominate the old northwest runway, and Airway Road – also known as Colonel Glenn Highway – borders the south.

Area B is home to the Air Force Material Command Center Headquarters. AFMC directs almost 77,000 military and civilian employees throughout the country, many of them scientists and engineers with an emphasis on "high technology". The Aeronautical Systems Center, the Air Force Security Systems Center, and the Material Systems Group all fall under the command of the AFMC. Also located in Area B is the Air Force Research Laboratory, the Air Force Institute of Technology, the National Air and Space Intelligence Center, the Defense Institute of Security Assistance Management, and the Defense Technical Information Center – the clearing-house for the collection and dissemination of scientific and technical information flowing in and out of the Department of Defense research and development system.

Several times, Brian had boarded a plane at the base and been delivered to another part of the country. There he would assist in some component of an operation, often with no idea of the eventual consequences of his assignment. Sometimes he was able to put the pieces together from media reports, and more than once he had felt regretful about the outcome, especially when someone had died – but it was always in the name of national security. Brian did what he was told and kept his mouth shut. *This* assignment – keeping an eye on a man driving a late model, metallic orange Camaro and visiting 567 Bobtail Court – was mundane, and Brian wondered what it could possibly have to do with national security.

Watching the house without much interest, his thoughts drifted to Sarah. Her memory was always with him. Losing her was the worst thing he'd ever experienced – like he'd been cut in half. It didn't matter to him that Sarah had been a Chinese operative. He had convinced himself that she loved him and that they'd been of like mind – ready to stop living on the edge, ready to settle down, to be *normal*. But it had all been taken from him by his own government – probably by his own employer.

Brian's mind moved beyond Sarah and into a familiar dark place, to the things he had done over the years that he was not proud of, things he had been directed to do by his employer, BlackSnake. One assignment in particular seemed to haunt him more than the others. Four years ago, he had unwittingly participated in the assassination of a Black cop from Mississippi. He'd never found out the reason for the hit, and he certainly had no idea that it was connected to the surveillance of 567 Bobtail Court.

23

Two Binders

"*You* have the binders? Jesus, Martin!" Burke said too loudly, leaning forward quickly and nearly tumbling out of his chair. Martin leaned back instinctively to get out of his way, but Burke righted himself with a hand on Martin's knee.

"Yes," said Martin after Burke had settled himself. "Two thick, navy-blue binders, with nearly a thousand pages of Henry's handwritten notes."

"Good lord! Did you read them?"

"Of course, I did," said Martin. "Henry didn't say *not* to, and I'm sure he expected me to. Fortunately, his cursive is very neat and legible, and he only wrote on one side of each page. It's all on lined notepaper, and there are quite a few excellent drawings. Henry was a scientist remember, and some of what he wrote is quite complicated."

"And it's for *real?*" Burke asked, excitedly. "I mean, is it *true?* Do you believe it, Martin?"

"Well, I certainly have no reason to believe it's *not* true. And yes, I believe every word of it. Henry was a good scientist. Being a scientist myself, and having done research at the base for many years, some of it was not completely new to me. But Henry had much greater access to the material that Blue Book warehoused, *much* greater, and some of what he wrote about it is very disturbing. I wasn't shocked by all of it – hell, we'd all heard the rumors and speculation from the beginning. But some of it *is* shocking. Henry spells it all out pretty clearly." Martin threw his arms into the air. "And *lo and behold* . . . the ufologists and the conspiracy theorists got a lot of it right."

"*What?*' Burke was stunned. "You mean about the CIA cover up . . . and flying saucers? Roswell . . . little green men . . . Hangar 18 . . . the Green Room . . . Area 51 . . . *all that?*"

"Well, yes. And a lot more that no one has ever heard of. Except that not all of the recovered vehicles are saucers, and none of the little men are green. In fact, according to Henry, not all of them are even men – *some of them are ladies!*"

Martin continued, "Apparently, there's *quite* a collection of little bodies – and not just from Roswell. Seems there were more crash sites than anyone knows about, not just Roswell and Aztec, and Kecksburg, and all of those in the United States. Crash debris has been collected from Shag Harbour in Nova Scotia, Sweden, Brazil, the U.K., Australia – and some of these were very old sites containing skeletal remains. According to Henry, although the bodies share some similarities, they're not even all of the same alien race!"

"C'mon Martin," Burke said incredulously. "Are you shitting me?"

"No, I'm *not* shitting you, John," Martin assured him. "Henry writes about all the reverse engineering that was done, all the technology that we tapped, and the technology we couldn't figure out – everything. I actually learned the outcome of some of the research I had done on what everyone had referred to as *memory metal*. It's an alloy that can be deformed when cold but returns to its shape when heated. Anyway, I imagine our scientists have figured out more since Henry's time – and since I retired."

Am I dreaming this, Burke thought?

"And it's all – all this stuff – it's still at Wright-Patt?" he asked.

"According to Henry it is, or *was* anyway, at least when Blue Book closed shop in 1969 and Henry left. He was sworn to secrecy under the threat of death, by the way."

"Jesus," Burke mumbled.

"Henry wrote that during his time there, Wright-Patt was the *only* place in the country where UFO-related material was housed. He says the whole Area 51 thing is a lot of baloney – smoke and mirrors – just to take the public's eye off of Wright-Patt. Same with Fort Worth down in Texas. That's where the CIA wanted everyone to think the debris from Roswell went back in 1947, but that was bullshit, too. Everything came here. And it stayed here – for a while in the famous Hangar 18. But since the late 1950's it's most likely been in the box."

"The box?"

"Yes. The box. It's a complex in Area B that no one talks about. I was inside twice, for consultations. Five floors down. But I'm sure it's even deeper than that. Apparently, some portions of the box are at the highest restricted access levels of any government facility in the country – higher than at nuclear weapons facilities. Higher than top secret. Even above the SCI level, I've been told."

"What's SCI?"

"Oh, *sensitive compartmental... information*," Martin replied, "or something like that. Maybe it's *compartmented*. Anyway, as far as I know, I've never met anyone with clearance at that high a level."

"Jesus Christ, Martin. This is all pretty hard to believe. Do *you* believe it?"

"Look, John . . . that's *exactly* what the CIA wants you to think. That it's all too outlandish to believe," said Martin. "They've spent over sixty years hiding this information, and according to Henry they are fully capable of doing whatever they have to do to keep the public thinking that it's all nonsense. Henry was a major pawn of that policy, and I think he became a *victim* of that policy. I think the CIA made good on their threat."

"But what about the Chinese threat? If *they* didn't end up with the binders, where do they fit into all of this? Or do they?"

"I'm guessing they're still very interested," said Henry. "They'd probably like to know where the binders are. The fact is, John, the State Department and the Department of Defense are very concerned about the Chinese – much more concerned than they appear to be to the general public. They fear China tremendously, both economically and militarily. And the Chinese are always looking for any edge they can find. They are *extremely* interested in our military technology. Yes, I suspect the Chinese could still be lurking about. But who knows?"

"Who knows, is right," Burke said, nodding. Both men were quiet for several moments.

"Are the binders here, Martin, in your house?"

"Why, I thought you'd never ask," said Martin with a slight grin. "But no, they're not here. After Henry died, I wasn't sure what to do with them, so I hid them on the base – right under their noses, so to speak. I'm an emeritus professor at the Institute, so they let me keep an office at the school, and I still have some access to Area B. I hid them where no one will ever find them. But there's a bit of a problem."

"Which is . . .?"

"Well, when I found out that Charles and Michael Johnson were flying up to see me, I retrieved the binders, locked myself in my office and made copies of everything. I hid the copies again, and kept the originals to give to Charles when he came up. I figured he should have them."

"But Charles never came," said Burke, realizing as he spoke what was coming next. "Oh, Jesus."

"Yes," Martin said, nodding. "I gave them to Michael Johnson."

24

Charles and Alex

Late in the afternoon, the day after Burke left Hattiesburg, Alex Johnson revisited Charles Robinson at the house on Adeline Street. They had formed a bond the day before, possibly a perilous bond, and Charles was not surprised when Alex knocked at his door. He liked the boy, as he had liked Michael Johnson, the boy's father. But Mike was dead, and Charles blamed himself for having gotten him involved. Both Charles and Alex had lost their fathers. *And for what?*

Alex just wanted to hang out, he told Charles. He'd spent most of the day mowing lawns, until his boss decided that it was too hot and sent the crew home. But Charles got the feeling that Alex wanted to help him – maybe even to protect him. They sat in Charles' office room and chatted, both of them avoiding any talk of Burke's visit, and Charles showed Alex some of the books he'd collected over the years about the Tuskegee airmen, pointing out old black-and-white photos of Henry Robinson. Alex had some of the same books in his father's collection, but he'd never paid them much attention. Charles dug out a boxful of service medals that Henry had earned from World War Two and the Korean War.

As Charles was putting the medals away, Alex got up and pulled a book from an upper shelf – the book that held the letters Charles had shown them the day before. Without speaking, he pointed to the book and then to his lips, shaking his head. Charles understood. He nodded, then sat quietly as Alex reread the letters silently. When he finished, Alex put the letters back in the book and returned it to the shelf.

"Can we go outside for a while?" he asked.

"Good idea," said Charles. Alex held the front door open for him, and they sat facing each other on the porch.

"Do you really think your house is bugged, Mr. Robinson? Even out here?"

"I don't really know if anything is bugged," Charles replied. "Possibly just the phone. Maybe my cell phone. Who knows?"

"Maybe you should change the locks on your doors. I could help you do it. I want to do it at my house too, but I'm afraid it would freak out my mom."

Charles smiled at the boy's concern and felt terrible that he'd now gotten Alex involved. He realized that Alex was feeling vulnerable, worrying about something that no young man should have to worry about. His father had been murdered – possibly by his own government – just as Henry Robinson had been. *How is an eighteen-year-old supposed to feel about that?*

"Thanks, Alex, but I just did that not too long ago. I even thought about putting in a security system, but I think if anybody really wanted to get in, they could figure out a way around it. But you shouldn't worry about it too much – if anything happens it's going to happen to me. I doubt that you pose much of a risk to whoever is behind all this."

"But I know some stuff now," Alex reminded him.

"You do," said Charles. "But I think if they did anything, they would just try to scare you a little." *I hope to God I'm right*, he thought to himself.

25

Let's Go Krogering

Burke looked at Martin in disbelief.

"Yes, I put the binders in a plastic Kroger bag, and Mike took them with him that afternoon," Martin said. "He asked me if I wanted to join him at the museum the next morning, and I left it that I would call him."

Burke's mind raced back to the Michael Johnson file. This new information didn't make any difference. Burke knew they hadn't found the binders in Michael Johnson's hotel room. Or in the rental car. *Or in the river.*

"We never saw the binders," Burke explained. "Whoever killed him must have taken them."

But *who* took them? The CIA? The Chinese? Whoever it was had also wanted Michael Johnson dead – he knew too much. And what about the copies that Martin had made and hidden somewhere on the base, somewhere in Area B? Did Mike's killer know about the copies?

"The copies are still hidden," said Martin, anticipating Burke's train of thought. "At least the last time I checked. That was about six months ago, and I imagine they're still there."

"Does anyone else know the copies even exist?" Burke asked. "Did Mike know?"

"No, I never told anyone, not even Mike."

But Michael Johnson knew enough, and now he's dead, thought Burke. Henry Robinson had known too much. Who else? Martin? He knew a lot about Blue Book, but he's still alive. It seems that up until

115

now he'd been sufficiently frightened into silence. And now, perhaps Burke himself knew too much. He knew more than Charles. And what about young Alex? *He knew something too,* Burke thought. The boy had found an unused airline ticket in a book, and because of that, the lid had come off this can of worms. Burke's initial interest had merely been to try and solve a four-year-old cold case, but now he found himself thoroughly bound up in a much larger, possibly dangerous situation.

Martin waved a bee away, and Burke looked at the old man. He didn't seem like he could be a threat to anyone, let alone the governments of the United States or China. Four years had passed since Michael Johnson's death, and Burke wondered if Charles – and Martin – had been watched all that time. Charles certainly thought so. *But what about now?* There was no way Burke could know. He could only hope that whoever took the binders got what they were after and didn't know about the copies – that after four years they had lost interest in Charles and Martin. Alex and Burke had come late to the game. *Maybe no one even knows about us,* he thought.

"Do you think you're being watched, Martin?" Burke asked.

"I have no idea," said the old man with a sigh. He slowly pushed himself out of the chair. "I think I need to lie down for a bit."

They went back into the house and stood together at the front door. Burke promised to keep in touch and asked Martin to call him if anything out of the ordinary came up. Martin picked up a piece of the mail that was lying on the small table – an electric bill from Dayton Power and Light – and pulled a pen from his shirt pocket.

"Here," he said. "Write your number down for me."

When Burke drove out of Bobtail Court, the black SUV that had been parked on Buckhorn Drive was gone. Burke was thinking about the binders that Michael Johnson had driven away with four years ago, wrapped in a plastic Kroger bag. Despite the gravity of what Burke had just learned from Martin, an old Kroger jingle popped into his head, and Burke absentmindedly sang it out loud . . .

"Let's go Krogering . . . Krogering . . . Krogering . . . let's go Krogering, the happy place to shop."

26

Completely Nuts

Back at his house in North Dayton, Burke spent the rest of the afternoon helping Maggie with some gardening, struggling the entire time to keep from telling her what was going on with the Michael Johnson case, and more specifically, what he had learned that morning from Martin Novak. His visit with Martin had been disturbing, and the information the old man had shared was hard to believe. Burke was torn. He didn't know whether to laugh out loud at the whole situation, or believe that Martin was right when it came to taking all of this UFO stuff seriously, and that the CIA had managed to shut down the collective imagination of almost the entire American public. But Charles Robinson and Martin Novak weren't just a couple of nut-job conspiracy theorists. *Anyone* would believe them, Burke thought. And the four-year-old image in his mind of Michael Johnson's cold, pale corpse lying on the bank of the Mad River was as real as it gets.

Jesus, was it all just *completely nuts*? Would *anyone* believe him? Did he believe it *himself*? Burke tried and tried to sort it out. But Martin was right – the CIA had managed to convince the vast majority of the American public that it was absurd to even consider the existence of extraterrestrial alien flight. Those who did so must not be taken seriously. They were to be considered misinformed, and branded as silly, or gullible, even pathetic . . . possibly psychotic and dangerous. The CIA had been created back in 1947 to deal with rising Cold War tensions, but almost immediately they found themselves dealing with the increase in UFO phenomena. Since then, they had been spectacularly successful in belittling any serious scientific investigation into what had once been a grave concern to the American government. *And it still is,* Burke thought. Michael Johnson and Henry Robinson may have been victims of this grave concern.

Burke watched Maggie as she dead-headed a petunia plant. He was worried about getting anyone else involved, at *least* until he figured out what was going on and what to do about it. What started out simply as a haunting, cold case investigation into the death of a fellow cop, had turned into this unimaginable, troubling situation that left Burke not knowing what to do next. He was uncomfortable with it. In all of his years at the DPD he had never found himself in such a position. He didn't know what to do next.

His instincts told him to take the investigation to a higher authority. He had worked with some of the FBI agents out of the Cincinnati office, in particular Lamar Presley, the special agent in charge. When Burke had asked for Lamar's help during his initial investigation into Michael Johnson's death, Lamar's superiors in Washington had inexplicably denied him permission to involve the Bureau in the case. But Burke and Presley had collaborated on several other cases over the years, and they had gotten along just fine. Is it possible that Presley would hear him out and not laugh in his face? Would he have any interest in helping out an old colleague? *No, Presley and the FBI would probably blow me off as being completely nuts,* Burke thought. Or, they might even go straight to the CIA with the information. Most likely they would do both. Who then? *What the hell should I do, goddammit?*

"Are you OK, Johnny?" Maggie wiped her brow with the back of a gloved hand. "Ever since you got back from wherever you went this morning, you've seemed a little distracted."

"I am distracted," Burke admitted. "This case has gotten a little weird and I'm not sure what to do. I'm dying to talk about it, but for the time being I don't think I should."

Maggie had actually heard this before – many times in fact, over the course of their marriage. She knew Burke was reticent by nature, but usually when he'd kept something from her it was because of the grim details or the disturbing nature of a particular investigation. She thought she already knew most of the details of the Michael Johnson case, but now she was worried that Burke had stumbled across something more sinister.

"I just hope you aren't doing anything dangerous," she told him. "I breathed a big sigh of relief when you retired, and if we don't get to enjoy a long, quiet, happy old age together . . . well . . . I don't know what I'd do."

"You'd *kill* me," Burke laughed, and gave her a hug.

"No, you know what I mean," Maggie said. "Just don't do anything stupid. Why don't you talk to Kevin about it?"

Burke had thought long and hard about that already. Kevin was the obvious choice, and Burke knew he would eventually have to tell his son what was going on. *Just as soon as I figure it out myself,* Burke thought.

"I *will* talk to Kevin at some point," Burke said. "And don't worry. I'm not in any danger. I'll get this straightened out sooner or later."

He wasn't lying to Maggie. All things considered, Burke did not believe that his life was in jeopardy. But, did he think it might be in the near future? Despite his long career as a homicide cop, Burke was optimistic by nature. Yet, things were different this time. It all felt like such a goddamn dream.

The next day Maggie and Burke would be playing golf with Jim and Kathy McGowan. Burke was looking forward to some mindless fun and a chance to forget about UFOs for a few hours. At the same time, he wondered if he should talk to Jim about the case. McGowan was a retired USAF brigadier general. He had worked at the Pentagon before he retired to Dayton, and was now on the board of directors at the Air Force Museum. Burke and McGowan knew each other as teenagers, growing up in Riverside, near Wright-Patt, and had been reacquainted just the summer before in the midst of Burke's last investigation. Their friendship had grown stronger ever since. Burke thought he could trust him.

27

The General

The following morning, as they walked the long fairways at the Community Golf Club, Burke told Jim McGowan about being sucked back into an old, cold case. When Burke told his friend that he'd applied for an Ohio investigator's license, the general chuckled.

"A *private dick?* Heh."

They pushed their three-wheeled golf carts ahead of them, stopping occasionally to make a shot, and were usually out ahead of their wives who had been hitting their drives from the ladies' tee box. Maggie and Kathy had also become friends, and they walked side by side, chatting away.

McGowan wasn't familiar with the Michael Johnson case – the death had taken place several months before he and Kathy had moved back to Dayton. Burke explained how the case had gone completely cold four years ago, and that despite a total lack of evidence to the contrary – a total lack of evidence *period* – the DPD homicide squad had all suspected foul play.

Without naming names, Burke told McGowan about Michael Johnson's son from Hattiesburg and how he had tracked Burke down and asked for his help. McGowan listened intently as Burke told him about the unused airline ticket and the connection that was made to the wheel-chair bound son of a former Tuskegee airman. He especially didn't mention Charles Robinson by name – no doubt McGowan would have remembered "Chuck" Robinson from high school. He didn't mention Henry Robinson, his mysterious death, Project Blue Book, Martin Novak or the China incident, but . . .

"There's an element to this whole thing that involves the Air Force, Jim," Burke said as they walked.

"The Air Force?" The general seemed surprised.

"Yeah. I can't really talk about it just yet, but I was wondering if you could get me onto the base sometime soon, just to look around. In Area B if possible. I wouldn't be snooping around, I'm just curious about something that's come up."

Burke had often been on the base as a teenager, but always in Areas A and C. He'd visited high school friends in the elegant Tudor-style houses on the tree-lined streets of the Brick Officer's Quarters. There was a movie theater on the base, two golf courses, the Officer's Club, and a gym where Burke and his friends would horse around and make fun of the old, fat retired officers sweating away in the steam room. The outdoor Olympic size pool, complete with a diving platform, overlooked the Patterson Field runway, and from poolside they could watch the thunderous takeoffs and landings of the Strategic Air Command's B-52 bombers – loaded with atomic bombs – and the KC-135 tankers that provided them with fuel to keep them airborne twenty-four hours a day. Burke had fond memories of the base, but he had never entered Area B.

McGowan hit a high, long iron shot that landed softly on the green. "Sure, I can get you on the base, he said, shoving the club into his bag. "Why not? You'll be my guest. I'll have to get a pass for you which means I'll have to fax in a copy of your driver's license. We *could* register right at the gate, but we'd be sitting there waiting until they ran your license through the system. I guess security really tightened up after 9/11. Hell, remember what it was like when we were kids? Remember the bumper stickers?"

Burke remembered. Back then if you lived or worked on the base, whether you were in the Air Force or a civilian, you sported a black and white decal on the front bumper of your car that got you access through the entry gates. The stickers varied, but the guards could identify an officer's vehicle and would automatically salute as the car passed in through the gate. Burke and his young friends were often mistakenly saluted as they entered the base in somebody's father's car. Everyone in the car would snap off a mock, exaggerated salute as they roared off into the base, laughing at the pissed-off guard.

"Yeah, it was pretty loose." Burke smiled, thinking back. "I remember a big sign that you read on the way out. *What you see, and what you hear, when you leave, leave it here.*"

McGowan laughed. "I guess they figured that didn't quite cut it anymore," he said. "After 9/11, they started checking IDs on all the Air Force bases. I think they still had decals here, but that ended completely a few years before we came back to town. Now *everyone* gets thoroughly checked out. They even do random vehicle searches."

At the next hole, both men hit good drives and started walking down the fairway. Burke decided to take a chance.

"So, tell me, Jim," he started nonchalantly. "What do you know about a building in Area B called the box?"

The general stopped dead in his tracks. Burke stopped as well and waited for McGowan's answer, not totally surprised to see the look of consternation on his friend's face. Burke had been weighing whether or not to even mention the box, but in the end his curiosity got the better of him. McGowan's reaction had been worth it.

"What *about* the box?" the general asked, without a trace of a smile.

"Well, tell me about it," Burke said. "What is it? I heard something recently about its existence and wondered what you knew about it."

They started walking again, and Burke could tell that McGowan was working on an answer to the question. As a homicide detective, he had asked a lot of questions and could tell when someone was weighing his words. It didn't always mean that he was about to be presented with a lie.

"I don't know what you heard," Jim said finally, "but you probably know as much about it as anyone else. All I know for sure is that the box is a highly secured location, and nobody talks about it. I've heard that a private security company is under contract to keep an eye on things there – not the usual Air Force personnel like everywhere else on the base. I've never met a single soul who's been inside – at least no one who ever admitted it to me."

"Do you have any idea what's in there – or what it's like inside?"

"Just what everyone else has heard – that it's deep and leads to tunnels that connect it to other buildings throughout the base. Hearsay and rumors, that's all I know about it."

Burke was inclined to believe that his friend was talking straight. Between the general's description and that of Martin Novak, the box appeared to be impenetrable and unknowable to most of the people connected to the base. Burke considered his next question carefully.

"What about UFOs?" he asked.

"Oh, Jesus," McGowan said, stopping again. "Look, John . . . like I said, hearsay and rumors, that's what I know. On the base it's always been a big no-no to talk about it, or even joke about it. I've been warned that if you do, and the wrong person finds out – you'll be off the base PDQ."

"But what rumors, Jim? What have you heard?"

"Hell, the same goddamn things you find all over the internet," said McGowan. "Little alien bodies in refrigerated rooms, wrecked flying saucers, secret labs, autopsy rooms – all the same bullshit that the conspiracy nuts go on and on about."

Burke thought he knew the general pretty well. They were deeply connected through some unfortunate, dark, life-altering events that had taken place when they were both very young, and in the short time since they had become reacquainted, a lot had passed between them. Burke was now trying to read McGowan's reaction. He couldn't tell if the general was embarrassed by his questions, that *maybe he feels sorry for me for being such a gullible, clueless idiot for even bothering to consider the subject of UFOs.* On the other hand, McGowan probably knew more than he was willing to say. Either way, it didn't really matter. McGowan was his good friend.

"So, is it true that people have been fired for talking about it?" Burke asked. "Are there rumors about people just disappearing from the base – or *being* disappeared – anything like that?"

"Yes," said an exasperated McGowan as he started walking up the fairway. "Yes. There are rumors like that. Jesus, John. C'mon – let's play golf."

28
A Simple Plan

Saturday night. Moonless sky. The man had been in the house briefly that afternoon while Martin Novak was grocery shopping, and had devised a simple plan. He knew that Sylvia Novak was away for a few days, playing in a bridge tournament in Cleveland, and that Martin was alone. Through a living room window, he watched Martin put down the book he was reading and turn off the lamp. The old man got up and turned out the other lights, checked the lock on the front door, and disappeared down a short hall that led to the master bedroom suite on the first floor.

After donning latex gloves, the man crept to the back of the house, easily picked the lock as he had done earlier, and made his way into the garage where he concealed himself behind Martin's car. He listened carefully for any sound coming from the house.

The door that led from the garage into the house was not locked, and the man entered quietly. He stopped to listen. A combination mudroom and laundry area led to the kitchen. He went through the kitchen and into the living room, stopping at the bottom of the stairs. A nightlight dimly lit the open foyer, and he saw the unopened box of light bulbs that he'd seen earlier. As he was about to move to the other side of the stairs, a door opened and more light entered the hall and the foyer. Stepping back quickly, he concealed himself behind a sofa.

Martin walked into the foyer carrying an empty coffee mug. He passed through the living room, went to the kitchen and turned on a light. The man was glad to see that Martin was still fully clothed. *This just got easier,* he thought. From where he was hidden, he could hear the old man rinse the cup and set it in the sink, then shuffle off to the laundry room in his slippers. *He's locking the back door,* the man thought. Coming back through the kitchen, Martin turned off the light and retraced his steps to the living room.

He was on Martin in an instant, jamming the small, powerful stun gun into Martin's back, and heaving the old man's body over his shoulder all in one motion. Martin did not struggle, and the man carried him up the stairs to the open landing. He balanced Martin over the railing, and then dropped him head first onto the foyer floor, wincing at the sound of Martin's head striking the tiles. Hurrying back down the stairs, he slipped through the kitchen, into the laundry room and out the back door.

In the garage he found the eight-foot aluminum stepladder that he'd spotted that afternoon. He carried it into the foyer and opened it up right below the chandelier, just to the left of Martin's body, being careful not to step into the small pool of blood that had already formed near the old man's head. He climbed the ladder and removed two bulbs from the chandelier. Back down on the floor, he gave the top of the ladder a push, directing it away from Martin. Stepping back, he watched as it fell, striking and slightly damaging the sheetrock wall and knocking over the small table, breaking a ceramic bowl and scattering mail and the contents of the bowl across the floor. He dropped one of the bulbs he'd removed, shattering it, and placed the other in Martin's hand, folding the fingers around it. He noticed that the hand had already begun to cool. Lifting the shirt from Martin's back, he checked to see if the unusual stun gun had left its small mark – more of a slight bruise really – and it had. After checking the scene one last time, he switched on the chandelier and went back to the garage, leaving the same way he had come in. He locked the rear garage door behind him.

29

Area B

It was a pleasantly warm Monday morning, and Burke drove the Camaro with the top down. He turned on the radio to the news – *George Zimmerman, Trayvon Martin, Yasser Arafat, Polonium-210, Syria, Bashar al-Assad, Wimbledon.* Burke switched off the radio and drove in silence through Riverside, past his old neighborhood, and into Beavercreek. McGowan was waiting when Burke drove up, sitting at the top of his front porch steps and leafing through a magazine.

Burke had faxed his driver's license to the general the night before, and McGowan forwarded it to the base, requesting a visitor's pass. Wright-Patt was designated a "closed" base, and no one got in without a sponsor and an escort. McGowan carried the appropriate Department of Defense ID card, but all vehicles entering the base were subject to inspection coming in *and* going out.

"I'll drive," McGowan said. "There's less chance we'll have to stop and be searched. We can take the Ford – a lot of the guards already know the car."

"Sounds good," said Burke.

"Here's a guide to the base," the general said, handing the magazine to Burke. "You can keep it. There's a little info about Area B in there."

McGowan owned a gleaming, light blue 1964 Ford Galaxie 500XL convertible, with a white ragtop and white interior. Burke was more of a Chevy man, but he thought the car was a beauty, and he and Maggie had enjoyed going out with the general and Kathy several times in the Ford. McGowan backed the car out of the garage, put the top down, and hopped out to finish the job.

"Are you going to tell me anything more about what this is all about?" he asked, as Burke helped him snap the vinyl cover in place.

"I'd love to tell you, Jim, but I can't right now. I will eventually, though, I swear."

It was a short drive from Beavercreek to the base, and the route took them past the spot where Michael Johnson's body had snagged on a log, four years ago. "That's where we found Michael Johnson's body." Burke pointed it out to McGowan. "Over on that far bank."

Jim nodded. "And you never solved that case, you say?"

"Not yet." Burke stared at the river. "Not yet."

Turning in at the main gate for Area B, the general pulled the car off to the side of the entryway and put it in park.

"I have to tell you, John," he said, turning to Burke, "I feel a little funny about doing this, not knowing what you're up to. All those questions about UFOs and the box – that's more than a little weird. But mainly, it's because I know they don't fuck around on this base when it comes to security. It sounds to me like somebody already told you more than they should have – and knowing that this has something to do with the possible murder of a cop – well, I just wish you could tell me more."

"Look, Jim," Burke said, "I know it's an odd request, and I certainly would understand if you decided to turn around right now, but I swear I just want to look around – strictly out of curiosity. I've never been in Area B. But hell, it's not that important that I get on the base at all, and I'm fine if we don't. Really."

"No," said McGowan, shaking his head. "We'll go. But like I said – this is serious shit here. The Department of Defense does not fuck around. Dick Cheney and Don Rumsfeld – they're scumbags. I had to deal with both of them when I was at the Pentagon. They may be gone, but believe me, they left their mark. If for some reason you went and got yourself involved in something that the DOD doesn't *want* you to be involved in – my advice to you is you'd better think twice about it. Hell, John, you're just some old retired cop who doesn't mean *shit* to these guys. They don't give a shit about the entire goddamn Dayton Police Department!"

"I appreciate the warning, Jim," Burke said. "And, as you say, this case is *definitely* more than a little weird, In fact, it's a *lot* weird. I've learned some stuff that's pretty hard to believe. But one thing I do know, two men are dead – and one was a cop. And my goddamn head feels like it's going to explode every time I try to make sense of it. At some point I hope I can share it with you, but right now you'd probably think I was ready for the nuthouse."

"*Two men?* Now it's *two men?*" McGowan shook his head.

Oops, thought Burke. "Listen, Jim, I've got to play this close for now."

McGowan stared straight ahead with both hands on the steering wheel. Finally, he glanced over at Burke, again shaking his head.

"Just let me know if I can help you out with anything," he said. "You know you can count on me. And don't do anything stupid, all right?"

"I appreciate that, Jim. You know I do."

"Well, as far as *they* know," McGowan said, nodding toward the gate, "you're just coming in here as my guest – as a *tourist* – that's what I put on the request for your pass. So, let's go do this and get it over with."

McGowan put the car into drive, and they passed between the old, abandoned guard booths, one on each side of the entry road. The stone construction and the red ceramic-tiled roofs of the booths seemed quaint to Burke – left there as a reminder of days gone by perhaps – a time before 9/11 when the World Trade Center was turned into a pile of rubble. The new, modern booth was located in the middle of the entry road, shaded by a white, curved, double wing-like steel canopy. Several airmen wearing standard USAF battle camouflage uniforms were visible inside the glass and block, steel-roofed booth. One young airman emerged as McGowan stopped the car.

"Morning, General," he said, saluting smartly. "Nice day for a drive."

"Thanks, airman," said McGowan, returning the salute. "We're just doing a little sightseeing this morning – thought I'd show John around the area. I applied for a visitor's pass last night – to save you guys some work."

"Yes, sir. Let me check and see if we have that," the young man answered, now looking directly at Burke. "Sir, do you have your driver's license?"

Burke fished the license out of his wallet and handed it over. "And I'll need to see your DOD card, General, and the registration for the car," said the airman with a shrug. "Sorry, sir, but you know how this works. Just pull over to the right while I run these through – it'll just take a minute."

McGowan indeed knew how it worked. He took the card and registration out of his shirt pocket and handed them to the airman, who returned to the booth. He pulled the Ford over and turned off the ignition.

"This won't take long. See those buildings?" McGowan said, pointing to a pair of white, three-story buildings off to his left across a large parking lot. "That's the headquarters for AFRL – the Air Force Research Laboratory – and next to it is the Aeronautical Systems headquarters."

"Those brick buildings over there are part of the Propulsion Directorate," McGowan went on. "It's also part of the AFRL – jet engines, spacecraft propulsion, that kind of stuff. I hear they're working on a new weapons' bay and a smart-weapon system for the B-52. Hard to believe the old Buffs are still relevant, isn't it?"

"Buffs?"

"Yeah, *Big Ugly Fat Fuckers* . . . B-52s," said the general. "Hell, my old man was flying them over fifty years ago. Remember when we were kids, and SAC was flying them out of here all day and night?"

Burke remembered well. During the Cold War years, just a couple of miles from where they were right now, his childhood home would shake hard enough to rattle the dishes when the huge B-52s lumbered into the sky, four in a row, loaded with nuclear bombs destined for cities in the Soviet Union . . . if need be.

"Across Loop Road there, that's a research and development facility – one of many – and that's Acquisitions and Weapons Systems, that complex straight ahead," McGowan said, pointing. Burke took it all in, then put on the reading glasses that hung around his neck. He thumbed through the base guide that McGowan had given him.

"What the hell is taking them so long?" said McGowan, looking over his shoulder toward the guard booth. Just then the young airman came out of the booth and crossed the road.

"Sorry about the wait, sir," he said, handing the IDs and passes to McGowan. "Computer glitch. But here are your passes. Please wear them at all times. You'll be returning them on the way out. Enjoy the base, Mr. Burke."

"Thanks," said Burke, taking the pass from McGowan.

"Good to see you, sir," the airman said, saluting. The general returned the salute, and the young man turned on his heel and walked back to the booth.

"*Computer glitch* my ass," said McGowan, looking over at Burke. "They don't *have* computer glitches on this base. Maybe your reputation precedes you – *Mr. Burke.*"

"Bullshit," Burke said with a grin, hanging the lanyard around his neck. "They don't know me from Adam." He forced the smile, but Burke was more than a little unsettled by what the general had said.

McGowan drove slowly along Loop Road. Off to the right, the Air Force Museum, ball diamonds, and soccer fields stretched across many acres. McGowan pointed out the buildings he knew, passing the Acquisitions Complex on the left, and Burke was surprised to learn that his friend had no idea what went on in many of the buildings. They passed a long series of hangars and followed Loop Road where it curved to the left and passed Gate 22B. This gate had also been recently upgraded with a modern guard booth and entryway. Colonel Glenn Highway and I-675 lay just beyond. Burke realized that there was much more to Area B than he had envisioned, with large, undeveloped open spaces and woodlots scattered here and there among the old and new – and many very modern – specialized buildings. The road curved again to the left, and McGowan pointed to the massive complex of buildings on the right, fronted by a twelve-story tall concrete tower topped with an array of antennae. Burke counted four large, white-domed sensors, and several other antennae, two of them dish-shaped and rotating, perched high on metal framed structures, or on rooftops throughout the complex.

"That's the AFRL's Sensors Directorate complex," said the general, slowing down and stopping so that Burke could take it all in. "A lot of these buildings are brand new, just finished. I think there's something in that guide that explains their mission."

Burke put on his glasses and opened the guide. He found the entry about the complex and read it aloud:

The Air Force Research Laboratory's Sensors Directorate mission is to ensure unequaled reconnaissance, surveillance, precision engagement, and electronic warfare capabilities for America's Air and Space Forces by developing, demonstrating and transitioning advanced sensors and sensor technologies. These technologies will enable continued U.S. warfighting dominance across the entire electromagnetic spectrum.

"Jesus Christ," Burke said, looking up at the tower.

"No shit," said McGowan. "There's some NSA money in there too – from what I've heard."

They continued on Loop Road which became P Street and passed between two more large building complexes. McGowan stopped the Ford again. "That's the Institute of Technology campus," he said, pointing to the right. Burke guessed that somewhere on that campus is where Martin had hidden the copies that he'd made from Henry Robinson's binders. "And that's the Materials and Manufacturing Directorate, that complex on the left. Some serious geeks in there. Aircraft, spacecraft, missiles, rockets, ground-based weapons systems – you name it. Hell, if you can dream it up, they've probably already designed it."

Burke looked at the complexes, stretching out all around him. *The war machine*, he thought. He'd always taken Wright-Patt for granted and hadn't given it much thought. As far as he could tell, most of the people in Dayton felt the same way – the base had always been there, but nobody knew much about it. Burke had known a lot of civilians who worked at Wright-Patt, and they almost never talked about what they did there. *What you see and what you hear, when you leave, leave it here.* But now, just barely inside the gate, he was beginning to understand the scope of work that was going on here – had *been* going on for over seventy years – and the amount of tax-payer dollars that must be involved. *And this is just one base*, he thought. Burke was enough of an historian to know that in Dwight Eisenhower's last speech in 1961 as President of the United States, he had coined a phrase – "military industrial complex" – and warned the world about its looming threat. *The war machine.*

"Tell me something, Jim," he said, "What do you think about all of this? I mean, how much goddamn money is getting dumped into this place? No wonder the national debt goes up two billion dollars every goddamn day. I mean – do we really *need* all this bullshit? It's insane, don't you think?"

"Of course, it's insane!" McGowan almost shouted. "The whole goddamn world is insane! We're just trying to stay ahead of whatever's coming next! And things have changed since we were kids, John. Hell, people bitch about gridlock – how the President and the Senate and Congress can't get anything done. But *forget* about those guys – they aren't running this country anymore. The Department of Defense and the Pentagon, the CIA, the NSA, defense contractors, the oil companies, Wall Street – even Silicon Valley to some extent – *that's* who's runnin' the show. It's money, and it's power, and it all makes me sick. Hell, when I retired from the Air Force, I had multi-million-dollar job offers from over thirty different corporate defense contractors – mostly weapons makers."

The two men sat in the Ford and didn't speak. It was too much – too incomprehensible – and too depressing to dwell on. Burke was reminded of a warm summer night long ago, when he and a couple of his buddies were "sleeping out" in his suburban backyard, maybe two miles from where he and the general were sitting right now. He remembered how he had stared up at the Milky Way, lying on his back in an old Army surplus sleeping bag, trying to wrap his head around the prospect of an endless universe. At one point he'd felt like his head would burst, and he actually became disoriented. That night sky had been incomprehensible – wondrous and depressing at the same time. It was how Burke felt now, sitting there next to McGowan in the Ford.

The general put the car in gear and they continued the tour of Area B, slowly passing several large facilities unknown to McGowan, and crossing a road called Faraday Way.

"Named after General Frank Faraday," McGowan said. "He was the director of the Department of Defense's Strategic Defense Initiative. Remember that? *Star Wars* – Reagan's wet dream? Weapons in space that would protect us against nuclear attack? Project was a *total* bust. But what the hell, the guy got a road named after him anyway."

"What about China, Jim?" Burke said, suddenly remembering what Martin Novak had said about China and the Department of Defense. "How does China figure into all of this?"

"Bingo!" McGowan nodded. "It's *all* about China, John. The D.O.D. is scared shitless. Everything *else*? Afghanistan? Iraq? The fucking *war on terror*? Hell, that shit going on in the Middle East is just a goddamn sideshow – nothing but field training and weapons testing for what's coming down the pike."

"Jesus, Jim."

"Yeah, and who the hell cares if we waste five or six thousand kids while we're at it." McGowan waved dismissively. "*Iranian nukes? North Korea?* Do you really think we give a shit about the Iranians and some fucking nut job in North Korea? Well, maybe a little, but it's really *all* about China. I think the DOD is just waiting for the slumbering giant to awake."

"You mean a *war?*" said Burke. "A war with *China?*"

"You tell me," the general said with a shrug. "Nobody knows what the hell China's up to. Yeah, they signed the non-proliferation treaty. Yeah, they're trying to improve their human rights image. *Bullshit!* Right now, the DOD thinks the Chinese may have as many as three thousand armed nukes ready to go, all hidden, all underground, but nobody really knows for sure. In ten more years, that could easily double. *And,* we think they're stockpiling chemical weapons. Hell, they already have the world's largest standing army, and they'll soon have the largest economy and military budget in the world. And they're smart, John. As far as technology goes, they're gaining on us fast, and what they can't figure out – they buy it or they steal it. Whatever works."

"Christ." Burke shook his head, thinking of the blue binders.

"No shit," McGowan said. "That's why we keep trying to make nice with a dirt bag like Vladimir Putin. If and when the shit hits the fan, we'll probably need his help."

McGowan passed a large, nondescript windowless building and turned into a parking lot. He parked the car facing the north side of the building and turned off the ignition. Burke wondered why they were stopping.

"Well . . . there it is" the general said, nodding toward the building, "The *box*. Pretty much dead center of Area B. Take a look and then we should probably move on. I don't want to make anyone nervous."

Burke took it in quickly. The white building was solid concrete, three or four stories tall, hard to say exactly with no windows. Two sections of it were a story higher than the rest – *elevator shafts*, Burke thought. The whole building was maybe 200 feet wide, a little narrower the other way, and the roof appeared to be flat. He noticed one entry area on the west side of the building, and another on the side facing the parking lot. Four sets of surveillance cameras were mounted on this side of the box alone. He looked around at the parking lot and saw maybe thirty cars there, including a row of five identical black GMC SUVs, with fully tinted windows and government license plates, parked at the east side of the lot. They were exactly like the one he had noticed parked near Martin Novak's house, when he had visited the old man.

Odd, Burke thought, that there was no security fence around the box. Then he realized that he hadn't noticed *any* fences in Area B, other than those around construction sites and the barbed-wire topped, chain-link perimeter fence that encircled the entire area.

No one came out or went into the box in the few minutes they sat there. McGowan finally started the car, pulled out of the lot and headed north. He pointed out a few more different complexes, and they were heading back toward the main gate when a black GMC SUV passed them quickly and pulled in front of them. When a row of blue lights flashed through the rear window of the SUV, the general stopped immediately.

A young man emerged from the SUV and approached McGowan's side of the car. He was wearing khakis and a navy blue, long-sleeved polo shirt. His hair was cut short and arm muscles bulged through the shirt. An ID tag hung from a lanyard around his neck. Removing wrap-around sunglasses, he saluted McGowan and apologized for the inconvenience. "Standard security policy, sir."

Burke was suddenly aware that he had seen this young man before. It was similar to the feeling he'd had when he met Charles Robinson in Hattiesburg several days earlier. Charles had been an old acquaintance, but this was different, and Burke couldn't nail it down.

The young man looked at the general's ID tag and then walked around to Burke's side of the car. He looked at Burke's tag and asked to see his driver's license. He studied the license, then Burke himself, before handing it back. Burke tried to get a look at a name on the young man's tag, but he couldn't make it out.

"Thank you, Mr. Burke," said the security agent, clearly addressing Burke and not the general. "We noticed you stopped in a parking lot on G Street and we want to know your interest in that area. This is standard security, I can assure you."

"We were just looking around," said McGowan, taking over. "I was showing off Area B to Mr. Burke here. He's never been in here before. I pulled into that lot just to get off the road for a few minutes."

"Very good, sir," the young man said. "I apologize for any inconvenience, sir. Nice ride by the way – sir." He saluted once more, patted the front fender of the Ford, walked back to the SUV and sped off.

"Something tells me that wasn't *standard security*," McGowan said, looking over at Burke. "I think we've worn out our welcome. Let's get the hell out of here."

They stopped at the gate and returned the passes. Driving away from the base in silence, Burke was worried that McGowan was upset about having taken him into Area B. It did seem as though Burke's reputation – *or something* – had preceded them. Coming here may have been a mistake. Unfortunately, he'd learned nothing new that would help him with the investigation into Michael Johnson's death. But now he was on someone's radar – if he hadn't been already – and Burke hoped that he hadn't created any trouble for his friend. While McGowan's take on the Chinese was unsettling, as was his perception of a shadow government running the country unchecked, what troubled Burke the most was what the general said about the apparent ruthlessness of the Department of Defense.

"Don't worry about it," McGowan said, breaking the silence, as if he had been reading Burke's mind. "Just be careful, John, *whatever* it is you're up to."

30

Suitable for Framing

Burke had a rough night after the visit to the base, finally falling asleep after hours of tossing and turning. Around 9 a.m. he awoke in a sweat to one of his old, recurring nightmares. The dream always ended the same, with the brilliant white burst of a nuclear blast. There was no sound, just the blinding flash, and as the light faded slowly back to daylight, the top portion of a telephone pole, splintered where it had been broken off and now roughly in the shape of a crucifix, floated in slow motion through the blue sky. The severed electrical cables, still attached to the cross at the top of the pole, dangled and danced to the sound of a soft, whistling wind.

Burke couldn't remember the last time he'd been haunted by the dream. He always figured that the nightmare was a product of the Cold War, when he and his childhood friends had grown up hearing, time and time again, that if we ever went to war with Russia, Wright-Patt would be one of the first places to be targeted. Photographs and newsreels of nuclear explosions were everywhere back then – from *Life* magazine to the evening news. Images from Hiroshima and Nagasaki lingered in the press right through the fifties and sixties as the national debate about the morality of atomic weapons wore on.

Burke got out of bed and dragged himself to the kitchen. Maggie was already up and gone – to look for some new plants for the garden her note said – and Burke poured himself a cup of coffee. They'd spent the evening before playing Scrabble and watching a Reds game, and Burke had found it hard to concentrate after the day's visit to Area B.

He was conflicted over how much he should be telling Maggie about the investigation. Based on how unsettled he was himself, he decided to stay quiet for the time being. He knew Maggie was not happy with what he was doing, but she approved of his trying to help out young Alex. That much she could handle.

Getting breakfast together, it took Burke some time to shake the nightmare from his thoughts. As disquieting as it always was, he felt a slight affection for the dream – as if for an old friend. He found the morning paper on the dining room table and sat down with his coffee, glancing at the front page, and checking the sports section. Turning to the local news page, a small headline caught his eye:

Retired Professor Dies, Falls from Ladder in Riverside

Burke spilled his coffee, setting it down too quickly as he read on: *Martin M. Novak . . . found dead in his house . . . fall from a ladder . . . discovered by his wife . . . retired professor of nuclear chemistry . . . taught for many years at the Air Force Institute of Technology . . . death ruled an accident by the Riverside Police Department . . . foul play not suspected . . . autopsy pending as death was unattended.*

Burke broke into a sweat. He read the article three times before putting the paper down. He mopped up the spilled coffee, then read the article one more time. An accident, it said. *Yes, of course, just a terrible accident*, Burke thought. *Coincidental to my visit to Martin maybe, but just an accident.*

Burke's mind raced. *Martin could have died sometime that same day, after I left, maybe that night. I could have been the last person to see him alive. Did anyone see me at the house? Should I tell the police I was there? Hell, it was just a goddamn accident! An accident!* But no matter how many times he read the word, or said it to himself, Burke couldn't stop the feeling in his gut that *maybe it wasn't* an accident.

His cell phone rang, and Burke flinched. He jumped up and unplugged the phone from the charger on the kitchen counter. "Burke here."

"Morning, J.B. It's Scott Kaminsky."

Kaminsky was the Riverside police chief, and he and Burke had known each other a long time. Burke realized immediately that this was not a social call. He knew that his decision whether or not to get involved in the old man's death had been made for him. Someone or something had already connected him to Martin. This was going to be a bad day.

"Hi, Scott," Burke responded calmly, trying to control his anxiety. "It's been a while. How's it going?"

"Good," Kaminsky said. "Everything's good. How's retirement treating you?"

"So far, so good. Maggie retired, too. I'm spending all my time with her, and with Kevin's family. And playing lots of golf – not that it's helping my game much. What's up?"

"Well, I'm not sure if it amounts to anything, but we had this accident out here. An old man fell off a ladder and died – guy named Martin Novak. It was in this morning's paper. Maybe you saw it."

"Yeah, I was just reading about it."

"Anyway, the case fell to us, so I've been sort of tying it up, and I found your name and a number written on a piece of mail at the man's house. Did you know there are half a dozen John Burkes in the Dayton phone book?"

"Yeah, I knew there were a few." Burke struggled to come up with a story, something to put Kaminsky off, but nothing came.

"None of the numbers matched the one I found, and none of the addresses were in North Dayton," Kaminsky informed him. "Are you still out there?"

"Yeah, I moved back in with Maggie."

"Oh, that's great, J.B. Glad to hear it. Anyway, I found one of your old cards in my desk drawer. The phone number matched, so I knew it was you. Did you know this guy . . . Novak?"

"He was a friend of mine," Burke said. "Well, not a friend really, someone I just met a few days ago."

Burke decided that this conversation with Kaminsky needed to be face to face. And he wanted time to put some thought into what he should and shouldn't say.

"Scott, can we talk about this in your office? I could come over right after I grab some breakfast."

"*Breakfast?* Christ, J.B., it's nine-thirty. I guess you *are* retired." Kaminsky laughed. "How about twelve-thirty? I'll be tied up till then. We can go get some lunch . . . if you're hungry again by then, that is."

Burke forced a little laugh. "OK, I'll see you then. Thanks, Scott."

He cut up a banana into a bowl of Cheerios and poured a glass of orange juice, but he'd lost his appetite. *I should tell Scott about reopening the Michael Johnson case,* he thought. *I can tell him I applied for the P.I. license.* Burke knew Kaminsky would be amused by that. *I can tell him it's just this one case, that I got a new lead and a plea for help from Michael Johnson's son.* He figured he could tell Kaminsky that the new lead had led him to Martin Novak, but that was about it. *The accident was purely coincidental.*

Maggie arrived with a box of perennials, and Burke had time to help her plant them in the yard. He'd discovered that he actually liked gardening, something he'd never done with Maggie during most of their marriage. It was mostly flowers, but they did have a small vegetable patch with tomatoes and peppers, a couple of basil plants, and a few other herbs. Maggie seemed to love it when he was helping.

"You were kind of restless last night, Johnny," she said, waiting while Burke dug a hole. "You okay today?"

"I'm fine," said Burke. "I was just bummed a little. The visit to the base was pretty depressing. They're spending a lot of money there, and it doesn't seem like much of it's for a good cause – mostly just developing weapons. I guess I never really gave it much thought before, but it's pretty damn scary. It's even got Jim a little freaked out I think."

The day before, Burke had come close to telling Maggie everything about his investigation, but now Martin Novak's death meant that he couldn't. She would have insisted that Burke talk to Kevin and the DPD. Burke hadn't mentioned Martin's name before, and Maggie wouldn't connect it to Burke's case, even if she'd read the article in the paper.

"I'm meeting Scott Kaminsky for lunch," Burke told her. "I want to tell him I've reopened the Michael Johnson case. He may be able to help." Maggie knew that Scott had helped drag the Mississippi cop's body out of the Mad River four years ago.

Burke was changing clothes and getting ready to leave when the mail arrived. Maggie handed him a large yellow envelope from the Ohio Department of Public Safety. "This must be for you," she said with a smirk. "Looks *official*."

He opened the envelope and read the letter congratulating him *on the completion of his training and for fulfilling all of the requisite instruction . . . your Ohio Private Investigator license.* The envelope included a plastic, wallet-sized identification card, a paper diploma *suitable for framing*, and a handbook. Burke handed the letter and diploma to Maggie, broke the ID card out of the plastic holder, and slid it into his fat wallet.

"Too much shit in here already," he said, stuffing the card in.

"Speaking of *shit* – should I get a frame for this?" Maggie asked, curling her nose and holding the diploma out away from her, between a thumb and a forefinger.

"Thank you – *dear* – for your kind understanding," said Burke, with his own smirk.

31

Ol' Bessie

It was another scorcher in Hattiesburg, and Alex Johnson had the afternoon off. He'd arranged to visit the African American Military History Museum with Charles Robinson, and maybe help him do a little grocery shopping. Ever since John Burke had returned to Dayton, Alex visited Charles Robinson almost every day, riding his bike across town to the house on Adeline Street.

Charles answered the knock at his front door. "Come on in, Alex. I'll lock this door and we can go out the back."

They went in through the house and out the back door. A small landing and ramp had been built over the two short steps down from the house. Once down the ramp, Charles handed his keys to Alex and asked him to lock up.

"Jiggle the knob to make sure," said Charles over his shoulder. "And give that screen door a good kick at the bottom, will you? It's swollen up a little and won't close all the way."

Alex kicked the old wooden screen door closed and followed Charles down a ramp to a concrete walk leading to the back door of the garage. Another short ramp had been installed over the garage threshold. Alex unlocked the garage door, and Charles tapped the automatic opener button as he wheeled himself in. The overhead door opened into an alleyway, and daylight flooded the garage. Charles pressed a button attached to the wheelchair, and Alex watched as a wide door slid open on the side of the van. A bi-fold ramp unfolded out onto the floor of the garage.

"Wow! Cool! It's kind of like a drawbridge!" exclaimed Alex. Charles maneuvered the wheelchair up the ramp and into position behind the steering wheel. When he pressed another button, the ramp retracted and the door closed.

"Get in," Charles called to Alex. He maneuvered the wheelchair precisely, activating a bolt mechanism that locked the wheelchair into place. Alex hopped in and watched in amazement as Charles put on his seatbelt and backed the van out of the garage, using a control column that extended from just below the dashboard. He closed the garage with another button, and they headed off down the alley.

"Just like a joystick in a fighter plane," said Charles, smiling and pushing the hand-operated accelerator forward as they moved into the traffic on Hardy Street. It was only a five-minute drive to the museum, and Charles parked near the Vietnam-era M60 tank that was on permanent display out front.

"My Dad was a trustee here, and now *I* am," Charles said, as he extricated himself from the van. "I think Dad and Mike spent a good deal of time helping out around here." Charles understood that his budding friendship with Alex, and the bizarre circumstances that had brought them together – a generation removed from their own fathers – was not lost on either of them.

Alex had been to the museum several times with his father, but the last time had been over four years ago. It seemed to him that everything had been upgraded since then, and all of the dioramas and displays were very slick and first class. The cases and cabinetry, the lighting, the video and sound systems, the floors and finishes – all seemed very modern. Alex mentioned it to Charles.

"Dad left the museum a bundle in his will," Charles whispered. "I'm sure they will be eternally grateful."

They spent several hours wandering through the entire museum. Charles took special care to show Alex the displays that related to Henry Robinson's military career as a WWII Tuskegee Airman, and as a jet pilot during the Korean War. In a diorama honoring the country's **First Black Korean War Ace**, a mannequin depicted a saluting Henry, dressed in a Korean War era flight suit, standing in front of an F-86

Sabre jet, while a dogfight took place high in the sky above between another F-86 and a Russian Mig-15.

Charles introduced Alex to some of the staff, pointing out to them that he was Michael Johnson's son. Alex was pleased when several people shared their memories of his father, and one even remembered seeing Alex in the museum with his dad. When it was time to go, Alex promised the staff that he'd come again soon.

On the way back to Charles' house on Adeline Street, they stopped at the Sunflower Food Store on Hardy Street and did some shopping. Alex pushing a cart, following Charles as he wheeled through the store, picking things off the shelves and handing them back over his shoulder. At one point, Charles tossed a loaf of bread back over his head. "Incoming!" he shouted. Alex grabbed the bread out of the air and tossed it into the cart. This happened several more times before they finished shopping, and by the time they got to the parking lot, both Charles and Alex were a little giddy from the horsing around.

Back at the garage on Adeline Street, Alex waited while Charles closed up the van and lowered the overhead door, then carried the groceries up to the house ahead of the wheelchair.

"Here, give me the bags," Charles said, handing Alex his key ring.

"You'll have to lift that screen door a little when you pull it open," Charles said, but as Alex put his hand on the handle, they both realized that the door was already ajar. Alex looked at Charles, and then back at the door.

"I'm pretty sure I kicked the door closed when we left," he said.

Charles knew right away what Alex was thinking. *Someone had opened the screen door while they were gone and hadn't bothered to push it in tight.* Their lighthearted mood vanished, and when Charles saw the look of consternation on Alex's face, he waved dismissively.

"Somebody probably came by," he said, as convincingly as he could. "Don't worry about it. Could have been one of my students was in town and stopped to visit – or maybe a neighbor. See if the other door is locked."

Alex tried the inside door and it was still locked. He unlocked it and pushed it open. Charles' paranoia nearly got the better of him, and he considered drawing the Beretta from the side pocket of the wheelchair, but he knew it would only alarm Alex. "Let me go first," he said, and Alex stepped aside. They entered cautiously and looked around. No one was in the house, and everything seemed to be in place. Alex double-checked all the rooms and then helped put away the groceries. They moved to the front porch, and Alex went down the ramp and unchained his bike. He looked up at Charles on the porch.

"I hope we hear something from Captain Burke pretty soon," he said. "Are you worried, Mr. Robinson?"

"No," Charles lied. "And you shouldn't worry either, Alex. And don't worry about me. That business with the door – that could have been anything."

"Well, I'll try not to," said Alex. "But it's hard."

"Just pay attention, Alex. If anything happens out of the ordinary, you let me know right away. Okay?"

"Yes sir, I will for sure," Alex said, climbing on the bike. "But you be careful."

"Don't you worry, I've got Ol' Bessie here." Charles smiled, patting the side pocket of the wheelchair. "We'll be fine.

32

Orangey Red Hot Rod

Just past noon, Burke put the top down on the Camaro and headed for Riverside. The Riverside Police Department was located in the city office building, just across the road from Riverside High where Burke had once gone to school. He parked in a tiny patch of shade under the only tree near the building, and stepped into the air-conditioned police station. The dispatcher at the front desk greeted him warmly, and Scott Kaminsky came out and did the same. He led Burke back to his office, closing the door behind them.

"So, Scott, what can you tell me about this accident?" Burke asked.

"First, how about you tell me what you were doing there," said Kaminsky. "And *when* you were there. Nobody else seems to know you were there, by the way. I'm the only one who saw your name on that envelope. I *did* show it to Mrs. Novak – but she had no idea who you were."

"Well, believe it or not, I got sucked back into an old investigation," said Burke. "Maggie's not too happy about it. Neither is Kevin for that matter." He pulled the wallet out of his pocket, found the private investigator's ID card and tossed it on the desk in front of Kaminsky. "He made me get that."

Kaminsky looked at the card, and a smile crossed his face. "Well, well. John Burke – private dick."

"Real funny," said Burke, shoving the card back in his wallet. "Anyway, I'm sure you remember the Michael Johnson case – the cop from Mississippi?"

"Hell, yeah. Of course, I remember," Kaminsky said. "Three or four years ago. You never closed the case, did you?"

"Not really," said Burke. "But as you know, we never had anything to go on. Nobody knew what the guy was even *doing* in Dayton – including his own family."

"You flew down there with the body, didn't you?" asked Kaminsky.

"Yeah, I did. Anyway, his son came up here a little while ago looking for me. He was just a kid back when his dad died, but now he wants to know what happened. He found out something in Hattiesburg that got me interested enough to want to help him out."

"Found out what?"

"I can't tell you yet, Scott," said Burke. "I'd love to, but I can't – not yet anyway. But it led me to Martin Novak, and I went there a couple of days ago to talk to him. That's when I wrote my number down for him on that envelope. The accident is just some weird coincidence."

"Are you hungry, J.B.?" Kaminsky stood up. "I need some lunch. Let's go over to Clancy's. Okay with you?"

"Sure," said Burke. "I can eat."

Kaminsky spoke with the dispatcher at the front desk, signed some forms, and the two men stepped out into the summer heat.

"I'll drive if you want," said Burke, motioning toward the Camaro.

"Whoa!" Kaminsky said, feigning shock as he looked at the car. "What the hell *is* that? A Camaro?"

"You like it? It's my retirement gift to myself."

"Well, it explains one thing," said Kaminsky, grinning.

"What's that?"

"One of the Novak's neighbors reported that she saw an *orangey red hot rod* in their driveway a couple of days ago. Mrs. Novak said she didn't know anyone with a car like that," Kaminsky explained. "It's a beauty, J.B. But I better drive the company car – in case something comes up."

Clancy's Tavern was on Belfair Avenue, next to a Kroger store in a small shopping plaza not more than a stone's throw from the house where Burke grew up. It was the neighborhood pub, and over the years it had morphed into a sports bar, with plenty of large TV screens and video games. Inside, it was pleasantly cool, and "classic hits" came from the speakers overhead. Kaminsky said hello to the bartender and to a petite, young waitress named Ling, introducing Burke as "My buddy, J.B." At Kaminsky's request, Ling led them to a booth in the back near the old pinball machines, and took their orders — burgers, fries, and iced tea. As Burke watched Ling walk away from the booth, he realized that she'd put him in mind of someone. *I'll probably think of it later*, he thought. They chatted until the food arrived, and while they ate, Kaminsky told Burke about Martin Novak's accident.

33

The Accident

"The 911 request came in about one o'clock Monday afternoon," Kaminsky told Burke. "At the time, everybody but me was dealing with a tractor-trailer rollover on I-675."

The caller, a next-door neighbor, reported that Sylvia Novak had been gone for the weekend and came home to find her husband dead. She thought he'd fallen from a ladder. When Kaminsky got to the house on Bobtail Court, the garage door was open, and as he got out of his car a middle-aged woman came out of the house next door to meet him. She was quite agitated.

"Sylvia is over at my house," she said. "Martin is inside there, just inside the front door. I peeked in, and I'm pretty sure he's dead. It's horrible."

Kaminsky sent her back to her house to look after Mrs. Novak, just as the EMT vehicle he'd requested came speeding into the cul-de-sac. Kaminsky greeted the EMTs, and they all pulled on latex gloves and paper booties and entered the house together through the garage.

They found Martin in the front entryway, lying awkwardly, with a pool of dried, almost black, blood under his head. Kaminsky spotted Sylvia's small suitcase at the bottom of the stairs where she'd dropped it. A stepladder was lying on its side, small bits of broken glass littered the floor, and a small table had been knocked over. A package of light bulbs, pieces of mail, some keys, pens, markers, and a broken bowl were scattered nearby. Everyone agreed that it looked like an unfortunate accident. The EMTs quickly determined that Martin was quite dead, and following the protocol for an unattended death, Kaminsky called the Montgomery County coroner's office. He spoke with Catherine DiMarco, the chief coroner and head medical examiner, and she said she would send a team right away. Finally, Kaminsky called the dispatcher at his own office and explained the situation to her. She said that everyone else was still tied up out on the highway.

A small crowd of curious neighbors had gathered on the street, and the EMTs walked next door to offer some counselling and support to Mrs. Novak. Kaminsky asked the onlookers to keep away from the house, then he unrolled yellow crime scene tape between some trees and plantings in the front yard. After that, he went inside to study the scene and wait for Catherine's team to arrive.

He found that the back door of the garage was locked. Stepping gingerly around the mess in the foyer, he determined that the front door was locked as well. He made notes on everything he saw, including the light bulb in the old man's hand, and that the chandelier light was on when he arrived. He snapped a few photos, and then asked one of the EMTs to keep an eye on things while he went next door to talk to Sylvia. The EMTs had managed to calm everyone down, and Sylvia was sitting at a table with the neighbor woman, sipping water and clutching her purse.

"I just got back from Cleveland," she told Kaminsky. "From a bridge tournament. The girls dropped me off out front and I went in through the big garage door. I have an opener in here." She held up her purse. "I was a little surprised that Martin didn't come out to meet me. When I went in, I found him by the front door, and then . . . and then I ran over here."

Kaminsky explained that it looked as though Martin had fallen from the ladder while changing the light bulbs in the chandelier, because he still had a bulb in one hand. When he asked, Sylvia and the neighbor woman both said they had not turned on any lights.

"I bought those new bulbs just the day before I left," Sylvia said, crying quietly now. "I told Martin to leave it for the woman who cleans for us. I told him she could do it when she came, and I told him to stay off the ladder. I told him he was too darned old to be up on a ladder." She blew her nose into a hankie and sobbed, "Oh, Marty, Marty, Marty."

Catherine's forensic crew showed up. Kaminsky had told her on the phone that it just looked like an accident, and based on his appraisal, Catherine had sent the "B" team – mostly young recent college graduates working on their chops. The team went through the entire house, talked to Kaminsky, and they all agreed that it must have been an accident. The house had been locked from the inside, there was no sign of forced entry, no sign of a robbery, no sign that anyone else had been in the house, and no sign of a struggle. They examined the body where it lay and determined that the blow to the head was consistent with a fall from a high step of the ladder. Other than some bruises, no other significant marks or injuries were noted. Their best guess was that Martin had died sometime in the last forty-eight hours, pending a thorough examination of the body in the lab. Accident or not, they followed the protocol for an unattended death – took photos, dusted for fingerprints, and made a lot of notes. A female member of the team went next door, where she very sweetly asked Sylvia a few questions, and made a set of the old woman's fingerprints.

By the time the forensic team was finishing their work, the nearby tractor-trailer accident had been cleaned up, and traffic was back to normal on I-675. Squad cars from the different agencies began arriving at the cul-de-sac, nearly filling Bobtail Court. Just curious, they mostly said. At one point Kaminsky counted at least a half dozen police vehicles. He couldn't imagine what the neighbors must be thinking, and he politely asked everyone who didn't need to be there to clear out.

The EMTs agreed to take Martin's body downtown and deliver it to the coroner's building. Catherine DiMarco would determine if a full autopsy was warranted after a closer look in the lab. Her team left, and Kaminsky watched as the EMTs bagged the body. A small pocket knife fell out of Martin's pants pocket and landed on the tiled floor. One of the EMTs picked it up and looked at it curiously before handing it to Kaminsky. He noted the swastika, wrapped the knife in a piece of paper towel, and put it in his pocket.

A Montgomery County grief counselor arrived, and arrangements were made for Mrs. Novak to stay with one of her friends until a cleaning crew could come in and take care of the mess the next day. Kaminsky asked one of his officers to remove the police tape from the yard, and then he went inside and gathered up the mail that had been scattered on the foyer floor, leaving the rest of the mess for the cleaning crew. He made sure the house was locked, pushed the button for the garage door opener, and hurried to the door. Ducking down, he hopped over the safety reverse beam, and the garage door came down behind him.

* * *

"And that's when I saw your name on that envelope," Kaminsky explained to Burke, after recounting all that had gone on at Martin's house. "When I gathered the mail off the floor, it was written on the back of a DP&L bill. Anyway, I wrote it down, and then I pointed it out to Mrs. Novak when I gave her the mail. She said she didn't know a John Burke."

"Yeah, she wasn't there when I met Martin," Burke said. "She'd already gone to Cleveland to play bridge."

"Oh, and I gave her that pocket knife," said Kaminsky. "With the swastika. She was very surprised to see it – said she hadn't seen it in a long time. She said it was an old war souvenir somebody gave her husband, but she thought he'd given it away a long time ago."

Hitler's knife. Burke shrugged, acting as if the knife didn't mean much to him. When Kaminsky had first mentioned it, Burke immediately thought about the possibility of his fingerprints being on the knife. But the forensic team had already left when the knife fell out of Martin's pocket. "I'm surprised forensics missed it," Burke said.

"Like I said. I think it was the "B" team," explained Kaminsky. "Very young. Some of them looked pretty green around the gills."

Burke knew the feeling. He remembered how it felt forty years ago, the first few times he'd witnessed the aftermath of a gruesome death. He never got over it completely – nobody ever did.

"Another neighbor noticed your car a couple of days ago," Kaminsky said, grinning. "The 'orangey red hot rod,' she called it. Same woman said she saw some kind of white service van in the driveway the next day – with pipes or lumber or ladders – something on top. She didn't see the driver, and she didn't remember if it said anything on the side of the van. Other than that, nobody I talked to noticed anything strange. Sylvia Novak couldn't think of why the van would have been there, but hell, it could have been anybody."

Anybody. *Yeah, like an assassin,* Burke thought instinctively. "So, Scott," he said. "You think we can keep this just between you and me for a while? My being at the house, I mean."

"No problem, J.B. And you let me know if you need any help with this case. I have to admit I've thought about Michael Johnson more than once over these past few years – him being a cop and all."

They finished their lunches, both men picking absentmindedly at the last of their fries, and Burke insisted on paying. He handed his credit card to the young waitress, and again, the feeling that he somehow recognized her lingered as she walked away.

"She's a cutie," Burke said.

"Ling?" said Kaminsky. "Yeah, she's a sweetheart. Her Dad's a lieutenant colonel and her Mom's Chinese – from Taiwan actually. They met when he was stationed over there."

That's it! Burke sat up with a start, accidently kicking Kaminsky's leg under the table. "Jesus. Sorry, Scott."

He now realized why Ling seemed so familiar, and at the same time he knew why he'd had a similar feeling the day before in Area B, when the young security agent pulled them over. As Jim McGowan would say . . . *Bingo!*

34

Soft Target

Earlier, while Burke had read it in the newspaper, Brian Lopez heard the story of Martin's death on the radio. The accidental death of an old man in Beavercreek meant nothing to him – until he heard the address. *Bobtail Court.* No house number was mentioned in the newscast – just Bobtail Court. But Brian knew. A few days before, the old man now known to Brian as Martin Novak, *a retired professor of nuclear chemistry at the AFIT* according to the radio, had simply been what Brian's handlers referred to as a "soft target". Brian knew right away that the death had been no accident. Twice in the past few days he had been assigned to surveil the house located on Bobtail Court. The first time, he had been there to watch for the arrival of an orange, late model Chevrolet Camaro. He'd been advised to keep his distance – the driver of the car was considered a "hard target" – possibly capable of detecting the surveillance. Brian was to report when the car arrived and when it left. That was all.

The second assignment had been a day later. He'd gone back to the same location, assigned to follow the old man who lived there when he left the house. From a tapped phone call between the man and his out-of-town wife, Brian's handlers had learned that the man would be going out at some point that day to do some shopping. Brian hurried to Bobtail Court and parked in the same observation point where he had parked before, near the entrance to the court on Buckhorn Drive. He'd waited less than an hour before the garage door opened and the old man backed down the driveway and drove out of the neighborhood. Brian called in, and was told to shadow the man and report his movements every five minutes – *immediately* if his return home was deemed *imminent*.

The old man drove directly to the Kroger store on Belfair Avenue. Brian watched him enter the store, and sat back to wait. The parking lot was scorched from the afternoon sun, and Brian eyed Clancy's Tavern adjacent to the Kroger store – *an ice-cold beer would be good*. After he'd reported in to his station, four times in twenty minutes, the target came out of the store with a plastic bag in each hand. Brian called in again – *return is imminent*. He followed the old man back to the house, parking again on Buckhorn Drive. A white, E-Series Ford van, fitted with a roof rack holding lengths of PVC plumbing pipe and an extension ladder, turned out of Bobtail Court as the old man turned in. Brian caught only a quick glimpse, and he didn't recognize the driver of the van. He watched the target's car go up the driveway and disappear behind the descending garage door. Seconds later, Brian's cell phone rang and he was told to return to the station. When he got back to the box, he noticed the white Ford van parked in the lot.

35

Over His Head

Burke and Kaminsky left Clancy's and returned to the Riverside police station. Burke was in a hurry now. He threw a quick salute to Kaminsky and hopped into the Camaro. Kaminsky watched as his retired friend – now a private dick – drove out of the parking lot, shot across Harshman Road, and accelerated up and around the oval ramp toward the westbound lanes of Route 4 leading back into Dayton.

Burke had decided it was time to tell his son what was going on, even if he didn't really understand the situation himself. His mind was racing as he sped toward downtown Dayton. Ling, the waitress at Clancy's, had jarred Burke's memory. Late in the previous summer, when Burke had been immersed in the last investigation of his long police career – a horrible accident had taken place on Dayton's north side, not far from where Burke and Maggie lived. A young Asian-American woman – *part Chinese* – had fallen from a window in her seventh-floor apartment. *It was an unattended death*, Burke remembered.

Kevin had taken the lead in that investigation, and although the DPD's final determination was that the death had indeed been accidental, Burke knew that his son was still bothered by the case. *What was her name? Sarah?* The young woman's death haunted Kevin in very much the same way that Michael Johnson's death still haunted Burke.

At the time of the woman's accident, Burke had been grooming Kevin to take over as the next head of the homicide squad. Burke remembered offering some advice and direction to his son regarding the tragic death, and he'd agreed to sit in and observe an interview that Tarisa and Marco conducted with the woman's boyfriend. *What the hell was his name?* The boyfriend had already been ruled out as a suspect, but he'd been asked to come in to headquarters for an interview. Tarisa and Marco were a good team, and Burke remembered being impressed with the compassion they showed toward the distraught young man. *What the hell was his name?* Burke couldn't remember.

But he remembered the face. And he was pretty goddamn sure it was the same young man who had stopped them in McGowan's car in Area B, the day before.

Burke had to admit to himself that this turn of events excited him. The old instincts were still there, and it felt good. On the other hand, he still had no idea what the hell was going on, or how all of these pieces were going to fit together. Who killed Henry Robinson? Who killed Michael Johnson? Had someone murdered Martin Novak, or was it really just an accident? *Sarah? I'm pretty sure that was her name.* An accident? The boyfriend who stopped and questioned Burke in Area B? Were they all connected?

Burke sped into town. It was just after two o'clock, and Kevin would most likely still be in the squad room. Burke parked in the lot behind the police building and was putting the top up on the Camaro when he suddenly realized that he had to tell Charles Robinson about Martin's death.

Goddammit. If Martin's death was not an accident, then there was a reasonable chance that Charles could be in danger. Burke had to warn him. If their phones were being tapped, so be it. Burke dug through his wallet and found the phone number Charles had written down for him.

"Charles?" he said. "This is John Burke. I'm in Dayton."

"Hello, John," said Charles. "Good to hear from you. Alex and I have been wondering what you've been up to."

"Well, I'm afraid I have some bad news for you. Martin Novak is dead. It happened a couple of days ago, and I just found out about it this morning. It looks like he fell off a ladder and died from a head injury. That's what the police are thinking anyway."

"Good Lord, John! I can't believe it. Did you get a chance to talk to him before this happened?"

"I did," said Burke. "The day or two before he died. He asked about you. We talked for a long time and he shared some very disturbing information with me, but I don't think we should talk about it over the phone. I'm planning to come down to Hattiesburg in a few days and I can tell you everything then. In the meantime, I figured I had to at least tell you about his death."

"Sweet Jesus," Charles said softly.

"You need to be careful, Charles. Martin's death may look like an accident, even to me, but I'm going with my instinct here, and I think you could be in danger. This whole thing is a real mess and I'm not sure we'll ever be able to figure it out – but I'm working on it. And it may be a little premature to warn Alex. No point scaring the shit out of him and his mother."

"I agree," said Charles. "And you be careful yourself, John. Don't worry about us." He thought about telling Burke about the screen door incident from the day before, but decided against it.

"I'll see you guys in a few days," Burke said. "Be careful."

"Okay," said Charles. "We'll see you then."

* * *

Smitty greeted Burke at the front desk and passed him through the metal detector. Burke took the stairs two at a time, and found Kevin alone in the squad room.

"Hey, Pop," Kevin said, getting up from his desk. Father and son bumped knuckles and then hugged. "What brings you into town? How's your investigation going?"

"It's going weird," said Burke. "And that's what brought me into town. Where is everybody?"

"Yeah, it's pretty quiet in here today," Kevin said. "Marco's out tracking something down – Tarisa's here somewhere. Hey, did you ever get your PI license?"

Just then, Tarisa walked into the squad room. "*JOHN BURKE, PRIVATE EYE*," she said, in a deep, theatrical voice. She laughed and gave her old boss a hug. "Whatsa matter, Cap? You miss us?"

"Just you, Tarisa," Burke said, grinning. "The heck with the rest of 'em."

"Yeah, right," said Tarisa. "How's Maggie doing? You driving her nuts yet?"

"She's doing great," Burke said, laughing. "Turning me into a gardener."

"No shit?" Tarisa said. "You? A gardener?"

"Yeah – me a gardener," said Burke. "Hell, I've gotta do something. I can't play golf *all* the time."

"Must be nice," said Tarisa, shaking her head and laughing. She settled herself at her desk and began to type something on her computer keyboard.

"I did get the license, by the way," Burke said, turning his attention back to Kevin. "But we need to talk. You got time to take a walk? I need to get some exercise. And I've got a lot to tell you – it might take a while."

Kevin looked at his watch. "Yeah, let's go," he said. "You got this covered, Tarisa?"

"No problem," she said without looking up. "See you, Cap. Say hello to Maggie for me, okay?"

They left the building through a side entrance, and Burke stopped to grab his sunglasses and a vintage Cincinnati Reds ball cap from his car. They walked west down Third Street, past the county coroner's building, and under the overhead lanes of I-75. When they reached the Great Miami River, they headed north along a bike path that followed the river's eastern bank half-way around the city. As they walked, Burke told Kevin everything. Well, *almost* everything . . . about Charles Robinson and his father's death, what had happened in China, Martin Novak's death, Area B, the security agent he'd somehow recognized on the base, and the waitress whose appearance had put him in mind of the young Asian American woman who'd fallen to her death the previous summer.

"Sarah Sheldrake," Kevin reminded him.

They walked all the way to RiverScape Park, where Burke bought them each a lemonade at the snack bar. They sat under an umbrella at one of the small round tables that surrounded the wading fountain. Kids squealed and shrieked, running in and out of the jets of cool water shooting up from the ground. Moms and grandparents kept an eye on the kids from the shade at some of the other tables.

"We've had the girls down here a couple of times," Kevin said, speaking of Burke's two granddaughters. "They loved it."

Burke watched the children playing in the water and thought about Kevin as a little boy. *I wasn't around much,* Burke thought, knowing he'd been married to his job. *When I was, I didn't do enough. Thank God for Maggie.* But he knew that Kevin had turned out okay. He knew his son was well adjusted, happily married, and a good dad. *Thank God for Maggie.*

"Tell me something, Kevin," Burke said. "Do you like being a cop?"

"Jeez, Pop . . . you *know* I do."

Burke sighed. "Yeah. I did too."

Kevin looked at his father, but couldn't quite see his eyes through the sunglasses. The information his father had shared with him on the long walk was more than a little disturbing. He patted his dad on the back. "Don't go getting all philosophical and shit," he said. "I know this Michael Johnson thing has got you a little freaked, but we'll figure it out. Hell, I admit it's the craziest goddamn thing I've ever heard. I can see why you're rattled . . . but we'll figure it out."

We'll figure it out. *We.* Burke felt a great relief from having told Kevin *almost* everything, but the relief was tempered by the fear of having now involved his son in the case.

Fear. It was something that Burke did not have much experience with, even after almost forty years as a homicide detective. He'd always had some control over whatever was happening. But now he seemed to have none. Someone else seemed to be calling the shots, and he had only a vague idea of who that was. He didn't really know where to turn or what to do next. For the first time in his life, he felt like he was in over his head.

36

Sarah Sheldrake

As they walked along the river, back to police headquarters, Burke asked Kevin to remind him some more about the death of Sarah Sheldrake. The case was closed – ruled an accident – but Burke knew that Kevin was still troubled by the case.

"She was a stripper," Kevin sighed. "Twenty-four years old. She danced at a couple of the clubs in Dayton and one in Cincinnati. Her father lives out in L.A. and taught math at U.C.L.A. Her Chinese mother was one of his grad students. They got divorced after a couple of years, and when Sarah was ten years old her mother moved back to China. Sarah went with her, and her dad never saw either of them again after that. When we tracked him down, he said he didn't even know Sarah was back in the States."

"What about the mom? Did you contact her?"

"No way," Kevin said, shaking his head. "About the only thing the dad could tell us about the mom was her name and what province she came from in China. I think her name was Li Lin – or Lin Li, something like that. Anyway, Danny tried to track her down through the Chinese Embassy in Washington. They told him there were over two hundred thousand women in China with that same goddamn name. Sarah's dad paid to have her cremated here in Dayton, and they sent the ashes to him in California."

Sarah Sheldrake had fallen seven stories from a window of her apartment. Her fall was stopped by a chain link fence, and her head struck the edge of a dumpster, crushing her skull. From what Kevin's team could determine, Sarah had been standing on a chair, leaned out to wash a window, lost her balance and toppled out. Her mangled body was discovered in the morning by one of the other tenants. The homicide team found no sign of foul play, no forced entry, no sign of a struggle, and no discernible fingerprints or any other evidence in the apartment. The data recovery geeks in forensics had found nothing incriminating in Sarah's computer. In fact, they'd been impressed by how little it had been used.

"And the boyfriend – the security agent that I saw at the base yesterday?" Burke asked. "*Lopez,* you said? Is that his name?"

"Yeah, I'm pretty sure," said Kevin. "Brian Lopez. He showed up at the scene later that morning and completely freaked out. Marco and a couple of other cops tried to keep him away from the body, but he got a look anyway. Man, it was sad."

"But if I remember, he was nothing more than a person of interest," Burke said. "You never really suspected him."

"Well, he was such a mess that we were pretty sure he didn't do it," said Kevin. "And he gave us a number to call at the base to verify that he'd been at work. I talked to an officer there, and he got back to me later and verified that Lopez had been on the base all that night. The officer said there were half a dozen others who could verify it, and security card swipes, and camera footage. They had it covered. And one of the other tenants in Sarah's apartment building had seen Lopez kiss Sarah at her door and leave earlier that afternoon."

"But you had him come in for questioning," Burke said. "I sat in on that interview – Tarisa and Marco handled it. That's where I remember Lopez from – from that interview. I remember him being pretty torn up."

"Yeah," said Kevin. "And Tarisa and Marco both had a vague impression that he was also pissed off. But pissed off at what? At who? When they asked him about it, Lopez wouldn't go there. He said he was just mad that Sarah had died."

"I remember," said Burke.

"But, Pop," Kevin said, stopping on the path, "how the hell does all of this fit together? I mean Michael Johnson and Novak, yeah – but

Sarah Sheldrake and Lopez? I don't see how they fit in. Sure, Sarah was part Chinese and lived in China, but so what? And Lopez works at the base. Again, *so what?* I just don't see how they could possibly tie in to Michael Johnson's death."

Burke knew that Kevin was right. It *was* difficult to connect these four people based on nothing but circumstance. But there were some odd similarities, especially between the deaths of Martin Novak and Sarah Sheldrake, and they weren't lost on Burke. Both deaths – *falls* – had been ruled accidents. The scenes were both extraordinarily devoid of any evidence that would suggest they were anything other than accidents. *Too clean*, Burke thought, *too goddamn clean.* Burke had never closed the Michael Johnson case, but even *that* death could have been ruled an accident, based on lack of any evidence suggesting foul play. But Burke's instinct told him otherwise. That's what it had told him four years ago, and it told him the same thing now. *They're all too clean.*

"It's just a feeling," he said.

Kevin had heard his father say that before, and he'd almost always been right. *He's a damn good detective,* he thought.

"Well, I will say, this whole thing is the craziest shit I've ever heard," Kevin said, as they walked. "And you need to tell Mom what's going on, don't you think? She'll probably think you're nuts though."

"I will," said Burke, grinning. "And you're right – she will."

They were almost back at police headquarters, just passing the coroner's lab, when Burke stopped. "I need to talk to the coroner if she's around – about Martin Novak's death." He nodded toward the lab building. "Do you need to O.K. that with her?"

"I guess I should," said Kevin. "But go ahead. I'll call Catherine and let her know you're on your way in." Burke watched as Kevin pulled a phone from his pocket and walked away.

"I'll be up to the squad room in a minute," Burke called to his son. "I'd like to look through Sarah Sheldrake's file."

* * *

Burke entered the coroner's building and chatted briefly with the woman at the security desk. He asked if Catherine was still in the building, and the guard thought so. She was about to check when Catherine pushed open a door and stepped into the reception area, holding a phone to her ear and laughing. "Thanks, Kevin," she said, and slipped the phone into a pocket of her lab coat. She hugged Burke.

"*Magnum, P.I.!* Long time no see."

"Jesus," said Burke, rolling his eyes.

"Sorry, J.B." Catherine said, stepping back, still laughing. "I've got *no* problem with it. What can I do for you?"

"I wanted to ask you about Martin Novak," said Burke. "The old man who fell off the ladder out in Riverside?"

"Sure. Come on back. We just finished with him this morning. Pretty routine. Did you want to see the body?"

"Not really." Burke shook his head. "I'm done looking at bodies. Just tell me about it."

Burke followed Catherine to her office, and she had him pull a chair up to her desk. She quickly found the file and opened it on the desk in front of Burke.

"Blunt trauma to the head. Cracked it open pretty good," she said. "Skull fracture, brain damage and bleeding, external hemorrhage. All consistent with a fall off a ladder. The chandelier was pretty high, and we figure he probably fell ten or twelve feet."

Burke looked at the photos. *Poor Martin,* he thought. The pictures taken in the vestibule matched the description of the scene that Kaminsky had given him. In one photo, he spotted the DP&L envelope on which he'd written his name and number.

"We all agree it was an accident. No indication otherwise," Catherine said. "No forced entry, house was locked from the inside, no sign of anyone else present. Prints didn't show us much. Martin and Sylvia Novak were the only clear ones we lifted."

"I'm guessing you didn't do an autopsy," Burke remarked.

"Just blood tests and toxicology, and it was all clean. We decided a full post mortem was unnecessary."

"Scott Kaminsky told me there wasn't any sign of a struggle," said Burke. "Did you find anything?"

"No sign of struggle on the body. Just the typical old man stuff. Small contusions on his arms and legs, sun damage, liver spots. Oh, and one odd little contusion on the lower back that could have been anything – a thorn prick, or an old insect bite, we couldn't tell."

She sifted through the photos of Martin's body that had been taken in the lab, pulled one out and put it on top of the pile, pointing to a close-up of the small bruise.

"Could have been anything," she repeated.

Burke looked closely at the photo. He could see that Catherine was right – *could have been anything.* But the photo, together with that simple, pedestrian phrase, jogged something deep down in Burke's memory. Staring hard at the photo and hearing the phrase in his head, Burke searched his memory. Finally, he got it. He made the connection.

"Thanks, Catherine," he said, standing up. "This all helps."

"So, J.B.," said Catherine, "Do you mind if I ask what your interest is in Martin Novak? Kevin said you were working on a cold case. Anything I would remember?"

"Probably not," Burke said. "It was almost four years ago. A dead cop from Mississippi named Michael Johnson. I don't think you were working here yet."

Catherine shook her head. "Well, anyway, let me know if I can be of any help – anytime. Oh, and good luck with the new career," she said with a smile and a wink.

37
Silhouettes

Burke trotted the short distance from the coroner's lab to the front entrance of the police building. Smitty buzzed him in and he hurried up to the squad room. It was late afternoon, and Tarisa and Marco had finished their shift. Pete Scoff and Bones were there and they were happy to see their old boss. Burke took some more ribbing . . . *private dick . . . Magnum . . . shamus . . . bounty hunter.* He was getting used to it.

Kevin had pulled the file on Sarah Sheldrake's death and set Burke up at an empty desk in a corner of the room. "I'm going home," Kevin said. "You be careful."

"Thanks, Kevin," Burke said. "Oh, one more thing – the Michael Johnson autopsy report. I need to see that."

"Help yourself." Kevin nodded toward the files. "You know where everything is."

After Kevin left, Burke found what he was looking for and took it back to the desk. He'd taken the Michael Johnson file home several days earlier, but hadn't bothered reading the coroner's report. In Catherine's lab, when Burke saw the photo of the *odd little contusion* on Martin Novak's back that *could have been anything* – he knew he'd seen something like it before. He searched through the Michael Johnson photos until he found it – a *small contusion* on the right side of the dead cop's lower back. Labelled as *inconclusive*, the mark looked a lot like the one Burke had just seen on the right side of Martin Novak's lower back. Catherine had not been the chief medical examiner at the time of Michael Johnson's death, but Burke could clearly recall the words of the previous coroner describing the bruise: *It could have been anything.* They were probably both right, Burke thought. It could be anything – maybe nothing.

But it could also be *something,* and Burke's instinct told him that it was. He put the Michael Johnson report aside and opened the Sarah Sheldrake file. Kevin had already told him most of what was in it, so Burke thumbed through the file quickly. He was mainly interested in Brian Lopez, and when he found a good, clear copy of the young man's Ohio driver's license, Burke was thoroughly convinced that the person in the photo was the security agent who had stopped him and McGowan in AREA B the day before.

He read through the transcript of the interview that Tarisa and Marco had conducted with Lopez, recalling most of it. Kevin's typed notes on the case were impressive – very thorough and well written, Burke thought. The information Kevin had collected from a liaison officer at Wright-Patt, proving that Brian had been on the base at the time of Sarah's death, was extensive. The officer had provided several time-marked security camera photos of Lopez, one showing him entering a building on the base, another of him walking down a hall. There were two printed read-outs from pass-through security systems, one a biometric facial recognition system, and the other from an ID card swipe. Both were also time-marked. There were emails between Kevin and the liaison officer. One mentioned that Brian Lopez was employed through a private security firm doing contract work on the base, another that he'd been working there since June of 2007. The officer had declined to give Kevin the name of the company, citing security reasons.

Burke wrote down some notes and made a copy of Brian's driver's license. The address listed on the license was Tibet Drive. It was out in Huber Heights, a sprawling suburb of small, look-alike brick ranch houses located just to the northeast of Dayton. Begun in the mid-1950s, Huber Heights had grown so vast that in 1981 it had incorporated as a city. Whenever he'd driven through Huber Heights, Burke always thought about the old song, *Silhouettes,* about a guy looking in a window through a drawn curtain at what he thinks is the shadow of his girlfriend making out with some other guy, until he realizes he's on the wrong block at the wrong house. *Huber Heights.*

Burke got up and put the autopsy report back in the Michael Johnson file. He was about to do the same with the Sarah Sheldrake file, when it occurred to him that he hadn't looked at *her* autopsy report. He knew the death had been particularly grim, and he wasn't really sure that he wanted to see the photographs again, but he was curious about one thing – there seemed to be similarities in all three deaths, and in two of them there was the *odd little contusion* that *could have been anything*. Would he find it again?

Returning to the desk, he set the gruesome photographs aside and read through the report. There was no mention of anything similar to the little contusion. Burke looked at the photos, and there was certainly *nothing* little about the injuries that Sarah Sheldrake suffered when she fell from her seventh-floor window. Kevin's description of the body had not been exaggerated. She'd landed with her midriff straddling the top of an eight-foot-high chain link fence, right at one of the vertical fence posts. Her head had struck the edge of a dumpster parked close to the fence. The fence had torn open Sarah's stomach and she'd been partially disemboweled. Her skull was cracked wide open and horribly misshapen. Burke could look no further, and he closed the report and put it back with the file. *Poor, poor Sarah.*

It was late afternoon now, and Burke called Maggie to let her know he would be heading home after he made one more stop. He'd call her if he got held up. Burke bumped knuckles with Pete and Bones and left the squad room. He threw a quick salute to Smitty, and pushed through the front door. Squinting in the harsh sunlight, Burke shielded his eyes and nearly ran into someone on the sidewalk.

"*Shamus!*" It was Lisa Fowler, a veteran crime reporter for the Dayton Daily News. Lisa had reported extensively on Burke's final case as a cop. "It's been a while."

"Christ almighty!" Burke said, shaking his head. "Does everybody know?"

"Word travels fast out here on the street, J.B.," Lisa laughed, and Burke gave her a heartfelt hug.

Lisa had covered many of Burke's investigations over the years, including his final case as a Dayton homicide detective. It was a crime involving the coverup of abusive clergy by the Catholic Church, and as a result of her reporting, Lisa was asked by a major New York publisher to expand the case into a book. She had interviewed Burke many times in the past year, and they had become quite close.

"Lisa, Lisa," Burke said. "How the hell are you?"

"I'm fine. Really good actually. The book is finally done. I mean *done* done. I'm off to New York tomorrow to meet with my agent and editor. And the *New York Times* wants me to write another article, something about a big abuse case that's going to trial soon. But what about *you*? *Private detective*? What the hell?"

"No big deal." Burke waved dismissively. "Something's come up that I decided I wanted to look into – an old case that never got solved."

"Anything I'd remember?" Lisa asked, eyebrows arched.

"Oh, you'd remember it all right. But I can't talk about it yet."

Lisa scowled. "What's Maggie think about this little turn of events?"

"Not too happy," Burke said. "But she gets it. She always does."

Burke and Lisa chatted for a while, and she asked him to let her know if his investigation turned into anything.

"You'll be the first to know," he promised, waving as he headed for the parking lot.

The interior of the Camaro was hot from sitting in the sun, and Burke dropped the top and drove out of downtown in the direction of Huber Heights – *"America's largest community of brick homes!"*

38

Huber Heights

Once in Huber Heights, Burke found Tibet Drive in a plat where all of the street names began with the letter T. The houses all looked alike on Tibet Drive – brick ranches with a front door, a living room picture window, two smaller windows high up just under the eaves, and a single car garage door. From what Burke could tell, the main difference was that some of the houses were topped with hip roofs and some roofs were gable-styled. The landscaping of the postage-stamp-size lots varied from house to house, but not much.

Humming *Silhouettes*, Burke drove slowly along Tibet Drive until he found the address listed on Brian Lopez's driver's license. The garage door was open, and two men, probably in their mid-thirties, were holding cans of beer and sitting on the open tailgate of a late model pick-up truck parked in the short driveway. Burke parked at the curb in front of the house, got out and approached the men. They seemed to be more interested in the Camaro than in Burke.

"Hi guys," he said. "I'm looking for Brian Lopez."

"Nice ride," said one of the men, nodding toward Burke's car.

"Oh, thanks," Burke said, looking back at the car. "Is this his house?"

"Not anymore," said the other man. "He sold it to me back in May."

"Any idea where he moved to?"

"Not really. He said he was going to buy something fancier – with more privacy."

"So, you have no idea how to get in touch with him?"

"Nope. He didn't talk much."

"That's for sure. I live next door," said the other man, pointing to the house on the left. "And I never really talked to the guy the whole time he lived here – about four years I think it was. He just said 'Hi' when I saw him. That was pretty much it."

"And you don't know where he moved to?" Burke asked.

"No idea," said the neighbor. "You a cop?"

"Not anymore," Burke laughed. "Do I look like a cop?"

"Yeah, kind of. Except for the Camaro."

"I was a detective in Dayton," Burke told them. "But this is just personal. Do you guys have any idea where I could find Brian?"

"Not really," said the neighbor, both men shaking their heads. "Like I said, he was pretty private. He kept funny hours. I think he may have worked at the base, but I'm not sure. You could try there."

"Did he ever have any company that you noticed?"

"Just this one girlfriend," said the man. "And she was *extremely* hot – a stripper. But the poor girl croaked last summer – fell out of a window, I heard. Man, what a waste."

"How do you know she was a stripper?"

The neighbor turned and looked over at two women who were sitting on lawn chairs, smoking cigarettes, just inside the open garage door at the next house. *The wives*, Burke guessed. Looking back at Burke, the man leaned forward and lowered his voice.

"I saw her strip a few times," he said. Both men laughed and bumped knuckles.

"Okay then," Burke said, grinning. "Thanks for your help. You guys take it easy."

"We'll take it any way we can get it," the neighbor said, winking. The two men laughed and bumped knuckles again. Burke was amused to be included in their little conspiracy.

He walked to the Camaro and was about to get in when the neighbor called out and motioned for him to come back. Burke saw him look over his shoulder again, toward the wives. When Burke approached, the neighbor spoke quietly.

"You might look for Brian in the strip clubs," he said, winking again. "I think that's where he spends a lot of his time. I've seen him in a couple of them."

Burke got back in his car and drove out of Huber Heights. Just before he turned on to Old Troy Pike, he pulled over and checked the expiration date on Brian Lopez's driver's license. It was good for another two years, and Burke knew that having the DPD run a registration check would be a dead end, the address would be the same. He could call the base, but he doubted that they would have any interest in handing out personal information on a contract security employee, especially to a private investigator. *You might look for Brian in the strip clubs.* Burke put the Camaro into gear and was looking forward to getting home. It had been a long day, and he knew that it probably wasn't over yet.

* * *

Maggie made some hamburger patties and a salad while Burke fired up the gas grill. Watching the burgers, he sipped a Jack Daniel's on the rocks. He was preparing to level with Maggie, and he knew she would not be happy. They ate on the screened-in porch at the back of the house, and for the second time that day, Burke laid out the investigation.

He did not reveal to Maggie his instinctive belief that Martin Novak's death was not an accident. Burke knew that Maggie would understand what such a possibility could mean – that maybe Burke's own life was also in danger. Other than that, he told her everything – or *almost* everything – from Alex's discovery of the unused airline ticket right up to his chat that afternoon in Huber Heights. As the bizarre dimensions of the investigation unfolded, Maggie sipped a glass of red wine and asked a lot of questions, variably shaking her head in disbelief or horror. It had gotten quite dark when she finally got up and lit a couple of candles.

"Kevin's right, you know," she said, pausing to blow out a match. "This is the craziest thing I've ever heard."

"Yeah, and I'm not sure what the hell I should do," said Burke. "I'm stumped – and I don't like it."

"Well, I know *exactly* what you should do," Maggie said firmly. "You need to tell somebody what the hell is going on."

"But…"

"But nothing, Johnny," said Maggie. "I know you're probably worried about somebody thinking that you're nuts – thinking this whole stupid thing is nuts. I mean *polonium-210*? And *UFOs*? The *Chinese*? The *CIA*? Yeah. I agree. It *is* pretty nuts. But people are dead, Johnny. Michael Johnson, and this Henry what's-his-name in Hattiesburg. Not just dead, but maybe killed. Maybe even Martin Novak. And that poor girl! Who knows what will happen next!"

So much for that, Burke thought. *I should have known she'd figure it out*. Maggie knew him better than he knew himself most of the time. And she was right, of course. He had to take this whole thing up the ladder to a higher authority.

"What about your buddy down in Cincinnati, the FBI guy," Maggie suggested. "Presley? Is that it?"

"Lamar Presley," said Burke with a nod. "I thought about him. He'll definitely think I'm nuts, but I think I could trust him. Whether he'll be able to help is another matter."

They sat quietly in the candlelight. Maggie had never seen her husband so conflicted about a case. "Johnny," she said, taking his hand across the table. "Do you think you're in danger yourself?"

"Hell, I don't know," he said with a shrug. "Every time I start to think that's a possibility, I end up thinking the whole goddamn thing is so absurd that I shouldn't worry about it. But I don't want *you* to worry. I'll call Lamar tomorrow. I should probably go down to Cincinnati and talk to him in person."

"Good. That makes me feel better." Maggie got up from the table. "I'm going to clean up. Should we play some Scrabble?"

Burke shook his head. "If you don't mind, I'm going out to see if I can find Brian Lopez. I can't help thinking he's tied into this somehow. If his old neighbor in Huber Heights is right, maybe I can track him down in one of the strip clubs."

"Oh Johnny, really?" Maggie said, grimacing. "Tonight?"

"Sorry, honey, but I've got to work on this and get it done before it drives me nuts. Don't worry. I'll be careful."

While Maggie was in the kitchen, Burke went into their bedroom and took a shoebox down from the top shelf in his closet. Unwrapping an old towel, he inspected his 9-millimeter Glock service pistol. Two empty magazines and a box of shells were in another box on a shelf in Maggie's closet. Burke had taken the gun to a shooting range only once since he'd retired.

"Fuck this," he said. He wrapped up the pistol, put it back in the box and returned the box to the closet shelf.

39

Boilermaker

From Maggie's computer, Burke printed out a list of adult clubs in the Dayton area. He left his house at nine o'clock and drove with the top up on the Camaro – too many bugs at night – taking I-75 south to Kettering, where several of the clubs were located. His first stop was Maxie's Cabaret. The parking lot was about half full, and Burke parked and went in. Before he could get to the bar, a friendly young woman in a bikini introduced herself and offered to make him feel right at home. Burke thanked her, proceeded to a bar at the side of the stage area, sat down and ordered a beer. He showed the photo ID of Brian Lopez to the bartender who served him, and asked if Brian ever came in.

"You a cop?" the man asked.

"Not anymore," Burke replied. "I just need to talk to him."

"He comes in, sometimes. Just to drink. I haven't seen him tonight. Maybe later."

Burke took a look around the club and didn't spot the man he was looking for. He thanked the bartender and left without drinking his beer. The same scene played out, more or less, in two other Kettering clubs, and in one a little farther south, in Miamisburg, called Felicia's Lounge. The bartenders were all familiar with Brian. He was a regular, but he wasn't there.

Burke drove back into Dayton and took Route 35 east toward Riverside. There were two infamous low-rent clubs near Wright-Patt that had both been shut down more than once over the years, mostly for illicit sexual activity, underage drinking, and drug dealing. Burke's perception of Brian Lopez was that the young man was a little higher class than these places, but he checked them anyway – with the same dead-end results. The staff in both places said they didn't recognize the photo. Burke didn't know if they were telling the truth, or they just didn't feel like cooperating.

It was getting late and Burke was tired. There were a couple of high-end clubs in north Dayton, not too far from where Burke and Maggie lived, and he headed back into town. The Scarlet Club was set back from the road on North Dixie Drive. Burke parked in the front lot.

He was greeted at the door by a hostess with large breasts and a mostly bare cleavage, wearing a very short skirt. He told her he'd just stopped in for a drink, and she led him to the bar, away from the cages and the stages in the entertainment lounge. Before she could walk away, Burke showed her the ID picture of Brian Lopez and asked if she had seen him that night. The hostess looked at the picture, then up at Burke. Her friendly expression disappeared, and she was about to say something when the bartender intervened.

"I've got this, Vicki," he told her. He turned to Burke. "Can I see that?" Burke showed him the ID.

"You a cop?" the man asked casually. He picked up a towel and began wiping a beer glass.

"Not anymore," Burke answered, just as he had done several times that night already. "I just need to talk to him."

"What about?"

Burke wanted to tell the bartender that it wasn't any of his goddamn business, but he knew how far that would get him. It was obvious that both the hostess and the bartender had recognized the picture, and Burke sensed they were being protective of Brian.

"Sarah Sheldrake," Burke said, taking a chance. "I'm investigating her death."

The bartender continued wiping glasses and didn't speak. He walked down the bar and drew a pint of beer for another customer. When he came back, he leaned across the bar toward Burke. "Brian's a good guy," he said quietly. "He didn't have anything to do with Sarah's death. It was an accident."

"I know that," said Burke. "And I have some information that Brian might be interested in hearing."

"They were in love. Brian met Sarah here. It really messed him up – her dying I mean."

"I know," Burke said. "I was a cop at the time."

He waited patiently while the bartender dried a few more glasses. Finally, the man folded the towel and set it on the bar. He leaned forward again and nodded toward the stage area.

"He's in the back," he said. "All the way in the back corner."

"What's he drinking?" Burke asked.

"Boilermaker," said the bartender. "Jim Beam and a pint."

* * *

Brian Lopez sat in the darkest corner of the Scarlet Club. He'd already had one more boilermaker than he usually drank in a night, and was thinking about having another. Alcohol seemed to be the only antidote for the pain he was feeling, and the pain was now paired with a fierce anger. Like the whiskey and the beer, it was a dangerous mix.

He'd recently found out the truth about Sarah's death. His own government – probably even his own employer – had been responsible. Her death had meant only one thing to Brian – that any chance for a normal life had been snatched away from him. And just that morning he'd discovered that he had unwittingly played a part in the death of an old professor, a man he didn't know and bore no grudge against. Apparently, his own government was again responsible. It wasn't the first time he'd been part of something *necessary to the vital interests of the country* that had shamed him to his soul. But it would be the last.

Brian kept a Beretta M9 semi-automatic pistol, loaded with a fifteen-round magazine, under the driver's seat of his pickup truck. It was the same weapon he had carried in Iraq and Afghanistan when he was a soldier. Back when he was a good American. He had served his country unconditionally for over ten years now. He always did what he was told and kept his mouth shut. He'd been paid well, yes, but he knew now that he had been betrayed. His blind loyalty to the American government had turned him into a criminal. And they had taken Sarah from him. The torment was too great to bear. He could walk out to his truck right now and put an end to it.

* * *

Burke held a glass of whiskey in one hand and a pint of beer in the other as he made his way through the crowded section of the club, dodging the whistling, cat-calling drunks and the young women working the room. The lights on several small stage areas lit the front of the club, but the house lights were dimmed at the back, almost off. The tables there were empty except for a lone man at the table farthest away from the stage area. In the darkness, Burke didn't recognize Brian Lopez until he reached him. Brian was leaning back in a chair with his hands in his lap, staring straight ahead. The empty glasses from his last round sat in front of him.

When Burke set the drinks down, Brian looked up at him slowly. Until then, he hadn't seemed to notice Burke's approach.

"Hey, Brian," Burke said. "Do you mind if I buy you a round?"

Burke watched the young man's eyes squint as he tried to focus. He sat up in the chair and looked at Burke without smiling. He was a little drunk, Burke could tell, and not very happy.

"Thanks," Brian mumbled. He picked up the glass of whiskey and tossed it back. "Do I know you?"

"Not really," said Burke. "But we've met a couple of times. You pulled my friend's car over a couple of days ago – out on the base. A '64 Ford convertible – light blue. Do you remember?"

Brian continued to squint, looking at Burke's face. He took a sip of the beer, spilling a little as he picked up the glass.

"Yeah," he said. "I remember. Nice car."

"My name's John Burke. Mind if I sit down?"

"Go ahead."

Burke sat down across from Brian. The young man leaned forward and continued to peer across the table at Burke's face.

"I remember you," he said, slouching back in the chair. "John Burke."

"I also met you last summer," Burke said. "When Sarah Sheldrake died. I was a cop."

Brian sat up straighter at the mention of Sarah's name. He took another long drink of beer, set the glass on the table, and pointed at Burke.

"I remember," he said. "You're a cop."

"Yeah, I *was* a cop. But I retired. Now I'm a private investigator."

Brian sat back in his chair and seemed to be considering what Burke had said. He opened his eyes wide and then rubbed them with his fingers, trying to clear away the fog. Pushing the beer glass away from him, he leaned forward, crossed his arms and rested his elbows on the table. "Are you investigating Sarah's death?" he asked.

"Not really," said Burke. "I'm working on two other deaths that I think are related to each other. But there may be some relationship to Sarah's death as well."

"Sarah's death was an accident," said Brian sternly, reaching for the beer.

"I don't think you believe that." Burke's eyes narrowed. "I think you know more than you shared with the police last summer."

Brian stared at Burke for several seconds, sighed deeply, and scooted his chair back. Leaning forward, he rested his forehead on his crossed arms. Burke waited a full minute without saying anything, and then realized that the young man was crying. He reached across the table and put a hand on Brian's shoulder.

"It's okay, Brian," he said. "I'm just trying to figure this out. Maybe you can help me. Hell, maybe I can help *you*."

Brian sat up and wiped his eyes with the back of his arm. He took a drink of beer, trying to compose himself. "I . . . I know who killed Sarah," he said quietly, at last. "And they'll probably kill me if they find out I talked to you about it."

"Christ!" Burke exclaimed, probably a little too loudly. "Who? Who killed her?"

"I don't know what *person* did it," Brian said. "I mean, whoever pushed her out the window – I don't know that. But somebody from the CIA set it up. They thought Sarah was a spy working for the Chinese."

"Jesus Christ!" Burke half whispered. He looked around, but no one was paying them any attention. "A *spy*, Brian? Do you believe that?"

"I didn't – not until a few days ago." Brian shrugged in resignation. "Now I think she probably was."

"Wait. You just found this out?"

"Yeah. Somebody sent me a bunch of emails and letters and stuff – on a CD. I have no idea who sent it."

Burke could hardly believe what he was hearing. He wasn't sure what he'd been expecting, but this was a complete surprise.

"Brian, do you work for the CIA?"

"Not directly," Brian said, shaking his head. "I work for BlackSnake. It's a private security contractor."

"I've heard of it," said Burke. "They were involved in some nasty shit in Iraq. So does BlackSnake work for the CIA?"

Brian was about to say something when he sat up quickly and finished the beer in several gulps. "I should shut up," he said. "I should go."

Burke leaned back and watched the sudden change in Brian's expression. He knew that the young man realized he'd spoken too freely.

"Let me drive you home," said Burke. "You might be drunk."

"I'm okay, sir," said Brian, standing up. "I'll be fine. Thanks for the drink."

Burke watched Brian navigate the room and make his way out the front door of the club. Their conversation had sobered him somewhat, Burke knew. Brian had even called him *sir*. But he was disappointed that the meeting had ended so suddenly. He wasn't quite finished with Brian Lopez and followed him to the door. He watched through a small diamond-shaped window as Brian climbed into a late model pick-up truck. Burke slipped out the door and hurried to his car on the other side of the parking lot, keeping an eye on the young man.

But Brian did not start the truck. Burke could see him sitting there and watched as he leaned forward and rested his head on the steering wheel. *He's crying*, Burke realized. Finally, after almost five minutes, Brian started the truck and pulled out of the lot. Burke followed at a discreet distance. Brian seemed to be driving steadily as he headed south on North Dixie Drive. He turned left on Wagner Ford Road and then right onto the ramp for I-75 south. Driving fast, he took the interstate to Route 4 and then headed east. Burke had no problem keeping up. Brian drove alongside the Mad River until the highway veered left. He passed north of the Eastwood Lake Metropark, crossed over Harshman Road by the Riverside Police station, and then exited onto Route 444, right near the spot where Michael Johnson's body had been found in the river below Huffman Dam. Route 444 passed between the dam on the left and the Wright Brother's Memorial up on the right, just skirting Area B and the Air Force Museum. Burke could see the massive building that housed Air Force Materials Command Headquarters on the left as they passed Area A, just before Brian slowed and turned right onto Dayton Yellow Springs Road. After several miles of suburban sprawl, the road entered the countryside that lay between Fairborn and Yellow Springs, a seven-mile stretch of mostly old farmhouses surrounded by fields and woodlots.

Halfway to Yellow Springs, Brian slowed and turned into a long driveway that led to one of just a handful of large, newer houses that had sprung up along the road over the last twenty years. The house sat between two farms on a lot carved out of a cornfield, probably a hundred yards off the road. There were no other houses within a quarter of a mile in either direction. Brian's next-door neighbor in Huber Heights had told Burke that Brian wanted to move somewhere with more privacy. He had succeeded.

Burke watched the lights go dark on Brian's truck, and drove on by. He turned around at the next farm. Coming back, he passed the house again and continued on toward Dayton, the same way he had come. Now he knew where to find Brian Lopez, and he would try to talk to him tomorrow. All Burke wanted now was get home and crawl into bed next to Maggie. He felt as if he hadn't slept in a week.

40

Cease and Desist

The following morning, Jim McGowan sat reading the *Dayton Daily News* in the living room of his house in Beavercreek. It was starting off as a fine summer day, but thunderstorms were supposed to roll through southern Ohio sometime that afternoon. Kathy was off playing golf in a woman's league she belonged to, and McGowan had a board meeting at the Air Force Museum scheduled for later in the morning.

He looked up from his newspaper when a black SUV with heavily tinted windows pulled into the driveway. McGowan noticed the U.S. Government license plate. A middle-aged man got out of the SUV and walked toward the house along the concrete path. He was wearing tan khaki slacks and a white short-sleeve shirt with a navy-blue tie, loosened at the neck. His head was shaved bald, and before he could knock, the general opened the door.

"Howdy," McGowan said. "What's up?"

"General James McGowan?" asked the man.

"Guilty," McGowan replied, extending his hand. "Who are you?"

The man saluted but did not extend his hand. He removed and folded his gold-framed aviator sunglasses and put them in his shirt pocket.

"I'm afraid I can't tell you my name," he said. "I'm from the Department of Defense, and for reasons for which I am sure someone like you can understand, I need to remain nameless."

"What do you want?" McGowan asked, the friendliness gone from his voice.

"It's about your friend, John Burke."

"What about him?"

"We're hoping you'll speak to him for us."

"About what?"

"About the investigation he's conducting."

"I don't know anything about it," said McGowan. "I don't know what the hell you're talking about."

"Well, be that as it may, General McGowan, we hope that you will convey to Burke our desire that he cease and desist with his investigation. Certain elements of our national security could be at risk if he continues, and we think that this request – delivered by you – may be more effective than if we spoke to him ourselves."

McGowan glared at the man. He wanted to cold-cock him, right there on the porch where he stood. The man took a step back, possibly sensing what the general was thinking. But McGowan knew better. He knew how the DOD operated, and now he fully realized, without even knowing what Burke was up to, that his friend was in *way* over his head. This man was offering Burke an *out*. McGowan guessed that the DOD had no idea how little *he* knew about Burke's investigation, but he knew that this visit was meant to be a warning to both of them. He knew the DOD was not doing this out of the kindness of its heart. *It had no heart.* They were merely trying to avoid having to take any extreme measures.

"I'll see what I can do," said McGowan.

"Thank you, General," the man said, saluting again. "Have a nice day."

McGowan watched the man walk back to the SUV and drive away. His only thought was, *John is in deep shit.*

* * *

Burke slept late, later than he wanted to. He'd planned to get up early and return to the house on Dayton Yellow Springs Road, there were a lot of questions that he wanted to ask Brian Lopez. Maggie was already up and gone, playing golf in a women's league with Kathy McGowan and some of her other girlfriends. Burke drank two cups of coffee and ate a bowl of Cheerios. Back in the Camaro, he drove east out of Dayton. He tuned the radio to WYSO in Yellow Springs – *same old shit* – decapitated bodies and drug wars in Mexico, phone hacking in England, dozens killed in Syrian civil war, Wimbledon results. One item in particular caught his attention – Raul Castro was visiting China. After what Jim McGowan had told him about the level of fear the Department of Defense had regarding Chinese intentions, Burke could imagine that they were paying pretty close attention to this visit from the Cuban president.

He gave up on the news and was about to switch to an oldies station when his cell phone rang. It was Jim McGowan.

"Hey, Jim, how you doing?"

"I was doing fine until I just had a little visit from some goddamn bald-headed goon who said he was from the Department of Defense."

"Good lord! . . . Hold on, I'll pull over." Burke's breakfast flipped in his stomach. "Okay. When?"

"Just now," said the general. "We need to talk, John. Whatever the hell it is you're up to, they want it to stop."

"Fuck!" *Fuck, fuck, fuck.* "Okay. I'm out your way now, but I have to talk to someone first. If I find him it might be a little while before I get to you. If he's not home, I'll be there soon."

"I'll be here," said McGowan. "In the meantime, you be careful. You're in some deep shit here, pal."

Burke realized he'd broken into a sweat. He thought about driving straight to the general's house and giving up on trying to talk to Brian Lopez. Maybe it *was* time to end this crazy goddamn investigation before someone else ended up dead. Before *he* ended up dead. But he couldn't just stop. He knew Jim McGowan was right, that he was in deep shit. But Burke also knew – *when the shit gets deeper, you'd better dig faster.*

A few minutes later, he was on Dayton Yellow Springs Road. From the road, Burke could see that Brian Lopez's pickup truck was still parked in front of the garage at the end of the long driveway. Burke pulled in. Now that it was daytime, he could see that the house was a large, clapboard-sided two-story, with an attached two-car garage. There were three gables facing the road and a columned porch all the way across the front. It was a newer house, designed to resemble an old farm house. Burke parked behind the pickup and walked to the front door. He rang the doorbell and waited. When there was no response, he knocked loudly and rang the bell again.

Something that Brian had said the night before troubled Burke at the time – *They'll probably kill me if they find out I talked to you about it.* He remembered those words now, and pounded on the door again. No answer. In desperation, he kept pounding.

"What do you want?" Brian finally shouted through the door.

"It's John Burke, from last night," Burke shouted back, relieved to hear Brian's voice.

"I know who it is," yelled Brian. "How'd you find me?"

"I followed you home last night."

"Jesus. What the hell do you want from me?" Burke thought he detected some resignation in Brian's voice.

"I just want to talk," Burke called out. "C'mon Brian, open the damn door."

Burke heard the dead bolt turn, and Brian opened the door. Standing there in plaid boxer shorts and nothing else, the young man squinted against the daylight. He lowered his head.

"Look, I opened my big mouth last night," he said. "I was drunk. I don't want to talk to you about Sarah."

"I don't want to talk about her either," Burke said. He'd thought about this moment, and now Burke fired what he knew might be a wild shot. "I want to talk about an old man named Martin Novak."

At this, Brian's head snapped up. His eyes narrowed and he glanced over at the orange metallic Camaro parked in the driveway. He looked back at Burke. His jaw clenched twice, and he swallowed.

"You know who I'm talking about, don't you, Brian?"

The young man stepped back and motioned for Burke to enter the house. When he stepped inside, Burke sniffed the musty, closed-up air. The interior was very dark, considering the sunlit day outside, and Burke noticed the heaviness of the shades on the windows.

"I'll get dressed. You can sit in there," Brian said, pointing toward a living room. Burke went into the darkened room and looked around. *Spartan* – that was the word that came to his mind – and the bareness of the room reminded him of the way he had lived for years when he and Maggie were split up. There was a set of living room furniture – two recliners, with one end table and one lamp between them, and a matching sofa. Nothing hung on the walls, and there were no plants, photographs, knick-knacks, books, magazines – nothing. The furniture looked as though it had never been used. Brian reappeared wearing baggy shorts and a t-shirt.

"I'll make some coffee," he said. "Let's go in the kitchen."

Burke followed him to the kitchen and sat down on a stool at a tall countertop. Brian started a pot of coffee and sat down across from Burke on another stool.

"Did you see me there?" Brian asked. "At Bobtail Court?"

"I saw the black SUV with government plates," Burke said. "Just like the one you were driving when you stopped me and General McGowan on the base."

"We have five of those SUVs – all identical," said Brian. "How do you know it was me?"

"How did you know it was Bobtail Court?" Burke responded.

"I heard it on the radio," Brian said, barely skipping a beat.

"Why would you remember a fact like that?" Burke asked.

Brian stared at Burke and Burke stared back. He knew he *had* the young man, and he knew that Brian knew he'd been had. Burke had been a homicide cop for most of his life, and he could play this game all day.

"Anyway, it's just a hunch," he said, lightening up. "But my hunches are usually pretty good. And I could tell you recognized my Camaro – just now, out front."

Brian got up and poured them each a mug of coffee.

"Milk or sugar?" he asked.

"Just black," Burke said.

Brian sat down and stared at the coffee mug he held between his hands on the countertop. He sat like that for a long time, without speaking, and when he finally looked up, his eyes were moist. "I need help, sir." It was a desperate plea.

Sir. He called Burke *sir*, just as he had the night before. Burke knew that this was an involuntary form of address for a lot of people with military backgrounds. But it was almost always used respectfully.

"How can I help you, Brian?" Burke asked. "What can I do?"

Brian began to cry, and Burke reached across the counter and patted the young man's arm, just as he had done in the strip club the night before. "It's okay," he said. "It'll be okay."

Brian stood up and started pacing the kitchen floor. He tried to talk, but the crying had quickly turned to sobbing and Burke couldn't make out what he was saying. Brian's shoulders shook, and he put his hands to the sides of his head as he continued spluttering out the words that Burke couldn't make out.

"They'll kill me...they'll kill me." That much, Burke understood.

Burke got up and walked around the counter. He put his arms around Brian and held him, patting his back in an attempt to comfort him. Brian stopped talking and sobbed on Burke's shoulder. Burke had witnessed breakdowns like this before, and he knew they were often born out of fear. This young man was afraid.

Brian suddenly pulled away from Burke, grabbed a dishtowel and wiped his face. He stood up straight, eyes open wide, trying to compose himself.

"I'm sorry, sir," he said. "I'm sorry that happened."

"It's okay," Burke said. "Don't worry about it. Drink some water." Burke sat at the counter and watched Brian gulp down a glass of tap water.

"Who's going to kill you?"

"I don't know," Brian said quietly. "Maybe . . . maybe nobody."

Brian was back-pedaling, Burke knew, trying to talk himself into believing that everything would be okay.

"Look, Brian," he said. "Maybe I *can* help you. Maybe you can help me. I think I might be in trouble with the same people you're afraid of. Who is it Brian? Who *are* you afraid of?"

"*How* can you help me?" Brian said desperately. "Nobody can help me."

"Look, I can try," said Burke. "I have a friend in the FBI, in Cincinnati. He may be able to help you. I'm going down to see him tomorrow." Burke knew it wasn't much, but it was all he had. He watched as Brian rubbed his face with his palms and scratched at the back of his neck, considering the offer.

"BlackSnake," Brian said at last. "They won't let me leave. I'm worth too much to them. And I know too much. If they want to, they'll just set me up – same way they set up Novak. It'll look like an accident and that will be the end of it."

"You *know* they set up Martin Novak?"

"Not for sure," said Brian. "I never know anything for sure. But that's how it works. You never know everything – just your own little part."

"And you were part of it?"

"Yeah," Brian said. "I was assigned to watch out for you – when you went to the house. I didn't know who you were, but I knew what you were driving. And then the next day I was sent back there to follow Novak when he went out. And I'm pretty sure somebody else went into the house while I was keeping an eye on him – probably just to scope it out."

"Was that somebody driving a white van by any chance?" Burke asked.

"Yeah. How'd you know that?"

"A neighbor saw it," Burke said. "Who was in the van?"

"No idea. I passed him, but I didn't get a good look. The van was in the parking lot when I got back to the box."

"In Area B?"

"Yeah. That's my base."

"How do you know Martin was set up?" asked Burke.

"I *don't* know for sure. But when I heard about his fall on the radio – well, I know how this stuff works. They probably brought somebody in from out of town to take care of the old man." Brian looked down at his coffee mug and grew quiet. He sighed, and looked up at Burke. "For all I know, it's the same guy who killed Sarah last summer," he went on. "Same set up. Same kind of op. It made me sick when I heard about the old man."

Burke thought back to the interview he'd attended in the DPD squad room almost a year ago, with a distraught Brian Lopez, angry and grieving over the death of his girlfriend. And then he thought even farther back. Burke played another hunch.

"Maybe it's the same guy who killed Michael Johnson four years ago?" he said, watching closely for Brian's reaction.

Brian shot a quick glance at Burke. He stood up, walked over and picked up the coffee pot, topped off their mugs and sat back down.

"They sent two of them to deal with Michael Johnson," he said. "Two Bobs. I never saw them before, and I never saw them again."

41

Four Years Earlier: Riverside, Ohio

Brian met the two men in Area B, in the parking lot next to the box. They looked to be around his age, maybe a little older. He would be their driver, as well as take direction from them. Grinning, they introduced themselves as Bob and Bob. Big Bob was about six feet-four and little Bob was maybe six feet. They were clean shaven with short cropped hair, and both dressed in jeans, polo shirts, and sneakers. The smaller man wore his shirt untucked, and Brian noticed a slight bulge under the front of the shirt – probably a handgun. When they asked Brian his name, he told them it was Bob. They all laughed, shook hands, and agreed that it was a remarkable coincidence. Brian guessed that they were probably former special ops, like himself.

It was a muggy night, a little before nine o'clock, and the sun had set half an hour earlier. Brian got behind the wheel of the black SUV, and they drove out of Area B. He was told to drive to the nearby Save-A-Lot grocery store, just minutes from the base.

"Unless you know where there's a closer pay phone," said Big Bob, who rode shotgun. Little Bob sat in back. Brian thought about it, and decided that Big Bob *knew* it was the closest pay phone – *they must have scoped it out earlier.* Brian was instructed to park the car near the front of the store, and Little Bob got out and walked to the phone, just inside the lobby area. Brian watched through the glass as Little Bob made a call. He could see him talking to someone, even laughing.

"Good to go," said Little Bob, getting back in the car. "I got a room number." Brian was told to drive back the way they had come, and then head west toward Huffman Dam. Two miles later, just after Kauffman Road joined up with Route 444, Big Bob told Brian to slow down.

"Pull in at the next right, then curve around to the left," said Big Bob. Brian turned on to Marl Road, followed it west, and stopped after a hundred yards where the road ended at a vehicle barricade. From here, the road narrowed and became part of the Huffman Prairie Bikeway that passed over Huffman Dam. "This is where we'll rendezvous later. When you pull in, just turn off your lights and wait for us. There'll be another car parked here – but don't worry about it. Okay, let's go."

Brian got back on the highway for a short stretch, and just before it crossed over the Mad River, he angled off onto Springfield Street, circumventing Area B down a long hill, and passing Bong Street that led into the Air Force Museum.

"Go to the hotel," Big Bob said, pointing to the right. It was almost dark now, and Brian turned right into the Comfort Suites, just across the street from the museum. He was directed to the far end of the crowded parking lot, as far from the main entry as he could get, and pulled into a spot. The lot was well lit, and both Bobs looked around in every direction.

"You take off as soon as we get out," Big Bob told him. "We'll call your cell when we're finished – half an hour tops, so don't go far. Pick us up at the dam. What's your number?"

Brian watched as the two Bobs got out and hurried around the north end of the building. He checked the time – 9:17. Driving away, he took Springfield Street back toward the dam. Once on Kauffman Road, he drove to Skyline Drive and up the hill to the Wright Brothers Memorial. The place was deserted, and he parked in the empty parking lot. It was dark, but spotlights lit the tall, granite obelisk at the center of the park, honoring Dayton's most famous brothers. Brian retrieved a pair of night-vision binoculars from the back of the SUV and walked past the shrine to the overlook, high above Huffman Dam. He sat on top of a low stone wall, dangling his feet over the side, and waited for a call from the Bobs. He could only guess at what they were up to, and admitted to himself that he hadn't a clue. He watched the traffic passing below on Route 444, then focused the binoculars and looked down from the bluff to the rendezvous spot. It was only two, maybe three hundred yards away as the crow flies. There were no streetlights near the area on Marl Road and no lights along the bike path over the dam. Minutes later, a car coming from the west on Route 444 slowed down and turned left onto a service road that split the median, crossed over the westbound lanes, and angled into Marl Road. The headlights of the car went dark. *Was this the Bobs? Already?* Brian trained the binoculars on the car and watched as three men climbed out.

They immediately started walking north along the bikeway, toward the dam, one man ahead of the others. Brian thought the two men in back were Bob and Bob. The man in front was almost as tall as Big Bob, and at one point he stopped and turned around. Big Bob shoved him hard. He stumbled and kept walking. Brian couldn't be sure, but Little Bob's right elbow was cocked at a ninety-degree angle, and he may have been holding a pistol. Within minutes they stopped just above where the water flowed over a spillway and under the road. Big Bob appeared to shove something into the small of the other man's back – could have been a knife, could have been a stun gun, Brian figured. The man stiffened, and instantly the two Bobs bent him over the concrete guardrail, lifted his legs and shoved. He disappeared from sight, and Bob and Bob started back toward Marl Road. Brian watched as Little Bob pulled something from a back pocket, and gave a start when his own cell phone rang. "Come and get us."

Brian looked at his watch – he'd dropped the Bobs at the hotel just eighteen minutes ago. He drove down out of the park onto Kauffman Road and back to the highway. Turning onto Marl Road he immediately switched off the headlights. The lights from passing traffic made it possible to see where he was going, and he pulled up behind another car – a late model Pontiac Grand Prix with Ohio plates, probably the other man's car. Brian shut off the engine as he'd been instructed. The only sound now came from the cicadas and the crickets and the passing cars. Almost immediately, the two Bobs appeared out of the darkness, popping up from the steep, grassy incline on the right side of the car. Little Bob hopped into the backseat while Big Bob opened the trunk of the other car. He took something out, closed the trunk, and tossed the keys onto the driver's seat through the rolled-down window.

"Let's go," he said, getting into the car. Brian could see that Big Bob was sweating. He held a plastic Kroger bag on his lap, but Brian couldn't make out the contents. Executing a three-point turn, he drove out of Marl Road in the direction of Area B. Bob and Bob did not speak until they were back on the base and Brian had parked the car in the lot next to the box. They all got out.

"Thanks, man," Big Bob said, clutching the Kroger bag under one arm and offering Brian his hand. "We'll put in a good word for you."

"Yeah, nice work," said Little Bob, also shaking hands. He grinned. "See ya' in the funnies."

They walked swiftly to the entrance of the box that faced the parking lot, and disappeared inside, leaving Brian standing there alone, feeling the collected heat of the day rising up from blacktop. He wondered what the hell had just happened.

42

Case Fucking Closed

"That was four years ago." Brian swallowed the last of his coffee and set the mug on the countertop. "I heard it on the radio the next day," he said, looking up at Burke. "Michael Johnson – a cop from Mississippi. Then I saw it on the news. I saw you on TV that night, talking about it."

"And you knew it right away?" Burke asked. "That you had participated in Mike's death?"

"Yeah," said Brian. "It made me sick. It's the worst thing I ever did – driving for those guys. I should have quit BlackSnake then. I should have called you up and told you."

"Why didn't you?"

"It would have been pointless. BlackSnake would have ruined me. Well, the DOD would have ruined me. Cheney and Rumsfeld. They would have denied everything. They'd have said I was nuts, and that would have been the end of it – *case fucking closed*."

"So, you just kept your mouth shut?"

"Yeah." Brian closed his eyes and leaned back, rubbing the top of his head with both hands. "And now it looks like I did it again – with the old man, Novak. I helped set him up. And I found out about it the same way – *on the fucking radio*."

Burke tried to imagine Martin Novak's last moments – and Michael Johnson's last moments. The two Bobs had taken the big Mississippi cop at gunpoint, driven to the dam in Michael's own rental car, and tossed him over the railing. The autopsy report had said that his death was most likely a combination of head trauma and drowning.

"You realize this makes you an accessory to both crimes," Burke said. "Do you understand that, Brian?"

"Yeah, right." Brian rolled his eyes. "Crimes that the DOD will *never* let you prosecute," he said. "No matter what I say, no matter what I confess, the DOD will deny everything, and it will *all* go away. Believe me, sir, that's how it will happen."

Is he right? Burke thought. *No matter what?* He knew that at this point his options were extremely limited – that Brian's version of how things would play out was probably correct. In fact, Burke could think of only one option.

"Look, Brian," he said. "I told you I have this friend at the FBI office in Cincinnati. He runs the show there. I'll talk to him. He's a good guy and maybe he'll be able to help. It's a chance I have to take. It might be the only chance we have right now."

We. When he heard himself say it, the absurdity of the whole investigation came back to him. When he thought about the phone call from Jim McGowan, about the visitor from the DOD, Burke shuddered. He stood up and offered his hand. "I've got to go, Brian. But I'll call you. I'll talk to the FBI. Hopefully they'll be sympathetic to the situation. I'd love to be able to tell you that it's going be okay, but I can't. This is one goddamn mess, worse than you even know, so keep your eyes open."

Burke pulled out his cell phone. "What's your number?" He punched in Brian's number, and patted him on the shoulder. "Hang in there, Brian . . . and be careful."

"I appreciate it, sir." Brian took a deep breath and exhaled slowly. "Let them know I'm very sorry for what I did. I'll talk to them anytime they want. I'm ready to talk."

Burke noticed the lack of enthusiasm in Brian's voice. The guy seemed tired. Burke had seen it many times before. Confessions often left people with a great sense of relief. But he also detected a hint of resignation in Brian. *Resigned to what?* Burke was worried that Brian might even harm himself. They went out to the front porch, and this time it was Brian who patted Burke's shoulder.

"Be careful, sir," he said. Burke was getting tired of people warning him to be careful.

* * *

Burke drove on back roads from Fairborn into Beavercreek. Jim McGowan met him at his front door and invited him in, taking a quick look up and down the street before closing the door. Burke noticed his friend's wariness.

"You are fucked, my friend," the general said, closing the door. "What the fuck is going on?"

"You wouldn't believe the half of it, Jim," said Burke wearily. "And I'm really sorry I dragged you into it. I know you'd like to know what the hell's going on, but as much as you want to know, the less I tell you the better off you may be right now."

McGowan looked at Burke and shook his head. "I told you, John, these guys don't fuck around. They'll come after you."

"I've become highly aware of that," Burke said. "I'll tell you this much, Jim – three people have been murdered here in Dayton. Assassinated, terminated, whatever you want to call it – and there may be a fourth murder involved, years ago, down in Mississippi. From what I can tell, they were all committed in the name of national security."

"John, look – this is the CIA. This is the fucking *Department of Defense*! What the hell do you imagine you can do about it?"

"I'm going to talk to the FBI. The district chief is a friend of mine – in Cincinnati – Lamar Presley. I think it's my only chance at this point."

"That's pretty goddamn risky, I would guess," McGowan said, shaking his head. "Hell, they could lock your ass up right then and there if they decide to."

"Like I said, it's my only chance. I think Lamar will help."

"Well, you better do something quick," said the general. "These guys are on you like white on rice."

"I'm sorry I got you involved, Jim. I sure as hell hope it doesn't cause you any trouble. I'm really, *really* sorry."

"Don't worry about it, John. But you've got to be careful, pal – maybe even arm yourself. That may sound a bit extreme, but I would if I were you."

"Fuck." Burke suddenly felt overwhelmed. There was a chair in the foyer and he plopped down in it. The idea that his life might be in danger was almost too much. "Fuck."

McGowan guessed what his friend was thinking. "I'll come with you if you want," he offered.

"No, no," Burke countered immediately. He stood up. "Thanks, Jim, but I'll be fine. I'll call you if I run into trouble."

* * *

Back in the Camaro, Burke headed into Dayton. *Arm yourself.* Jesus. He found himself checking the rear-view mirror. When he stopped for gas, he located Lamar Presley's cell number in his phone and started to dial. *Maybe not a good idea*, he thought. He noticed there was a pay phone attached to the front of the station. He finished filling up and parked the car, found some coins, and dialed Lamar's number, reading it from his cell phone. The FBI agent picked up.

"Presley."

"Hi Lamar. John Burke here, from the Dayton Police Department."

"Hey, J.B.! Good to hear your voice. I thought I heard you retired last year?"

"I did," said Burke. "But I got dragged into an old case from a few years ago. Do you remember the Black cop from Mississippi – Michael Johnson? We found him in the river?"

"Oh yeah, I remember," said Lamar. "You wanted some help with that, but I couldn't get the okay from upstairs. And you know, I never *did* get a good explanation."

"Well, I think I might have one for you. But I need your help. I'm in deep shit here. I think the CIA is on my ass and I need to talk to somebody about it. I thought maybe you boys in the Justice Department could help me out of this mess."

"Well, J.B., you've come to the right place," Lamar said, laughing. "You know we like to fuck with Big Brother whenever we get the chance."

"I'd like to meet with you. I could drive down right now if that works for you," said Burke.

"That's going to be tough today, J.B. I'm slammed here," Lamar told him. "How about first thing in the morning? Can it wait till then? Say . . . eight o'clock? I can make sure security knows you'll be here."

"Yeah, I guess that'll have to work," said a disappointed Burke. "Thanks a bunch, Lamar. I'll see you then."

He drove out of the gas station and headed for downtown Dayton. When he got to the police building, he found Kevin at his computer in the squad room. Danny and Jamal both got up from their desks and greeted Burke. He endured some more ribbing.

"I was going to call you," Kevin said, pulling Burke aside finally. "How'd you make out with Brian Lopez?"

"I'll tell you all about it," said Burke. "Did you eat lunch yet?"

"Not yet," Kevin said. "Let's walk down to Lucky's."

Lucky's was nearly empty, and over sandwiches and iced tea, Burke told Kevin about his conversations with Brian Lopez. He didn't, however, tell him about Jim McGowan's visit from the unidentified DOD man.

"Jesus, Pops! Lopez is an accessory to *murder*," Kevin almost shouted. He was angry. Burke put a finger to his lips, but Kevin continued loudly. "Hell – *two* goddamn murders! *And one was a cop!* We should haul his ass in right now. Even if the feds *do* just make it all go away – we still have to arrest him."

"Easy, Kevin." Burke looked around the lunchroom, but now they were alone. "I'm going down in the morning to talk to Lamar Presley," he said. "Let me talk to him first. Hopefully the FBI will have some advice on how to proceed. I don't think Brian Lopez is going anywhere in the meantime. He said he would help us, but he's kind of a mess right now, and I just hope he doesn't flip out. I think he's afraid someone is going to come after him for talking to me. Hell, I'm afraid he might even kill *himself*."

Kevin leaned back and threw his hands in the air. "How would they even know he talked to you, Pops? Jesus Christ . . . do you think they're watching you?"

"I don't know what the hell they're doing," Burke said with a shrug, not wanting to alarm his son any further. *But they probably are*, he thought.

"You should be carrying the Glock," Kevin warned him, just as McGowan had done. "And don't tell Mom – she'll freak. I'll go with you in the morning to talk to Lamar if you want."

Burke couldn't believe it had come to this. He was going to have to arm himself. Against his *own goddamn government*. He felt like he was going to puke, but he forced a smile and patted his son's hand across the table.

"Thanks, Kevin, but I'll be all right. I have no idea how Lamar will handle this – I just hope he doesn't think I've completely lost it. And don't worry, I won't tell Maggie. I think she's already a little freaked."

When Burke got home, he pulled the Camaro into the garage. Maggie was out in the back yard, deadheading the petunias. He called to her from the back door, saying he would be out in a few minutes. In their bedroom, he removed the Glock from the shoebox on the shelf and found the magazines and cartridges in another box in Maggie's closet. He filled the magazines, loaded one into the pistol, and replaced the boxes. Making sure that Maggie was still in the yard, he went out to the Camaro, put the pistol and the extra magazine in the glove box, and locked the car.

"Howdy, stranger," Maggie greeted him when he went outside. "Haven't seen much of you today. You were sound asleep when I left this morning."

"Sorry, honey," Burke said, giving his wife a hug. "I got in pretty late last night. How'd you hit 'em today?"

"I did all right," Maggie said. "Shot a ninety-five. How were the strip clubs last night?"

"Kind of depressing," said Burke. "But I found Brian Lopez. He was in the last joint I checked, of course. Right up here on Dixie Drive. The Scarlet Club."

"Was he able to help you at all?" Maggie asked, tossing a wilted petunia head into a basket.

"A little bit," Burke lied, hating having to do it. "I went to his house and talked to him some more, earlier today. The poor guy is still pretty messed up about Sarah Sheldrake's death."

"What about Michael Johnson's death? You were wondering if he might have had anything to do with it."

"Maybe," said Burke, lying again. "I'm going down to Cincinnati in the morning to talk to Lamar Presley about everything. I called him today."

"What do you mean – *maybe?*" Maggie asked, ignoring Burke's attempt to change the subject. She knew when her husband was fudging, and she knew that he usually did it to keep her from worrying.

"Well . . . he may have had something to do with Michael Johnson," Burke continued to fudge.

"Johnny," said Maggie, arching her eyebrows. "Did he, or didn't he?"

"Okay . . . he did," Burke finally admitted. "But he didn't kill him, and he can't confirm who did it. He'd been involved without even knowing what was happening. I stopped in at the squad room and told Kevin what was going on."

"So will Kevin have him arrested?"

"Not yet. We agreed I'd talk to the FBI first. They may want in on this."

Maggie sighed, but didn't ask any more questions, and Burke was happy to be off the hook for the moment. "How about we go to Jay's for dinner?" he suggested. "We could come home and watch the Reds game. Maybe play a little Scrabble."

And that's just what they did. Burke tried to forget the madness that had been his last week. He still found himself checking the rearview mirror on the way to the restaurant, but after a Jack Daniel's on the rocks and several glasses of wine with his seafood dinner, Burke was relaxed enough that he playfully danced Maggie out of the restaurant to the sweet, slide guitar sound of Santo and Johnny's *Sleepwalk,* cascading from the speakers above the bar.

But Burke barely slept that night. He was afraid. He was in deep shit, and he wondered if he could dig fast enough to survive.

43

Hattiesburg 911

Burke wasn't the only one who was having a rough night. Down in Hattiesburg, Charles Robinson was suddenly awake. He wasn't sure what he'd heard, but it came from the back of the house, maybe the kitchen. He looked over at the clock radio on the bed stand and saw that it was 3:56 AM. The only sound now was the usual white-noise hum from the air conditioner.

The streetlight on the other side of the street cast a faint light into the bedroom through the closed window shade. The night was warm and calm, and other than the AC unit, the only sound came from a whistle on one of the many freight trains that moved slowly through the center of Hattiesburg – the Hub City – in the middle of the night.

Charles' hearing was quite sharp, always had been. Again, a sound came from the kitchen area, this time a floor board creak that he was familiar with. Whoever was in his house had most likely come in through the locked back door, even though Charles was sure he had latched the security chain.

He knew that any attempt to get himself out of the bed and into the wheelchair would probably be heard by the intruder. Quietly, Charles reached into the large pocket at the side of his wheelchair and drew out the Beretta. The door into the room was about twelve feet beyond the foot of the bed. He scooted himself up against the headboard, flipped off the safety on the pistol with his right thumb, and cradled the gun in his lap with both hands. And then he waited.

Charles was calm, and his hands were steady. At this moment, he felt no fear, only anger. He had somehow been waiting for this moment. *These motherfuckers killed my father and now they are trying to kill me.* There was just enough light from the streetlamp so that Charles could focus his eyes on the doorknob and the edge of the door. He didn't know if he would be able to see the knob actually turn, but he was sure he could tell if the door moved, even slightly.

A car passed by outside, and a train whistled again. Charles strained to hear any sound coming from the other side of the door, and something, maybe another floorboard creaking beneath the hall carpet, was followed by a long silence. Then, the door opened, just a crack.

He inhaled, raised the pistol to what he figured was chest high and fired four quick shots through the door. The gun kick was easily absorbed by his powerful arms and the pillows at his back. Charles lowered his aim about a foot and fired four more shots. The roar of the gun after the long silence stung his ears. He heard a groan, and the door suddenly opened about half-way as the intruder fell to the hallway floor. In the dim light, as the smoke cleared, Charles could make out a figure slumped outside the door. He waited until he was sure there was no movement, then lowered the gun. His hands began to shake, and sweat poured down his forehead and into his eyes. Once he'd convinced himself that no one else was there, he set the gun down on the bed amid the scattered, spent shell casings, and wiped his face with a corner of the sheet. His ears were ringing, and the smoke and the smell of gunpowder was suffocating.

Charles sat quietly for several moments, then switched on the bedside lamp. He leaned toward the wheelchair and fished his cell phone out of another pocket. Sitting up, he dialed 911.

"Hattiesburg 911," a woman answered. "What is the exact location of your emergency?"

"I'm at thirty-three Adeline Street," Charles said calmly. "Someone just broke into my house. I fired several shots through my bedroom door and I think the intruder is injured, maybe dead."

"One moment, sir," said the dispatcher. Charles could hear the dispatcher talking to someone. An odd, unpleasant odor began to mix with the smell of gunpowder. Charles realized it was the stench of blood and eviscerated guts.

"Sir?" she said, coming back on the line. "We have officers on the way to that area already. We had a call reporting gunshots. Thirty-three Adeline you said? Is that correct?"

"Yes, that's right. "My name is Charles Robinson and I live here."

"Someone should be there shortly, Mr. Robinson. An EMT unit has also been notified. Is there anyone else in the house?"

"Just me," said Charles.

"Are you injured, sir?"

"No, I'm okay." He could hear police sirens approaching, and spoke very distinctly to the dispatcher. "Please tell the police that the back door may be open. I think the intruder came in that way. I will be in my bed in the middle hallway room. The intruder is lying on the floor in front of my bedroom door. I am paraplegic, and I will sit here and wait for them to arrive."

"One moment, sir," said the dispatcher, and again Charles could hear her talking to someone else. "They should be there any moment, Mr. Robinson," she said. "I'll stay on the line with you until they arrive."

"Thank you," said Charles. "Please tell them not to kick the front door in. I think the back door is open."

A police car squealed to a stop in front of the house, and flashing blue and red lights backlit the window shade. Charles heard a second and then a third vehicle pulling up outside. Through the partly opened bedroom door he saw a flashlight beam briefly illuminate one wall and the ceiling of the hall. Another vehicle, siren blaring, arrived out front. After several minutes, a male voice called into the house from the back door.

"Charles Robinson? Are you there? This is the Hattiesburg police."

"Yes, I'm here," Charles shouted. "I'm on the phone with 911. I'm okay."

A few seconds later, Charles saw light emanating from the kitchen. He could hear several muffled voices now, something about a bolt cutter, then a light went on in the living room.

"I'm in here," he called out. A few seconds later he could hear movement beyond the door, and the hall light went on.

"Jeez! What a mess," were the first words he could clearly make out. A helmeted, bullet-proofed police officer – pistol at the ready – peered into the bedroom.

"Are you all right, sir?" asked the cop.

"I'm fine," Charles said. "Is he dead?"

"The EMTs will let us know." The cop pointed toward the bed. "Is that your gun?"

"It's mine," said Charles. The cop stepped into the room, and using his little finger, he picked up the gun by the trigger guard and carefully set it down on the top of the bureau.

"All clear!" he called out, holstering his own weapon. Charles thanked the 911 dispatcher and hung up.

More cops and an EMT unit quickly filled the house. Propped up comfortably in his bed, Charles watched them work, answering all their questions. A gloved officer picked up the pistol from the bureau and looked it over. He carefully ejected a cartridge, removed the magazine, and set both the gun and the ammo back on top of the bureau. Charles knew he wouldn't be going anywhere in the wheelchair for a while, not until the body had been taken away. He could see that the hallway wall was splashed with blood, and the carpet under the fallen intruder was soaked. The EMTs quickly determined that the white male – dressed in a long-sleeved black T-shirt, black jeans and black sneakers, approximately thirty years old and carrying no identification – was thoroughly dead. Someone made a set of fingerprints from the corpse. A small handgun, fixed with a silencer and partially covered in blood, was found on the floor next to the body. A Hattiesburg homicide detective determined that the weapon was a .22 caliber Walther P22, with a Gemtech sound suppressor. The manufacturer's markings had been filed off from both the pistol and the silencer.

"Nobody would have heard that," he said, shaking his head. "Not even in the next room."

Someone realized that Charles would be trapped in his bedroom until the investigators were finished with the corpse, but when two of the officers offered to carry him and his wheelchair out to the living room, Charles declined. "I'm fine."

"Good shootin'," one of the cops said to Charles with a wink and a grin, inspecting the bullet holes in the door. Charles had fired eight times, and most of the shots had found their target. An officer carefully picked up the Beretta and the magazine from the bureau top, and put them into a plastic bag. "Ballistics will have to take a look at this, sir. I'm pretty sure you'll get it back," he said.

Another cop took pictures, including a close-up of the intruder's face. "Anyone you know?" he asked, showing Charles the digital image on the camera screen. One side of the face was covered with blood, but Charles was quite sure he'd never seen the man before. He answered truthfully all the questions the police asked him. All except one. He told them he didn't know of anyone who would want him dead.

John Burke and Alex Johnson, Charles thought. *They need to know.* But he didn't want to call them with all the cops around. The call would have to wait. At one point, Charles hoisted himself into the wheelchair and motored into the half-bath that was connected to his bedroom. It was a little after six o'clock and the sun had just come up. When he came out of the bathroom, he raised the shade in the bedroom and looked out at the three or four police vehicles that still lined the street. Charles got back into bed and actually managed to doze off.

A little later, someone nudged him awake. Charles wiped his eyes and looked up at a uniformed officer. "Sir," the cop said, "we're finished. There's a cleaning crew here and they'll take care of the mess for you. A victim service counselor will be out to talk to you later this morning. They'll call you before they come. And we may have some more questions for you. I'm sorry this happened, sir."

Charles could see that the corpse had been removed from the hall, and a man and a woman, wearing gloves and Tyvek coveralls, were scrubbing away at the carpet. The cop left, pulling the bullet-riddled door closed behind him.

* * *

At just about the same time Charles had finally nodded off down in Hattiesburg, Brian Lopez was driving home along Dayton Yellow Springs Road, tired and slightly hungover. He'd spent hours drinking at Maxie's Cabaret, just south of Dayton, and had fallen asleep in his truck in the club's parking lot. He'd woken up stiff and a little disoriented, but now he was almost home, and stopped at a traffic light.

Brian's Beretta M9 lay on the seat beside him. Ever since he'd talked to John Burke the day before, he'd kept the pistol close at hand. The ex-cop's apparent concern for him had convinced Brian that it was time to try to make a break from BlackSnake. He knew the break might come at a great cost to him. It might even cost him his life. But that grim thought had not kept him from his usual schedule, including drinking half the night away at a local strip club.

In his rearview mirror, Brian noticed another pickup. It slowed to a stop behind him at the otherwise deserted intersection. There were two men in the truck. The traffic light was about to change when the other truck quickly pulled out to the left, as if to pass. Instinctively, Brian reached for the Beretta, keeping an eye on the pickup. The last thing he saw was the muzzle flash of a .308 fully-automatic rifle.

44

Dead Man Walking

Burke turned off his alarm. When Maggie stirred, he kissed her on the forehead. She opened her eyes and smiled.

"I don't know when I'll get home," Burke said, getting out of bed. "You should go back to sleep."

"Let's be careful out there," Maggie reminded him. It was a catch line from an old television cop show – *Hill Street Blues* – and she had been quoting it to Burke for years.

"I'll try." He blew her a kiss. It was exactly seven o'clock when he backed the Camaro out of the garage. The FBI building was located on Ronald Reagan Drive in Kenwood, a bedroom community with a couple of large malls located about ten miles north of downtown Cincinnati. Burke would be there in just under an hour. He turned off Stanley Avenue, and drove up and around the on ramp leading to I-75. Just before he merged into traffic, Burke looked down to his right from the top of the ramp. A black SUV, with highly tinted windows, also turned off and headed up the ramp. *Shit.*

Traffic was already heavy on the interstate, and Burke checked his rearview mirror. There were too many cars and trucks behind him to make out the SUV. *Relax,* he said to himself, but continued looking back occasionally as he drove. Ten miles down the road the traffic began to stretch out a little, and when Burke looked in the mirror again, he saw what he thought was the black SUV, maybe a hundred yards back with five or six cars between them. He eased into the passing lane and sped up, looking back. The SUV soon followed, passing the other cars but maintaining the same distance. Burke passed a tractor-

211

trailer and moved back into the slow lane. The SUV followed suit, but continued to stay back. Burke slowed and the big truck went around him, blasting its air horn. The other cars also began to pass, but the SUV stayed in the right-hand lane, coming no closer.

Son of a bitch.

He accelerated the Camaro up to eighty-five mph and began passing the slower traffic. The SUV kept pace, hanging back. *Goddammit.* He cruised along for a while, trying to figure out if he could lose his pursuers. Soon he caught up to a group of five or six trucks that were closely packed and running at about seventy miles per hour. Burke saw a sign for the Tylersville Road exit, coming up in four miles, and he suddenly remembered a stunt he'd seen years before, on TV. James Garner, as a private investigator on *The Rockford Files,* had pulled it off in his gold Pontiac Firebird.

I can do this, Burke thought. He slowed a bit and pulled into the right lane, falling in behind the line of trucks. About two miles before the exit, he started to pass the trucks. The SUV followed at a distance, moving into the left lane behind him. As he approached the Tylersville exit, Burke was running even with the first truck in the line. He could see the SUV behind him, also in the passing lane, about four trucks back.

Just a hundred yards before the exit ramp, Burke accelerated. He shot past the first truck, crossed its path and angled for the ramp. The trucker blasted his horn, but Burke's timing was perfect. He charged up the ramp and watched as the line of trucks sped by on his left, blocking the SUV from sight, and cutting off its access to the ramp.

Jesus Christ! It worked! Son of a bitch!

Burke turned left at the end of the exit and followed Tylersville Road to the east for about five miles, all the way to I-71. Heading south, he crossed under I-275, the Cincinnati beltway. If the SUV was still in pursuit, this would be the logical spot for his pursuers to pick up his trail. He didn't see the SUV at the exit as he passed, and looking into his rear-view mirror, he didn't see it behind him.

Burke was getting close to the FBI building. *Can they track my cell phone?* He dug the phone out of his pocket, had it in his hand and was about to switch it off when a call came in. *Goddamn.*

"Burke," he answered. Fumbling with the phone, he nearly missed the exit for Montgomery Road.

"John, this is Charles Robinson."

"Hold on, Charles." Burke pulled over as soon as he got off the highway, and again checked the rear-view mirror.

"Hi, Charles," he said. "I was planning to call you a little later today. We need to talk, but right now I'm on my way to talk to the FBI. Things are getting pretty nasty up here, but I have a friend in the Cincinnati office who may be able to help."

"Well, it's gotten nasty here, too," said Charles. "Somebody tried to kill me this morning. He got into my house when I was asleep, and . . . and . . . well, I guess he was going to shoot me in bed. The police just left."

"Jesus, Charles," Burke said, turning off the ignition. "Are you okay?"

"I'm fine," said Charles. "But I shot him dead, right through the goddamn door of my bedroom."

"Good lord, Charles!" Burke knew that this was a brave man he was talking to. *Could I have done that?* he wondered.

"The son of a bitch was carrying a pistol with a silencer attached," Charles told him. "He had no I.D. on him, and somehow he managed to get into my locked house. I think he came in here to kill me. Probably planned to make it look like a robbery before he left . . . I don't know."

Burke was stunned. *These guys mean business.* He knew now that not only was his *own* life in danger, but if they went after Charles, they could go after Alex.

"You need protection, Charles," said Burke. "So does Alex Johnson – maybe even his mother. I'm going to call Luther Banks and talk to him about getting some police protection in place for you. I'll talk to the FBI and then I'll come down to Hattiesburg. Can you get me a phone number for the Hattiesburg Police?"

While Charles was looking up the number, Burke thought about Brian Lopez. He thought about Maggie and Kevin. *Maybe they all know too much.* Charles read him the Hattiesburg Police number and Burke punched it into his phone.

"Sit tight, Charles," said Burke. "I'll call Luther right now, and I'll be down there tonight or tomorrow so we can figure out what to do next. For now, I think we should keep this pretty close. I'm hoping the FBI will have some ideas, and depending on what they say, maybe I can fill Luther in when I get there. And you better keep that Beretta handy."

"It's gone," Charles said. "The police took it."

"Shit," Burke mumbled under his breath. "All right," he said, "I'll talk to Luther about it. Maybe they can post some guards at your house. Just sit tight, okay? I'll see you tomorrow."

Burke hung up and punched in the number Charles had given him for the Hattiesburg Police Department.

"Luther? This is John Burke from Dayton, Ohio."

"Hello, John Burke from Dayton, Ohio," Luther said. "What's up?"

"I just got off the phone with Charles Robinson. He told me about what happened this morning."

"Nasty business," said Luther. "Looks like somebody wanted him dead. But why did Charles call you?"

"Well, remember when I was down there last week, I told you that I was looking into Michael Johnson's death? And that his son Alex had come up with some new information? Anyway, it's a long story that I can't go into right now, but Charles and Alex are both involved, and their lives may be in danger. I'm at the FBI office in Cincinnati, and I'll be talking to the main man here in a few minutes. I have no idea what will happen after that, but I'll drive down to Hattiesburg no matter what."

"I could bring Charles and Alex into the station and put them under protective custody," Luther said. "Should I do that?"

"Or post some guards," said Burke. "That might be better. Let them stay in their own houses. Can you spare the manpower for that?"

"We can handle it," Luther said. "Don't you worry. Good luck up there, and I'll see you when you get here. I can't wait to hear what the hell is going on."

Burke could see the FBI complex, just across the highway. Crossing over I-71, he turned onto Ronald Reagan Drive and parked in a lot at the front of the main building. He locked the Camaro, and walked up to the security station at the front of the FBI building. His name and I.D. were checked against the guard's visitor's log. Lamar Presley had provided the necessary clearance forms, and once they were checked, Burke was searched and passed through a metal detector. Another guard escorted him into the building and led him to Lamar Presley's office on the third floor.

Lamar shook Burke's hand and patted him on the back. "You want some coffee? You look a little frazzled."

"Somebody was tailing me on the way down here," Burke said. "I think I managed to lose them."

"Well, if it's the CIA, you came to the right place, pal. But I'm guessing they're also following your cell phone."

"I thought of that, maybe too late. I should have turned it off."

"Doesn't matter whether it's on or off, J.B. The NSA knows right where that phone is."

"Shit," said Burke.

"Hey, it's *good* if they know you're here," Lamar said, grinning. "They'll probably back off once they think we're involved. They'll at least think twice about how to proceed. They probably just about shit when they realized where you were."

"Lamar, you have no idea what a relief it is for me to hear that," said Burke.

They sat down and made small talk for a while, and then Lamar recommended that they record the rest of their conversation. Burke agreed, and Lamar turned on a recorder. By the time Burke had laid out his entire investigation, an hour later, he was shivering. The mention of *Blacksnake* had particularly interested Lamar.

"Let me get you some more hot coffee," Lamar said, hopping up. A minute later he was back. Shaking his head, he set the coffee down in front of Burke.

"Fucking *BlackSnake*," he said with a sneer. "That's Dick Cheney's baby now. After the son of a bitch left the White House, he went to work for BlackSnake as an operations director. Rummy's working there, too."

Burke described the emotional confession that Brian Lopez made the day before – how he'd been involved in the deaths of both Michael Johnson and Martin Novak – and how he now feared that he'd be targeted himself.

Lamar sighed. "He's right. If they find out he talked to you about it, he's a dead man walking. I can almost guarantee it."

"Jesus, Lamar," Burke said. "Don't tell me that." Lamar merely shrugged.

Burke described the phone call from Charles, regarding the attempt on his life just that morning.

Lamar whistled, shaking his head.

"I called Luther Banks, the Hattiesburg Police chief," Burke explained. "He's a good man. Said he'd put some protection in place for Charles Robinson – and for Alex and his mother. I told him I would drive down after I left here. Charles and Alex are involved in this with me, and we have to figure out what to do next."

"Well, J.B.," said Lamar, "If it's any consolation, you've certainly got me interested. This might be the craziest goddamn thing I've ever heard. And believe me, I've heard some crazy shit. But I think I know you well enough to know you're on the level."

"Thanks, Lamar. That means a ton to me right now." Burke didn't try to hide his genuine relief.

"I'll share this tape with a couple of agents here that I trust the most, and we'll make a plan," Lamar said. "And I think I'll keep Washington out of the loop for now. It might cost me – but hell, they screwed me on this four years ago, so the hell with them. How much does the police chief in Hattiesburg know?"

"Not much," said Burke. "He knows that Charles and Alex might be in danger."

"Let's keep it that way for now. And you're right – I think Charles Robinson and Alex Johnson should be part of the conversation on how we proceed. Who else knows anything about this?"

"Kevin, my son, he knows the most. You know Kevin – he took over the homicide squad when I retired. And my wife. She knows about some of it."

"All right," said Lamar. "We should probably put some protection around them, just in case. I have a couple of agents at our satellite office in Dayton. I can call them."

"How about if I talk to Kevin?" Burke offered. "The DPD could probably take care of it."

"I'm good with that. And don't worry, J.B. Like I said before – if the CIA *is* involved, and they know you're talking to *us* – they'll back off."

"I hope you're right. Jesus, Maggie is going to be pissed off."

"Did you say you were *driving* down to Hattiesburg?" Lamar asked.

"Yeah, I thought about flying, but I did that trip recently. By the time I find a flight – get to the airport – transfer in Atlanta – rent a car at the airport – hell, I can almost get there faster driving. From here I think I can get there in about nine hours, maybe ten. Plus, I have my Glock with me, and I want to *keep* it with me. The paperwork for getting it on a flight would take forever."

"You're probably right," Lamar agreed. "I'd send you down in our plane, but it's in service. I could probably get something here in a few hours, though."

"Don't worry about it, Lamar," Burke said. "Really, but thanks a bunch. I'd go nuts sitting around waiting. This way I'll at least be doing something."

"Okay. Let me see your cell phone then," Lamar said. Burke dug the old flip-phone out of his pocket and handed it over. The battery cover was being held on with transparent tape.

"Nice," said Lamar, grinning as he inspected the phone.

"Yeah, yeah," Burke said. "It's an old friend."

"We can help with this," he said. "I can give you a new phone that the NSA can't track – *or* hack."

"No shit?" said Burke. "How do you do that?"

"Now, J.B.," Lamar said, laughing. "You know if I told you that I'd have to kill you. Do you want the phone?"

"Hell yeah I want the phone! Thanks, Lamar."

"I can have the lab transfer your address book into the new phone. It'll be a different number, so you'll have to call your contacts and let them know. Any calls you make or receive on the phone will be scrambled for anyone trying to listen in."

Lamar left the office with Burke's phone and was back a minute later, with a smile on his face. "The lab will bring the new phone up when it's ready – shouldn't take too long. And we'll keep *your* phone here," he said, laughing. "The CIA will think you moved in with us."

"I really appreciate this, Lamar."

"Not a problem. You know, now that I think of it, we could give you a different car, too. Whoever was following you probably high-tailed it outta here when they realized you were coming here, but if they *are* out front watching, we could send you out the back gate in one of our cars. What are you driving?"

"It's a – hell, maybe we can see it from your window," Burke said, walking over to the office window. They looked down on the front lot and Burke pointed out the car. "The orange Camaro," he said.

"Jesus, J.B.," Lamar exclaimed. "You might as well just put a big light on top that says HERE I AM."

"Yeah, it does kind of stand out," Burke agreed.

"How about if we put you in a nice *gray* Buick – with Ohio plates," suggested Lamar. "I may have to take a little heat for this – it ain't exactly standard ops for us. If I could deputize you I would, but I can't. But if you get stopped, a computer check will come back to us. And I can also have something official drawn up to carry with you." He mimed stamping a seal. "Come on, I'll go down and help you get your stuff out of your car."

"It's just the Glock," Burke said with a shrug. "This is all spur of the moment. I wasn't really planning on going to Hattiesburg until tomorrow."

They walked down to the front lot, and Lamar admired the Camaro. He helped Burke register the weapon at the security desk, and when they got back to the office, there was a new flip phone lying on Lamar's desk, and a phone number written on a sticky note. Burke memorized the number, folded the sticky and put it in his wallet.

"I'd better call Kevin and tell him what's going on," said Burke. "Maybe he can put a DPD car in front of his house, and one at my house." He sat down and called Kevin's cell number on the new phone.

"Kevin? It's your dad."

"Jesus Christ, Pop," Kevin said, sounding relieved. "I've been trying to call your cell phone. Where the hell are you?"

"Sorry, Kevin. My phones been turned off. I'm in Cincinnati – in Lamar's office."

"Yeah, I was about to call there. Anyway, I thought you should know – Brian Lopez is dead."

"*Dead?*" Burke jumped to his feet. "Jesus Christ, Kev!" He sat down again just as quickly as he had stood up, feeling faint from the shock of what he'd just heard. *It's my fault. I got this poor man killed.*

Lamar Presley's eyebrows arched as Burke motioned for him to get closer.

"The BlackSnake kid – Brian Lopez," he said to Lamar.

"Kevin, Lamar's right here. Tell us what the hell happened?" *Lamar was right . . . Dead man walking . . . And it's my fucking fault.*

"Somebody gunned him down about six o'clock this morning – out between Fairborn and Yellow Springs. Didn't you tell me that's where he lived?"

"Yeah," Burke said. "Did it happen at his house?" *Brian would still be alive if I hadn't involved him.*

"No, no – not at his house," said Kevin. "He was stopped at a light on Dayton Yellow Springs Road, where it crosses Xenia Road. Looks like somebody pulled up next to him and opened up with an automatic weapon – thirty or forty rounds. Danny and Jamal are out there now helping out. They said there were three-oh-eight shell casings all over the road."

"Any witnesses?"

"Not really," Kevin told him. "A woman in the house nearby heard the shots and then squealing tires. She thought it was firecrackers. There's just the one house right near that intersection. Nobody saw the other vehicle."

"Jesus," said Burke, deflated.

"Lopez's truck just drifted through the intersection and down into some trees," Kevin continued. "There was a loaded Beretta M9 lying on the passenger seat. He never even had time to pick it up."

Burke could only imagine Brian's last terrified moment. He'd come to like the young man. He felt sorry for him. Now, Brian would *never* have the chance to make the fresh start he'd longed for. *And it's my fault.*

"Pop? Are you there?"

"Sorry," said Burke, sitting up and holding the phone to his ear again. "Listen, Kev. Here's the deal. Lamar wants to work with us on this. He thinks that if the CIA is involved, they probably tracked me here to the FBI building. He thinks they'll back off, knowing I'm here. But he thinks we need to put you and your family under protection – and Maggie, too, just to be safe. He offered to do it, but I told him you could probably make that happen. Can you take care of it?"

"Sure," Kevin said. "But I'll have to let Major Winston in on this. All she knows for now is that you got your P.I. license and that you were working on the Michael Johnson case."

"Go ahead and tell Claire whatever you need to make her happy," Burke said. "And I think you should put an officer and a patrol car in your driveway and one in mine – twenty-four-seven – until this gets straightened out. And keep someone with you on your way home. Don't go anywhere without back-up. All right?"

"Okay. I'll take care of it. But what about you, Pop?"

"I'll be all right," Burke assured him. "Like I said, Lamar's pretty sure things will cool off now that the FBI is involved. He's giving me one of their cars, and I'm driving down to Hattiesburg from here – to talk to Charles Robinson and Alex. I called Luther Banks, the police chief in Hattiesburg. He's going to post some officers around them. And Lamar gave me a new phone that the NSA can't track. Let me give you the number."

Burke didn't tell Kevin about the attempt on Charles Robinson's life. With the shooting of Brian Lopez, Kevin would already realize that his Pop's life might also be in danger, but why add fuel to the fire. He gave Kevin the new number.

"I'll call Maggie," Burke said. "Let's not tell her about Brian Lopez just yet."

"Good idea," Kevin agreed.

"I'm really sorry about all this, Kevin," Burke said. "I'll keep you posted. And don't worry about me, I'll be fine. I've got my pistol with me – not that I think I'll need it."

"Okay," said Kevin. "Be careful, Pop."

Burke closed the phone and looked at Lamar. "You were right," he said. "About Brian Lopez."

"Yeah, and so much for subtlety. I guess they figured they had to get rid of him quickly." Lamar patted Burke's shoulder sympathetically. "Don't take this too hard, John. These guys are scumbags. From what you told me about Lopez, they would have done this eventually anyway."

"Yeah, but . . ."

"Forget it, John," Lamar admonished him.

"Okay," Burke mumbled unconvincingly. He wouldn't forget it.

Lamar patted his shoulder again. "I'll get someone to type up an authorization letter for you to carry."

After Lamar left the room, Burke tried to collect himself. He called Maggie and told her that the FBI was now involved – much to her relief – and that he was driving down to Mississippi to meet with Charles Robinson and Alex Johnson. She was not too happy about the idea of having a police cruiser parked in their driveway, but she understood. He didn't tell her about the intruder Charles shot to death that morning. He didn't tell her about being followed on the way down to Cincinnati. And he most certainly didn't tell her about the murder of Brian Lopez. What he *did* tell her, was that the FBI had given him a new phone – *for security reasons* – and he gave her the new number.

"Let's be careful out there," Maggie said for the second time that day. "I love you, Johnny."

"I love you, too. I'll call you later. And don't worry. I'll be fine."

45

Nice Shooting

Later that day, Charles Robinson was sitting at the desk in his office. He'd taken the textbook on nuclear chemistry down from a shelf, found the letters hidden in the book, and was once again reading the correspondence that he'd had with Martin Novak over four years ago. Two letters and a technical report from Dr. Jürg Bütler, the scientist from the lab in Switzerland, were also opened on the desk. *This is how it all began,* Charles thought.

A victim service counselor, representing the Hattiesburg Police Department, had called earlier, and Charles insisted that he was okay. He promised to let her know if he needed to talk to someone about what had happened. There was a floor fan humming in the hallway in an attempt to dry out the blood-soaked carpet that had been scrubbed clean earlier that day. The police cleaning crew had done a remarkable job of removing any traces of the shooting – except for the bullet riddled door – and Charles found the tangy smell of the cleaning solution mildly offensive.

A Hattiesburg Police cruiser was parked on the street in front of his house, and another in the alley out back. Luther Banks, the Hattiesburg Police chief, had called earlier and told Charles that he'd spoken with John Burke. Burke suggested that protection be put in place for Charles, and for Alex Johnson as well. Charles had chatted with the two officers about the shooting when they'd arrived, and offered them coffee. They checked out the bedroom door, and complimented Charles on how he'd handled the situation. Now they were back in their cars and Charles sat alone with the letters.

He remembered what young Alex Johnson had said just over a week ago upon reading the first letter from Martin Novak. *Cool. Very cool.* Charles had spoken with Alex and his mother on the phone earlier, explaining to them what had happened that morning, and that police protection was going to be put in place for all of them. When they heard about Martin Novak's death, Alex wanted to see Charles immediately, but Michelle Johnson insisted that her son stay right where he was. Charles agreed. He told them the FBI was getting involved and that Burke was on his way down from Dayton. Charles wondered if Alex thought that any of this was cool. Probably not.

It was almost noon, and although the weather was hot, Charles had turned off the air conditioner and opened the windows, hoping to air out the house. When he heard a car pull into the driveway, he put the letters back in the book and returned it to the shelf. He motored to the front door and got there just as Police Chief Luther Banks was about to knock. The Chief was holding a paper sack in one hand.

"Good afternoon, Luther," Charles said. "Come on in. How are you?"

Luther opened the screen door. "I'm okay. How are *you?*"

"Fine, thanks. But it was a hell of a morning," Charles said, pointing to the hallway. "Take a look."

Luther looked up and down the hall, stepped around the fan and carefully examined the eight bullet holes in the bedroom door. He whistled in amazement.

"Man, oh man," he said, shaking his head. "Nice shooting, sir. Those hollow points put some big-ass holes in that guy. One shoulder shot, one in the upper thigh and the rest between the sevens. Yessir, he was a real mess."

Between the sevens. Charles knew that Luther was referring to the numbers on the outside ring of the human body targets at the local firing range. And due to the expanding nature of the hollow point slugs, only one of the seven clean shots had passed on through the body of the intruder. The slug grazed the man's shoulder and had been found imbedded in the plaster and lathe of the hall wall. The shot that missed had penetrated the same wall and was found buried in the pages of a book that it knocked off a shelf and onto the floor in Charles' office.

"Ballistics said the slugs had already mushroomed when they hit him, after they passed through the door." Luther examined the holes in the wall, whistled again, and returned to the living room.

"Here's your gun, sir," he said, handing the paper sack to Charles. "I asked ballistics to speed it up so I could get it back to you. The magazine is in there, too."

"Thank you, Luther," said Charles. "I appreciate that. I just hope I don't ever have to use it again."

"Me, too," Luther nodded. "Did our victim counselor come by to see you?"

"She called – I told her not to come."

"Well, you make sure and call her if you think it will help. You might feel different down the road."

"I will," said Charles. "Who the hell was that guy anyway? What have you found out?"

"Not a damn thing, sir," Luther said, shaking his head. "That's what I wanted to talk to you about. We have no idea who he is. There's no fingerprint match on file – *anywhere*. When Captain Burke told me the FBI was involved, I went ahead and sent the prints to the field office in Jackson. So far, nothing. No matches anywhere. They said they were going to pass the prints on to Interpol, to see if they could come up with something. DNA samples won't help much, they said, not without somewhere to start. So, you never saw this guy before?"

"I've no idea who he was." Charles shrugged.

"You told one of my officers that you didn't know of anyone that would want you dead," said Luther. "Is that true, sir?"

Charles sighed and picked up the paper sack from his lap. He slowly removed the Beretta and the magazine from the sack, and slipped them into the pocket at the side of the wheelchair. Chief Banks waited patiently.

"No, Luther," Charles said, looking up. "It's not true. And it's all tied to poor Michael Johnson's death. Maybe my father's death, as well. And one of Dad's old friends was murdered this week, up in Dayton. John Burke said that was connected, too. That's about all I can tell you right now."

Luther shook his head and whistled again. "Man, oh man."

46

Secret Agent Man

Burke drove out through the back gate of the FBI complex in a drab, gray Buick sedan, and wound his way through a residential neighborhood until he found the main road that led to the entry ramp for I-71 south. The loaded Glock was on the passenger seat, along with an official letter of endorsement printed on FBI stationary.

Lamar Presley had treated Burke to an early lunch in the FBI cafeteria, presented him with the letter, and sent him on his way. The Buick was peppy enough, and Burke made good time through downtown Cincinnati, past Great American Ball Park where the Reds and the Phillies would be getting under way in about an hour, and crossed the Ohio River into Kentucky. He checked the rearview mirror every few minutes, but no one seemed to be following. *Maybe Lamar is right. Maybe they backed off.*

The interstate speed limit was seventy miles per hour – in Kentucky, Tennessee, Alabama, and Mississippi – and Burke kept the Buick right at eighty. He took I-71 to Louisville where he picked up I-65, and he managed to listen to most of the Reds/Phillies game on WLW out of Cincinnati. He drove south through Kentucky, and when he stopped at a rest area near the Tennessee line, he realized that he hadn't really been checking the rear-view mirror for maybe the last fifty miles.

While he was stopped, Burke called Maggie to let her know where he was and that he was safe, and then he called Alex Johnson and his mother, Michelle. He told them he was on his way and expected to get to Hattiesburg around nine o'clock. Michelle insisted that he stay at their house again, and Burke was happy to agree.

Somewhere south of Nashville, he stopped at a truck stop and filled the Buick's gas tank. He bought a toothbrush and a tube of toothpaste, some deodorant, a three-pack of boxer shorts, a four-pack of athletic socks, two apples, a ham and cheese sandwich with lettuce and tomato, some Oreos, and a large coffee to go. Just as he crossed into Alabama, searching around on the car radio, he tuned into a minor league baseball game that was just starting between the Birmingham Barons and the Pensacola Blue Wahoos. The Wahoos were a new Cincinnati Reds farm team playing their first season. Burke had always found that listening to a baseball game in the car made the time pass quickly. He felt somehow blessed at finding the game, and he listened all the way to Birmingham, where he headed south on I-59. Just past Tuscaloosa, the game ended – Billy Hamilton stole four bases and scored the winning run for the Wahoos.

Burke turned off the radio. The July sun was getting low in the sky, but wouldn't set for another hour, and he would be in Hattiesburg an hour after that. Traffic had tapered off, and Burke felt tired but relaxed. He'd long ago stopped worrying about being followed, but now, a casual glance in his rearview mirror revealed what he thought was a Black SUV coming up slowly behind him.

Son of a bitch. He maintained his speed, and the vehicle continued to come closer. Burke reached over and picked up the Glock. Steering with just his left hand, he held the pistol at the ready, and kept an eye on the approaching vehicle. He could see clearly now that it *was* a black SUV. There was no front license plate.

Damn! The vehicle moved into the left lane and began to pass the Buick. The windows of the SUV were tinted, and Burke couldn't see inside. Making sure no one was behind him, he hit the brakes hard.

As the SUV sped past, Burke saw the large red, stylized "A" decal on the back window. Another decal – *Go Tide!* – reassured Burke that the SUV belonged *not* to his pursuers, but to a University of Alabama football fan. He released the deep breath that he'd been holding, set the Glock back down on the car seat, and wiped the sweat from his eyes.

"Goddammit!"

Burke was angry. He reached out and pounded the passenger seat with a clenched fist several times, cursing with each blow. He knew that his anger was fueled by his fear. He had managed to relax on the drive for the first time in days, but the SUV had drawn him right back into the bizarre reality that he'd been living with for the past week. His hands were shaking and he was perspiring heavily.

When he saw a sign for a rest area, Burke got off the highway and parked the car. He sat in the Buick until he calmed down, then went inside and used the bathroom. He gulped down cold water from a drinking fountain and bought a bottle of water to take with him. Walking around the grounds of the rest area to stretch his legs, Burke called Maggie and Kevin to let them know that he was okay.

Back in the car, Burke spent the last two hours of the trip trying to put into perspective what had happened in his life – and the lives of everyone else involved in the case – over the course of the last week. Martin Novak, an old man, had died. Brian Lopez, a young man, had died. Both had been murdered. Burke had discovered that the death of Michael Johnson four years earlier and that of Sarah Sheldrake the previous summer – both long regarded as suspicious – had also been hit jobs, probably carried out by the same organization responsible for the deaths of Martin and Brian. The 2004 death of Henry Robinson – once the director of the USAF Project Blue Book – was most likely attributable to this same organization. Henry's son, Charles Robinson, had narrowly escaped an attempt on his life, shooting to death his would-be killer. Burke's own life had been at risk as well, and was possibly still at risk. Fortunately, Charles Robinson and Alex Johnson were now under police protection, as were members of Burke's own family.

Was the Chinese government involved in this mess? Burke guessed not. The CIA and the Department of Defense were definitely involved, and now the Federal Bureau of Investigation and the Justice department were about to step in.

Burke's new cell phone was lying on the passenger seat next to the Glock, and he flinched when it rang. It was the first time he'd heard the ring tone – Johnny Rivers singing *Secret Agent Man*. Lamar Presley's little joke. Burke opened the phone.

"Burke," he said.

"J.B.? It's Lamar Presley. How are you making out?"

"Everything's fine," said Burke, laughing. "Nice ring tone, Lamar. And thanks for calling. I'm almost to Hattiesburg."

"I thought you'd get a kick out of that. Anyone following you?"

"Not that I can tell. I really appreciate your help, Lamar."

"Listen, J. B., I'm flying down to Hattiesburg in the morning. I'll stop in Jackson and pick up Tina Hardaway. She's the new Special Agent in Charge at our Mississippi field office. She's a good, smart agent and she wants to help. And get this – turns out she went to the police academy with Michael Johnson when they were both just starting out in law enforcement. She knew about his death, and when I filled her in on everything, she was very interested. I sent her an audio file of our conversation. She talked me into calling our boss in Washington, and it looks like we're good to go. Hell, they could hardly ignore a mess like *this*."

"You *are* the man, Lamar. I'll talk to Luther Banks at the police station. Maybe we can all meet there. Call me when you get to Hattiesburg in the morning."

"Will do."

By the time Burke pulled into Michelle Johnson's driveway, he was exhausted. There was still a bit of light in the sky, and a police cruiser was parked on the street in front of the house. Alex came out to greet Burke, followed by Michelle.

"Thank you so much for coming, John," she said, starting to cry. She gave him a hug. "Thank God you're safe."

"I think it's going to be all right," Burke consoled her. "I think we're all safe now."

Once in the house, Michelle offered Burke a glass of wine or a beer, and he asked her if she had any whiskey in the house. She found a bottle of Johnny Walker Black and poured him a glassful.

"How about if I make you an omelet?" Michelle offered. Burke thanked her, made short work of the whiskey, and Alex opened a beer for him. While he ate, Burke began to tell the bizarre tale of the week that had passed since he'd last been in Hattiesburg. He spared them the description of Michael Johnson's death, as told to him by Brian Lopez, and said nothing about Brian's death that morning. At one point he leaned back and yawned.

"John," said Michelle, reaching out and patting the back of his hand, "you need to go to bed. We can talk more tomorrow."

Once in the guest room, Burke turned out the light and peeked through the window. The police cruiser was there. He put the Glock on a nightstand and got into bed. He was asleep almost instantly, and enjoyed the first deep sleep he'd managed since the last time he'd been in Hattiesburg, just over a week before.

47

Plausible Deniability

Burke was up early and immediately looked out the window. The police cruiser was there on the street. He showered, and was putting on the jeans and shirt he'd worn the day before when Alex knocked at the guest room door.

"Here's a clean shirt if you want it," Alex said, handing him a white polo shirt. "You can have it. It's a little big on me."

Burke put the shirt on. "Perfect fit." They bumped knuckles.

"You ready for some breakfast?" Alex asked.

"Absolutely. Oh, and it occurred to me last night, when I was talking to you guys, that I need to write everything down so I can keep it all straight. We'll be getting together with Charles and the FBI agents sometime this morning, and I'll have to go through it all. Maybe I could borrow your laptop and write things out."

"No problem, Cap," Alex said.

Burke called the Hattiesburg Police Department, and a dispatcher took his number and promised he would have Chief Luther Banks call as soon as he got in. They were just finishing breakfast when Burke's phone rang. Alex and Michelle looked at each other for a moment when they heard *Secret Agent Man*, and they both burst out laughing. Burke answered the phone, shaking his head and grinning.

"Hello, John? This is Luther Banks returning your call."

"Hi, Luther. I'm here in town. Got in last night."

"Glad you made it in, my friend," Luther said. "Now, how can I help?"

"Well, there are two FBI agents flying into Hattiesburg sometime this morning. One is the Special Agent from Cincinnati and the other is from the Mississippi district."

"Tina Hardaway?" said Luther. "I know Tina. Is it Tina? I just talked to her yesterday. Oh, she's a good one, John. Smart as a whip."

"Good, good," said Burke. "Anyway, I was wondering if we could all get together at the police station. I'm with Alex and Michelle Johnson, and we'd want to get Charles Robinson there, too."

"Shouldn't be a problem. We can set up in one of the conference rooms – plenty of room for all of us."

"Great! You *are* the man, Luther. I'll call and let you know when the agents get to town. Thanks a bunch."

Burke sat down on a couch with the laptop and began typing out the timeline of the events from the past week. Alex helped his mother with the dishes, and they all waited for the call from Lamar Presley. At ten o'clock Burke's cell phone rang, and he heard Alex and Michelle laughing in the kitchen, amused again at the ring tone. It was Lamar Presley.

"Meet us at the Hattiesburg Police station, on James Street," Burke said. "I'll call Chief Banks and Charles Robinson. We'll see you there."

Alex printed out what Burke had typed, and they all drove to the police station in the FBI Buick – with a police escort front and rear. Other police officers were posted to keep an eye on the house. Chief Luther Banks met them in the lobby, and Lamar Presley and Tina Hardaway arrived a few minutes later. When introductions were made, Chief Banks proudly pointed out that not only was Tina Hardaway the first female special agent in charge of the Jackson FBI office, she was also the first African American to hold the job.

Alex spotted Charles pulling into the parking lot in his handi-van, also with a police escort. He ran out to meet Charles while the others waited in the air-conditioned lobby, and after everyone had finally passed through security, Chief Luther Banks led them to a conference room on the second floor. A young cop named Zack set up a state-of-the-art digital recorder and showed Luther how it operated. An older, matronly woman appeared.

"This is Dot," Luther said, introducing her to the FBI agents. "She's a court stenographer. Said she'd be willing to take notes if you'd like."

"Absolutely," said Lamar. "Perfect. Thank you, Dot."

They all sat around a wide, oak-veneered oval table. With the help of the timeline he had written earlier, Burke began the long, twisted tale of what had begun simply as a cold case investigation into the death of Michael Johnson.

As the FBI agents had already heard most of the story, Burke's telling was mostly for the benefit of Alex and Michelle, Charles Robinson and Chief Luther Banks. Charles listened stoically, shaking his head from side to side, and occasionally adjusting his position in the wheelchair. More than once, Chief Banks sat back in his chair and whistled, muttering, "Man, oh man."

Alex and his mother sat wide-eyed, obviously shocked by much of what they heard. They clutched each other's hands, and both wiped away tears when Burke finally detailed what he'd learned about Brian Lopez, the two Bobs, and Michael Johnson's death. At this point, Lamar Presley decided that a time-out was in order. Luther had coffee, Cokes, and sandwiches sent up to the conference room.

After lunch, it was more of the same as Burke wrapped up – shock, dismay, disbelief, and head shaking. When he'd finished, everyone in the room, including the two FBI agents – and especially poor Dot – seemed wrung out. Lamar and Tina Hardaway each had a few questions, then no one spoke.

Suddenly, **BAM!** It sounded like gunfire, and everyone in the room jumped. When they realized it was just a back-fire from a passing truck, they slowly relaxed. There were a few nervous smiles, but no more questions. Luther turned the recorder off and leaned back in his chair, with a long sigh and one last *man, oh man.*

"Let's take a break," Lamar said, getting up. "Tina and I need to talk about all this for a few minutes."

The others sat in silence after the agents left the room, lost in their own thoughts. Burke could only imagine what they were thinking. Five minutes later, Lamar and Tina returned and sat down.

"Okay," said Lamar, "let me tell you what our agency is doing so far, and then we want you all to tell us what you want us to do."

"*Us?*" Alex piped up, motioning toward the others around the table.

"Well, you all have a big stake in this, Alex." said Lamar. "Tina and I think we could go several different ways. Right now, I have my agents from Cincinnati and Dayton meeting with Captain Kevin Burke at the Dayton PD." He nodded toward Burke. "Kevin is J.B.'s son. He's the head of homicide up there now. They'll re-open the investigation into Michael's death four years ago, and they'll also look into the deaths of Sarah Sheldrake, Martin Novak, and Brian Lopez."

"And speaking of Lopez," he continued, "we've already done a thorough search of his house, but there was no sign of that CD he received about Sarah Sheldrake's involvement as a Chinese agent. Tina's agents here in Mississippi will investigate the attempt on your life this morning, Charles, *and* the death of your father back in 2004. Fortunately, our head honcho in Washington has given us *carte blanche* on this whole thing."

"What about the CIA and the Defense Department?" asked Burke.

"As far as I know, no one has talked to them directly yet," Lamar said. "But they must have some idea of what's up. This whole thing smells like CIA, and if it is, let me warn you right now – they will most likely try to make it all go away, and they will probably be successful. Some of you may be familiar with the term *plausible deniability*. It's a little thing they invented back in the 60's."

"*Blame shift. Willful ignorance,*" Tina added. "Be prepared to hear it all, because you're going to hear a *lot* of it."

No one spoke for a moment as the reality of what the future might hold sank in.

"What about China?" Charles asked, finally.

"We've talked about that," Tina Hardaway said. "We'll check it out, but right now our gut feeling is that China's interest may have just been a catalyst for this whole thing. Sarah Sheldrake's presence in Dayton as late as last summer could mean the Chinese are still interested. But as Lamar said – the whole thing smells like CIA."

"But are we safe?" asked Michelle, visibly agitated.

Tina turned to her. "From the Chinese? We don't think you should worry about them for the moment."

"No, no! I mean the CIA! My God, they've already killed, what . . . five people . . . almost six!" exclaimed Michelle, pointing toward Charles.

"Well, we *think* you're safe," Lamar tried to reassure them. "As I said, the CIA knows that the FBI is now involved. They'll probably back off."

"*Probably?*" asked Charles, his eyebrows arching. "That son of a bitch – sorry – that guy who snuck into my house this morning was fully prepared to send me to kingdom come. Who the hell was he anyway?"

"No idea . . . so far," said Tina. "And I just talked to Interpol again this morning and they haven't found anything either. Apparently, he is – *was*, that is – deeply covert."

"I've gotta say, I'm still feeling a little jumpy," said Burke. He related the incident from the evening before, when the Alabama fan in the SUV had passed him on the highway. "I had the Glock in hand and was ready to fire."

"I understand," said Lamar, nodding. "And that's what I meant about you guys having a stake in this. Tina and I think there are two ways we can go. One, we can begin this investigation quietly, without confronting the Department of Defense and the CIA. We're fairly certain they already have us on their radar, and they may choose to sit back and see how far – *and how close* – we get. Two, we confront them right off the bat, in which case they will be forced to back off even further, and go into full blown denial. If *they* know that *we* know . . . and they know *what* we know . . . and they know that all of *you* know . . . well, we think that will pretty much guarantee an immediate end to any nefarious interest they might have in you guys. But either way, no matter what we do, they will eventually interfere in the investigation and most likely try to shut us down."

"Jesus, Lamar," Burke said, smiling. "You sounded a little like Donald Rumsfeld there for a second. 'If *they* know . . . and *we* know . . . and *you* know . . . and . . .'" Everyone laughed and seemed to relax a little.

Everyone but Alex. He was leaning forward, rubbing his knitted brow, and appeared to be deep in thought. After a few moments he cleared his throat, swallowed hard, and sat up straight.

"I think we should go to the press," he said.

Everyone looked at him.

"I . . . I think people should know what's going on *right now*," he said, tapping the table top with his index finger. "If the whole world thinks the CIA is responsible, then the CIA would be stupid to come after us."

He looked back and forth at the others around the table, then locked eyes with Lamar Presley, who stared back. When Lamar finally blinked, he looked over at Tina Hardaway. She just shrugged and appeared not to know quite what to say.

"Yes, option number three," said Lamar at last, winking at Alex. "We could – *indeed* – go to the press."

Alex broke into a wide grin, relaxed and sat back in his chair. Michelle smiled, and took his hand.

"Thomas Jefferson. He said something we learned in my journalism class," Alex said. "*When the press is free and every man able to read, all is safe.*"

A grinning Burke pointed his thumb at Alex and nudged Charles Robinson. "I think the young man has made a very good point," Charles said with a smile.

"I have to agree with my son," said Michelle.

Lamar looked back at Tina and sighed. "If you all don't mind, I think Tina and I should talk about this in private for a moment," he said. "We'll be right back."

Tina and Lamar left the room, and now everyone looked at Alex. Burke reached across the table and bumped knuckles with him, and then everyone around the table was laughing and bumping knuckles, including Dot, the court stenographer.

"You're a smart young man," she said to Alex.

48

All In

Ten minutes later Lamar and Tina returned to the conference room. Burke and the others were milling about, stretching, and plotting how to get the story into the press. They took their seats around the conference table, and Lamar took a long drink of bottled water before he spoke.

"Tina and I have talked about taking this directly to the press, and we talked about the possible consequences for you guys. And even though we've been given *carte blanche* from Washington, there will probably be consequences for us as well. But I'm retiring soon, like J.B. here," he said, nodding toward Burke. "I'm not too worried. But Tina's career could be affected."

"I told Lamar to let me worry about that," Tina said. "We need to do the right thing here and put an end to this nonsense. It was bad enough that they went after Henry Robinson and Michael years ago, but now it's time for it to stop. Lamar and I, we took an oath to defend and protect this country from foreign *and* domestic threats. And this is bullshit! Sorry, I don't know any better way to put it."

"But you all have to be ready for this," said Lamar. "It'll be a zoo, believe me. There'll be news trucks and reporters outside your doors for weeks. You will be blessed by some and vilified by others, and you're going to be called every name in the book – whacko, nut job, looney tune, conspiracy theorist – *traitor*. You might even end up getting keelhauled in front of a Senate committee hearing. It could get really ugly, and it may mark you for life. So, if you want some time to think about it, tell us now."

Burke, Alex, Charles and Michelle exchanged glances with one another, and then Burke responded.

"We talked about all that while you were out in the hall," he said. "We think we should go for it." There were nods all around.

"Okay then. We're all in," said Lamar, giving a thumbs up. "Now, my only press connections are at the *Cincinnati Enquirer*. Tina knows the folks at the *Clarion-Ledger* in Jackson. These are both Gannett papers, same as the Hattiesburg paper, I understand. If we hit one, we basically hit them all. But they don't have many boots on the ground, and mostly they get their news second-hand. I'm not sure what the *New York Times* would do with this, but we could give it a shot."

"I have a good friend at the *Dayton Daily News*," said Burke. "Lisa Fowler. She's a crime reporter there, and she's even had a couple of articles published in the *New York Times* this year. Maybe she could do something – in Dayton, or maybe even for the *Times*."

"I like that idea, J.B., and it's perfect." said Lamar, sounding excited for the first time. "Hell, this story has a lot more to do with Dayton than anywhere else. Do you think you can contact her?"

"I'll give it a try," said Burke. "I've got her in my phone."

Burke left the conference room and wandered down the stairs and out of the building. It was hot, and he sat on the lawn in the shade of a small tree and called Lisa Fowler's cell phone. It rang six or seven times and then Lisa's voice said to leave a message. Burke asked her to call him back ASAP. He got up and was heading back inside when the phone rang. It was Lisa.

"J.B.!" she said, "How the hell are you? Sorry I didn't pick up – you showed up as a restricted number."

"Oh, sorry about that. It's a new phone. But I'm okay," Burke said. "How are you?"

"Good. Great really," she said. "I just had a meeting with my agent and my editor, and yes, the book is really finished!" Burke had forgotten that just days ago Lisa told him she was going to New York.

"Way to go, Lisa," he said. "That's really great. Congratulations!"

"So, what's up?" she asked. "Did you come up with something on that cold case you were looking into?"

"Yeah, I'm afraid so," Burke said. "If you've got a few minutes, you might want to write some of this down."

He explained the situation as concisely as he could, without going into all the fine details. Lisa mostly listened, and Burke could imagine her scratching away on a notepad. When he finished, Lisa repeated the same thing Burke had heard already, more than once.

"This is the craziest shit I've ever heard, J.B." she said. "I'm just glad you're okay."

"Thanks, Lisa. So, what do you think?"

"Well, here's what I can do," she said, after a few seconds. "I just happen to have a meeting with an editor at the *Times* building in half an hour, about that upcoming trial for the abusive priest. I told you about it the other day when we met in front of the Safety Building. Anyway, I'll run this by her and see where it goes. I'll call you back as soon as I can."

Burke walked back into the police station, passed through security again, and returned to the conference room. Lamar and Tina stood in different corners with their backs to the room, talking on their cell phones. Chief Banks was gone, and Charles and Michelle were chatting. Alex had his head on the table with his eyes closed. When they realized Burke was back, the agents finished their calls, and everyone gathered at the table.

"I talked to Lisa Fowler," said Burke, thumbs up. "She just happens to be in New York right now and has a meeting with a *Times* editor in half an hour. She'll call me back after that."

"Wow!" said Alex. "How lucky is that?"

"No shit," said Tina.

"Okay then," Lamar said. "I guess there's no point everyone sitting around here. Tina and I can stay in town for the time being, and I'll let the Chief know. Call me as soon you hear something, J.B."

* * *

"Charles, why don't you follow us," Michelle offered, as they stepped into the oppressive, late afternoon heat outside the police station. "We could make an early dinner at our house, maybe stop at the Winn-Dixie and get some stuff for burgers."

"I would love that," Charles said, wholeheartedly. And he meant it. He felt safe among these newfound friends.

"I'll ride with Mr. Robinson," said Alex.

With police cruisers front and rear, they paraded back to the house, making a quick stop for groceries, beer, and wine. Burke and Michelle shopped while the others waited in the heat of the parking lot.

"Let's get enough so we can feed those poor officers," Michelle recommended to Burke.

Back at her house, Michelle insisted that Burke and Charles relax with a beer while she prepared the burgers and a big salad. She asked Alex to go outside and fire up the grill.

"Man make fire," Alex deadpanned, grunting like a caveman. "Woman make salad."

Burke and Charles laughed, and Michelle just rolled her eyes. They stayed inside to beat the heat, and when the burgers were ready, Alex delivered one to each of the very appreciative cops, along with ice-cold Cokes. Charles explained to Burke that in that part of the south, pretty much *all* soda pop was referred to as Coke.

It was just after five-thirty and Burke was helping Michelle clean up when his cell phone rang. It was the first time Charles had heard the *Secret Agent Man* ringtone and a broad grin cracked his face. Michelle and Alex laughed out loud.

"Hey, J.B. It's Lisa. I'm here at the *Times* with two editors. If it's okay with you I'll put you on speakerphone. They have some questions for you. Is that okay?"

"No problem, Lisa," Burke said. "Thanks for doing this. I'm with some of the other principals in this mess. I'll turn my phone speaker on so they can hear, too."

For the next forty-five minutes, the editors questioned Burke. They were polite but matter-of-fact, and in the end, it was suggested that Burke have an audio file of that day's meeting at the police station emailed to a secure address at the *Times*. They also wanted scanned copies of all the materials mentioned, including the unused airline ticket, the correspondence between Charles and Martin Novak, the letters and reports from the Swiss forensics laboratory regarding the polonium-210 poisoning of Henry Robinson, and a complete list of contact information for everyone involved, including Burke's son, Kevin. The editors assured Burke that there would probably be a lot of questions after they reviewed the audio file. If they received it that evening, they would listen to it and contact him in the morning.

"Okay, J.B. The editors are gone now," Lisa told Burke, staying on the phone. "Listen, they want me to work on this, and it could be big. I mean *really* big. You all better prepare yourselves for the aftermath."

"We've talked about that, and we're ready to go," said Burke, nodding to the others in the kitchen. "I'll talk to Lamar Presley about getting that file out right away. We can scan and send the other stuff. Thanks again, Lisa. You're the best. I hope you get another book out of this."

He hung up and immediately called Lamar Presley. Chief Banks had already had the recording turned into a file, and Lamar agreed to send it to New York right away, from his FBI email address.

"Tina and I will stay in Hattiesburg tonight," he said. "Call me as soon as you hear something from Lisa Fowler."

Alex jumped up and hurried to the guest room. He dug out the unused airline ticket from the same book where he'd first found it. Within minutes, Charles and Alex were aboard the handi-van headed for Charles' house on Adeline Street, with Burke close behind in the borrowed FBI car. One of the police cruisers followed, and Charles was surprised to see yet another cruiser already parked in front of his house.

"Just keeping an eye on things," said the young officer, when he got out of the car to greet them.

Once in the house, Alex helped Charles retrieve the letters that were hidden in the textbook. Burke called Luther Banks and Lamar Presley and wrote down their contact information. They scanned all of the material, including the ticket, and sent it off to the *Times* editors, along with a list of phone numbers and email addresses for everyone involved.

"Now we wait," said Charles, opening a bottle of beer and handing it to Burke. He opened one for himself, and poured a tall glass of ice water for Alex. They made their way out to the screened-in porch, and Burke and Alex sat in the same places they'd sat on that day when Burke had first confronted Charles. They sipped their drinks and sat for a while in silence, lost in their own thoughts. Charles finally spoke.

"So, tell me, John," he said dryly. "How was your week?"

Alex looked at Burke and stifled a laugh. Burke started to laugh at the absurdity of the question, and soon lost all control. The giddiness infected Alex and Charles, and before it was over, Alex was rolling around on the floor of the porch, doubled up and clutching his stomach, and both Burke and Charles had sweat and tears rolling down their cheeks. The officer in the car parked out front stared up at the scene on the porch, grinning.

"Jesus! I don't think I ever laughed like that in my entire life," Burke said, when he finally regained control of himself. "*Man,* that felt good!"

Charles wiped his face with a handkerchief. "Amen, brother, amen."

49

Some of Them Are Ladies

Burke and Alex finished their drinks and bid Charles a good evening, with a promise to call in the morning when they'd heard from New York. Accompanied by a police cruiser, they returned to the house in the Avenues, and Alex told his mother about the laughing fit they'd shared on the porch.

"I guess I'd better make a few phone calls," Burke said. It was a bit cooler now, and he sat in a lawn chair in the backyard and called Maggie.

She was understanding, as usual, and they talked for a long time about what would happen when, in her words, *the shit hits the fan*. It would likely be a media feeding frenzy and it would be awful, Burke told her. She joked that she was already getting used to having strangers watching the house, referring to the rotation of Dayton police officers who'd been parked out front since the day before.

Burke called Kevin, who took it all in stride. He told Burke that when the time came, the DPD was prepared to officially reopen the Michael Johnson case, and that several FBI agents were now working with them on the Brian Lopez homicide. As far as the local press knew, the FBI's interest in the case was just standard operating procedure – at least so far. Burke warned his son that the FBI would eventually want to get involved in the deaths of both Sarah Sheldrake and Martin Novak.

"And I'll let you know what the *Times* decides to do to with this," Burke said. "You may want to contact Mrs. Novak to let her know that her husband's death was more than just an accident – let her know before she hears about it in the news."

The hardest call that Burke had to make, the one he dreaded, was to his good friend Jim McGowan. Burke regretted getting Jim involved, and he'd thought long and hard about how to keep his friend's name out of this mess. In the end, he realized that for the sake of full disclosure it would be impossible. He'd gone ahead and told Lamar Presley and the others about McGowan taking him onto the base, and pointing out the building that Martin Novak had referred to as *the box*. He'd also mentioned the warning visit that McGowan had received from the mysterious representative of the Defense Department.

They talked for over an hour, and Jim was not very happy about any of it. But before they hung up, he told Burke that he could handle whatever came up on his end. He understood why Burke had done what he'd done. He told him that not only would this not sour their friendship, it would make it stronger.

"Don't worry, John, you're doing the right thing," McGowan assured him. "The shit will roll down the hill and the scumbags at the top won't get any on their shoes. They'll try to make you look like a fool, and you can bet on that. Just remember this, when it's all said and done, *you* will have done the right thing. That's what I'll remember. Fuck the fucking bastards."

* * *

Burke woke the next morning to Johnny Rivers singing *Secret Agent Man*. He was confused at first, not sure where he was. Guest room. Hattiesburg. He could smell coffee, and the clock on the end table said it was 7:01. Burke grabbed his phone.

"Burke."

"Good morning, J.B.," said Lisa Fowler. "I hope I didn't get you up."

"No way," Burke lied. "Did you guys listen to the file?"

"Unbelievable."

"Is that *good* unbelievable or *bad* unbelievable?"

"Everyone was shocked, J.B., and these guys don't shock easily, I'll tell you that."

"So now what?"

"Well, they want to set up a video conference. They want you all there, especially you and Charles Robinson and the FBI agents. On this end, it'll be two editors and a senior writer and probably a couple of staff writers. And me. They were thinking around nine o'clock this morning."

"Jesus, Lisa. Okay, I'll see what I can do," Burke said. "I'll make some calls and call you back. Thanks for making this happen."

Burke called Luther Banks, and the police chief reckoned that young Zack, the department's resident techie, could set everything up, no problem. Lamar and Tina were already up and agreed to head over to the police station when they'd finished breakfast at their hotel. Charles Robinson was ready to go.

While Burke showered, Michelle cooked up some grits and eggs and tossed together a fruit salad. Alex was excited and couldn't wait to get to the police station. He wolfed down his breakfast and waited outside for Burke and Michelle, chatting with the cop in the patrol car.

At the Hattiesburg police station, they all gathered in the same conference room where they'd met the day before. Zack had a camera set up across from the oval table, with six chairs bunched along the other side, a bottle of water on the table at each chair. A large flat screen TV on a tall rolling stand stood just above the camera. Alex was able to lend a hand, helping Zack figure out the patching between the camera and the TV and the police computer system. Everything was ready to go when Lisa called a few minutes after nine o'clock. Zack spoke to a *Times* techie, and before long, Burke, Charles, Alex, Lamar Presley, Tina Hardaway, and Chief Banks were looking across at a similarly bunched group of *New York Times* editors and writers, including Lisa. One of the editors introduced his group, and Burke did the same. After Zack made some adjustments on the camera, he sat down off to the side, out of the camera's view.

Again, Burke observed, the editors and writers were very matter-of-fact. They questioned Burke and the others for over two hours, without a break. When they were apparently satisfied, the editors said that all of the information would be considered. They thanked everyone, and said that a decision on "if and when" they chose to run with the story would be made very quickly – they would let them know within the hour.

When the TV screen went blank, there was a collective sigh from everyone in the room. Chief Banks excused himself and left the room, and the FBI agents checked their phones. Burke and Alex both leaned back and laced their fingers behind their heads. Burke looked around at the others and reflected on the events that had brought them all together. He thought about those who had died. Charles lost his father. Alex had lost his. Looking at Alex, he thought of his own son.

I could have been next.

When Burke's phone rang, he flinched, brought out of his reverie. Tina Hardaway was the only one in the room who hadn't yet heard the *Secret Agent Man* ringtone before, and she laughed out loud. The call was from one of the editors with a question about Charles' intruder, the man he'd shot dead. Burke handed the phone off to Tina. She talked to the editor, then gave the phone back to Burke. Within a minute it rang again. It was a different editor with another question, this time about Brian Lopez. He wanted to make dead sure the name of his employer was BlackSnake, and not one of several other private security companies with the word *black* as part of their name.

"I wonder how long this is going to take," mused an impatient Alex, as Burke hung up.

"They just want to get it right, Alex," Charles said. It hadn't been two minutes when the phone rang again. Burke imagined they were all getting a little tired of *Secret Agent Man*.

"It's me, J.B." said Lisa Fowler. "Tomorrow morning – front page – above the fold. That's the plan."

"Good lord," Burke said, giving a thumbs up to the others. "That was fast."

"The editors are expecting some serious pushback from the Defense Department. They're calling them right now, just to let them know what they've got, but they don't think it'll change anything."

"You're a dear girl, Lisa. I owe you one."

"No," Lisa said. "I think I owe *you* one. But I've got to go – got to get to work on this. I'll keep you posted."

* * *

The FBI agents agreed that police protection was no longer necessary. Lamar said he would deal with the Buick, and Burke managed to book a flight to Dayton that afternoon. He wouldn't be able to fly with the Glock, and Lamar offered to take it back to Ohio, certain that they would be seeing each other soon. Michelle drove him to the Hattiesburg airport, and Charles and Alex followed in the handi-van. Their parting in the terminal was quite emotional – they all agreed that it felt as if they'd been through a war together. They were a team now. They would support each other in the weeks ahead, and they'd talk soon – *after the shit hit the fan.*

Burke sat in a window seat and watched Mississippi fade away as the plane rose to altitude. He tried to imagine what lay ahead. How would he and the others be perceived by the general public? How thoroughly would the Defense Department and the CIA manage to wash their hands of the entire mess? Everyone with any *direct* knowledge of their wrongdoing had already been eliminated. Henry Robinson had died a mysterious death. Polonium-210? Not likely they'd say. Michael Johnson had fallen to his death at Huffman Dam. Could have been an accident, could have been suicide. Sarah Sheldrake had also fallen to her death – accidentally. Same with Martin Novak. Brian Lopez would be portrayed as a random victim – his killers would never be identified, same for the intruder who was shot dead by Charles. All the details that had been revealed to Burke – from Martin Novak and Brian Lopez – would now be considered nothing but hearsay. *His* hearsay. It would be his word against the word of the CIA and the Defense Department.

Son of a bitch.

As the plane levelled off, Burke leaned back with a sigh and looked up through the window. He'd always been struck by the deep blue of the high atmosphere. It was almost black. Beyond was outer space. Now he had to smile, thinking about the one detail he hadn't revealed to anyone – not to the *New York Times*, not to the FBI agents, not to Charles or Alex, not even to his own son Kevin or his wife Maggie.

Somewhere, *somewhere where no one will ever find them* – probably on the campus of the Air Force Institute of Technology in Area B at Wright-Patterson Air Force Base – Martin Novak had hidden the copies he made of Henry Robinson's revealing, detailed description of Project Blue Book.

. . . and none of the little men are green. In fact, not all of them are even men – some of them are ladies!

EPILOGUE

The day after Burke returned to Dayton, the *New York Times* ran their lead story under the following headlines:

Multiple Deaths Related to USAF Project BLUE BOOK

CIA Denies Involvement, FBI Investigating in Ohio, Mississippi

* * *

Closed In 1969, Controversial UFO Study Rears Its Ugly Head

The story, and several other related articles, were published simultaneously in the *Dayton Daily News*. In both papers, the byline credited the lead article to Lisa Fowler and two other writers. Lisa's name was listed first.

A forthcoming statement from the CIA denied any knowledge of the events. The Secretary of Defense said there would be an internal investigation, but he'd been assured by the director of the CIA that the claims made in the press were baseless, certainly paranoid and ludicrous, dangerous, and possibly traitorous. BlackSnake Security, LLC, regretted the death of one of their valuable employees, Brian Lopez, the victim of a random shooting. They claimed no knowledge of the other allegations.

By that evening, both Hattiesburg and Dayton were inundated with national and international press personnel and camera crews from all the major media outlets. The next day, due to the overwhelming interest from the press, the police protection that had been pulled from the homes of those involved, was put back in place.

Some of the national reporting was good. A lot of it – especially from FOX News – was scurrilous. Rush Limbaugh and Glenn Beck couldn't get enough. Charles was a *freak*, they said. Burke was a *sociopath*. The FBI had been *hoodwinked*. But the reporting didn't stop the Tea Party from contacting Burke. They were always looking for new, high-profile constituents willing to stand up to what they saw as a meddling U.S. bureaucracy.

In the days that followed, Lisa wrote profile pieces on John Burke, Charles Robinson, and Alex Johnson. She portrayed Alex as a smart young man who, at the age of fourteen, had been devastated by the death of his father, but had been brave enough to pursue the unsolved crime despite a dire warning. The day after the piece appeared, Alex received a phone call from the director of the admissions office at Cornell University and was told that they still had room for him in the fall, offering him a full ride. He got another call from the Cornell chapter of Alpha Phi Alpha, urging him to come to Ithaca. AΦA was the very first African American inter-collegiate Greek fraternal organization, founded on the Cornell campus in 1906.

Fortunately, the initial media and internet frenzy died fairly quickly, but not before a bipartisan group of U.S. senators had called for an inquiry into the allegations. The Senate Armed Services Committee considered a hearing, but in the end, an emergency session of the Senate Select Committee on Intelligence was scheduled, and Burke flew to Washington where he shared a hotel suite with Charles Robinson and Alex. To Burke's great relief, the committee had not invited Jim McGowan. Only Burke and Charles had been asked to appear before the committee, but Alex had offered to accompany Charles, and they made the fifteen-hour drive to D.C. in the handi-van, stopping overnight in Roanoke.

The Senate Committee Hearing turned out to be a mostly friendly affair. No one was subpoenaed, and everyone who was questioned had readily agreed to appear before the committee. Burke watched as

Charles testified. The senators were, for the most part, very polite and respectful. There was snickering in the room, however, whenever Charles tried to make a serious point about UFOs and Project Blue Book. Burke noticed that one Republican senator in particular seemed to lead the derision, laughing out loud several times.

When it was Burke's turn in front of the committee, the same senator continued to mock the proceedings. Twice he was asked by the committee chairwoman to behave. When it was finally the senator's turn to question Burke, he began with an attempt to impugn Burke's patriotism.

"Mr. Burke," he began. "According to my research, you have never served as a member in this country's armed forces. Is that correct?"

"That is correct, Senator."

"And I'm guessing that like me, you would have been of age to serve during the conflict in Vietnam, as I did. Is that correct?"

"Yes, that is correct, Senator."

"Mr. Burke, would you care to share with this committee the *reason* why you did not serve."

"Senator," responded Burke. "I'm sure that from your – *research* – you already know that I drew a high number in the draft lottery and was never called up."

"Yes, Mr. Burke," said the senator, smirking. "I did indeed already know that. But I'm wondering, why didn't you *volunteer* for military service?"

The chairwoman had heard enough. "Senator, I'm afraid I have to insist that you drop your line of questioning," she said. "I don't see it as pertinent to this proceeding. And I will also remind you that Mr. Burke came here of his own free will, and that you are bound to treat him with respect." There was a smattering of applause in the room which the chairwoman quickly quashed.

"Very well," said the senator, pouting theatrically and shuffling some papers in front of him before he continued. "Tell me then, Mr. Burke . . . tell me a little more about the . . . the . . . the *little green men* that are supposedly hidden away at Wright-Patterson Air Force Base."

When loud snickering broke out across the chamber, a broad grin creased the senator's face. Some of the other panel members were obviously annoyed by their colleague, and the chairwoman again quieted the room. She was about to speak when Burke leaned in close to his microphone.

"Excuse me, Madam Chair, but may I say something to the senator?" Burke pointed at his interrogator.

"By all means," she replied.

Burke cleared his throat and took a sip of water. He thought about what he was going to say, and then leaned forward, adjusting the microphone.

"Senator," he said, staring directly at the man, "you seem to think this hearing is one big joke. But I'd like to remind you that five people are dead – five American citizens who were most likely killed – *targeted* – by their own country. If you think that's so goddamn funny, then I guess we're finished here."

Burke stood up. He made a friendly nod toward the chairwoman, and as he turned to walk away, the rogue senator snapped, "Sit *down*, Mr. Burke! This panel will tell you when we're finished with you."

Burke stopped, paused for a moment, and then once again leaned in close to the microphone.

"Senator," he said calmly, "go fuck yourself."

There were gasps of astonishment, and then the room exploded with laughter and cheers. As he walked toward the chamber door, Burke locked eyes with the red-faced senator, like a batter trotting to first base, staring down the pitcher after he'd been beaned by a pitch. A reporter later pointed out to Burke that he was only the second person to ever walk out on an Intelligence Committee hearing. The same reporter gleefully informed him that it was the first time the *F bomb* had been so publicly dropped in a Senate chamber since 2004, when then vice-president Dick Cheney had used the exact same phrase.

"Well," Burke responded to the reporter, "I certainly wasn't trying to emulate *that* sorry son of a bitch."

Later, as the hearing continued, "the box" was described by the Commander of Wright-Patterson AFB as "just another highly restricted research facility." The Secretary of Defense declined an invitation to appear before the committee. He was not subpoenaed, but offered to send a representative who adamantly denied that the DOD was responsible for any of the deaths. A representative from BlackSnake Security testified, and also denied any connection between his firm and the deaths (the name of the company was changed shortly thereafter). The man who was shot dead by Charles Robinson was never identified. The two Bobs whom Brian Lopez had unwittingly assisted in the murder of Michael Johnson were never identified. Brian's murderers were never identified. The Department of Defense employee who'd visited Jim McGowan in an attempt to warn Burke off was never identified.

The Chinese government expressed righteous indignation at the suggestion that they had any interest in something as silly as UFO research. Within a month of the hearing, the Director of the FBI was forced to resign, but not before he had presented a special commendation to Lamar Presley, and promoted Tina Hardaway to Special Agent in Charge of the Atlanta office, for their work on the "Blue Book" case, as it had become known.

Former President Bill Clinton took a keen interest in the Blue Book case, and in an interview two years later on the Jimmy Kimmel Show, he admitted that during his presidency, he had ordered a review of all the information the U.S. government possessed concerning Area 51 and the Roswell crash incident. During the interview, Clinton stated that it seemed highly unlikely that we were alone in the universe, and he joked that a visit by aliens *". . . might be the only way to unite us in this incredibly divided world."*

ACKNOWLEDGEMENTS

Thanks to my wife and soul mate, Annie Campbell. To Greg Dearth, Emily Rhoads Johnson, Harry and Nancy Campbell, John Piccarella, Lamar Herrin, Cody Ann Cook, Cara Hoffman, Richard Campbell, Doyle Burke, and Vaclav Kostroun, Professor Emeritus, Cornell University, School of Applied and Engineering Physics.

Made in the USA
Monee, IL
04 January 2023

24320228R00152